P9-DSZ-768

Saving

Juliet

BOOKS BY SUZANNE SELFORS

Saving Juliet
Coffeehouse Angel

Saving
Juliet

Suzanne Selfors

WALKER & COMPANY NEW YORK

For my mother, Marilyn McLauchlan, who was *not*,
in any shape or form, the inspiration for the crazy mothers
inhabiting this novel. I just wanted to make that
perfectly clear. Love ya, Mom!

Copyright © 2008 by Suzanne Selfors
All rights reserved. No part of this book may be reproduced or transmitted in any form or by any means,
electronic or mechanical, including photocopying, recording, or by any information storage and retrieval system,
without permission in writing from the publisher.

First published in the United States of America in 2008 by Walker Publishing Company, Inc.
Paperback edition published in 2009

Visit Walker & Company's Web site at www.walkeryoungreaders.com

For information about permission to reproduce selections from this book, write to
Permissions, Walker & Company, 175 Fifth Avenue, New York, New York 10010

The Library of Congress has cataloged the hardcover edition as follows:
Selfors, Suzanne.
Saving Juliet / Suzanne Selfors.
p.   cm.
Summary: Seventeen-year-old Mimi Wallingford's stage fright and fight with her mother on the closing night of
Romeo and Juliet are nothing compared to the troubles she faces when she and her leading man are transported to
Shakespeare's Verona, where she decides to give the real Juliet a happy ending.
ISBN-13: 978-0-8027-9740-7 • ISBN-10: 0-8027-9740-7 (hardcover)
[1. Actors and actresses—Fiction. 2. Theater—Fiction. 3. Space and time—Fiction. 4. Stage fright—Fiction.
5. Interpersonal relations—Fiction. 6. Characters in literature—Fiction. 7. Shakespeare, William, 1564–1616
Romeo and Juliet—Fiction. 8. Verona (Italy)—History—16th century—Fiction. 9. Italy—History—
1492–1870—Fiction.] I. Title.
PZ7.S456922Sav 2008   [Fic]—dc22   2007018528

ISBN-13: 978-0-8027-9831-2 • ISBN-10: 0-8027-9831-4 (paperback)

Book design by Michelle Gengaro
Typeset by Westchester Book Composition
Printed in the U.S.A. by Quebecor World Fairfield
2 4 6 8 10 9 7 5 3 1

All papers used by Walker & Company are natural, recyclable products made from wood grown in well-managed
forests. The manufacturing processes conform to the environmental regulations of the country of origin.

This above all: to thine own self be true.

—William Shakespeare

Saving
Juliet

A few words beforehand.

I'm not going to begin my story with "Once upon a time," even though many of you will call it a fairy tale. Fairy tales are fantasies. Fairy tales are made up and my story is true. Every single word.

I'm going to call this a life-is-the-stuff-of-dreams tale, because that's what it felt like, at first. It felt like a dream, except I'm not the only person who was there and who remembers. Dreams simply do not happen in tandem.

My name is Mimi, and you might think I'm completely nuts after you read this. But I won't mind because it's *my* story and it saved my life.

Fine then. You can turn the page.

One

"All the world's a stage."

Ｍ𝐘 𝐒𝐓𝐎𝐑𝐘 𝐁𝐄𝐆𝐈𝐍𝐒 at six forty-five on a Saturday evening, one year ago. On that eventful night, winter pounced on New York City like a hungry tomcat. The temperature plummeted. Pedestrians hid their faces behind coat collars and scarves, hurrying home as heavy clouds loosened a flurry of dusty snowflakes that coated everything like polluted powdered sugar.

Why choose that particular moment to begin my tale, as opposed to five fifty-five or seven ten? Because winter's first snow transforms everything it touches, and so, too, was I about to be transformed. A bit of heavy symbolism to get things started.

I stepped out of my toasty limousine, thanking the driver as he held the door. The words *Wallingford Theatre*, composed of yellow lightbulbs, were reflected in the passenger window. The moment my boots touched pavement, my stomach turned queasy. It wasn't that I had eaten a rancid meal or was coming down with the flu—it was what I was about to do that made me feel sick.

You see, at that time I was a professional actor. But the job wasn't agreeing with me.

Despite the numbing cold, patrons formed a line that wound around the block. A fog of excited breath swirled above their heads. This was not the crowd of retirees who usually came to the Wallingford to watch classical renditions of Shakespeare's plays. Teenagers formed this line, girls to be exact, all dressed up in fur and velvet, fidgeting nervously as if they had to go to the bathroom. They didn't notice me. I wasn't the person who had inspired them to wait in line for three hours. If you had walked by, you might have thought that Jesus himself had come to town, such was the excitement.

I passed them quickly. A few parents recognized me. "That's Mimi Wallingford," one said to her uninterested teen.

"Who?"

"You know, the great-granddaughter of Adelaide Wallingford."

As long as I can remember, these words have followed my name: *great-granddaughter of Adelaide Wallingford*. Most people don't even bother to pause between my name and my place on the family tree. Never do I hear, "That's Mimi Wallingford, a very fine person," or "That's Mimi Wallingford, an individual." Never am I introduced without my superspecial tagline.

Since ticket holders had blocked the backstage door, a

pimply-faced security guy opened the lobby for me. With a whoosh of cold air, I entered. Some programs flew off a table and the chandelier tinkled. Pimply-faced guy quickly closed the door, shutting out winter's wrath. Shutting me into the place I had started to dread.

With the performance still an hour away the lobby stood empty. Ushers had not yet arrived, nor had bartenders or ticket takers. But behind the coat check counter, cackling laughter arose along with three threads of smoke. I loudly cleared my throat. After some shuffling and muttering the smoke disappeared and three elderly faces popped up. Everyone called these ladies the Coat Check Crones. They had worked at the Wallingford since before I was born. Like MacBeth's witches, they toiled and troubled over their work—knee-deep piles of outerwear.

"Hello, dear," one said in a sandpaper-y voice. She narrowed her bloodshot eyes. "You're not going to report us, are you?" The other two, equally ancient, leaned forward and waited for my answer.

"Of course not," I replied. I didn't care if they smoked, even though it was against theater rules. I actually enjoyed their rebellion, secretly wishing I had the nerve to conduct one of my own—one that wouldn't result in lung cancer.

"She's not going to report us," the second one said, smiling through yellowed teeth. "Such a nice girl."

"Who is she?" the third one asked, dementia nipping at her brain.

"Why, that's Mimi Wallingford great-granddaughter of Adelaide Wallingford."

The very same, the one and only. Descended from the clan that has graced the American stage since the early twentieth century. As of this writing, I am the last in the Wallingford line. "Our family's reputation rests on your shoulders," my mother often reminded me. Rests? There was no resting going on. Crushing, flattening, and squashing was more like it. Try carrying that load around. It's amazing I hadn't developed a Richard the Third hunch.

Before making my way backstage for wardrobe and makeup, I picked up the scattered programs. Not my job but I was stalling—trying to avoid the inevitable. I stood beneath a larger-than-life portrait of Adelaide Wallingford, hung high above the water fountain. Founder of the Wallingford Theatre, she peered down from her cobweb-laced frame with a tight smile, probably miffed by the threadbare carpet and fading wallpaper. The theater's heyday had long since passed. My mother, the current owner and manager, could barely keep the place running, let alone update the interior. People didn't seem to be as interested in Shakespeare anymore. But I've been told that the Wallingford was once *the* place to be seen, that dignitaries and foreign royalty had attended Adelaide's performances. They say she commanded the stage simply by standing on it. People often tell me that I look like her. Aside from her hefty bosom, we share the same wavy brown hair and green eyes. My mother calls it the "It" factor, a combination of talent and beauty. I'm not boasting, believe me. I wanted nothing to do with the "It" factor. *It* had totally screwed up my life.

Shrieks erupted outside because He, for whom they

waited, had pulled up in a stretch limousine. Without access to the stage door, he was forced to strut past the fans, basking in their admiration. They tried to take bits of him, anything they could manage, artifacts to carry around tucked in bras or enshrined in lockets. I folded my arms and watched the scene with a mixture of jealousy and awe. While I had a famous name, kids my age didn't know me. My fame resided with the geriatric crowd. But my peers knew him.

His name is Troy Summer and he had been cast as Romeo in the Wallingford's current production of *Romeo and Juliet*, specifically to attract new patrons. "Let's update Shakespeare," the board of directors had decided. "Let's give our show a mass-market tweak." So they brought in a teen idol from California.

"We can't afford him," my mother had argued. Troy's agent, eager to help his client break into acting, and knowing full well that Troy couldn't act his way out of a monkey cage, had agreed to a reduced wage.

Dressed in a trendy ski parka and dark glasses, Troy looked as handsome as ever. He greeted his frenzied fans then made his escape, thanks to pimply-faced guy who opened the lobby door. The chandelier tinkled again. I had no intention of letting Troy know that I had witnessed the display of hero worship. If his ego got any bigger, he'd need additional luggage to carry it around. I hurried from the lobby as the Coat Check Crones sighed in unison. Even they found Troy irresistible.

On that night one year ago, it took me almost an hour to prepare for the performance, a slower-than-normal pace due to my increasing queasiness. I'd had major roles before but during all my years of acting I had never felt an ounce of stage fright. But stage fright consumed me on *Romeo and Juliet*'s opening night—surges of anxiety that made me dizzy, waves of panic that made me want to flee. My heart raced, my skin flushed, and nausea doubled me over. When it came time to perform the role of Juliet, I became a basket case.

Why? I asked myself time and time again. Others offered their theories about nervous exhaustion and lack of confidence. It never occurred to me that it was Juliet herself who lay at the heart of my condition. I'm writing with hindsight, of course, which is a very powerful tool. But at that time I didn't pay much attention to Juliet. I was the opposite of a method actor—an actor who tries to get into the character's head and body. For instance, Bill, who played Tybalt, wore his costume 24-7, stopped bathing, ate only kidney pies, and read only books about the Italian Renaissance. I learned my lines but I never looked beyond Juliet's surface or imagined a life for her beyond the script. To me, she was just a lovesick girl who made the really bad choice of committing suicide. But, as I would later learn, she was so much more.

As I pulled on my lavender and gold costume, my hands began to tremble. Applause rolled down the hallway, followed by the narrator's voice. "Two households both alike in dignity, in fair Verona where we lay our scene," he said with an exaggerated British accent. That is the first line of Shakespeare's beloved tragedy.

I tiptoed to the wing and sat in a chair that was reserved

for me. A chair that allowed, I mean, *forced* me to see the edge of the stage and hear the audience's reaction. Placed there on my therapist's orders, to defeat that which had started to terrify me. "In order to conquer phobia, we must face it," Dr. Harmony had explained to the cast and crew a few nights into our run. A real touchy-feely kind of guy. "Like a supportive family, we will all help Mimi overcome her stage fright."

So in that chair I sat, rocking back and forth, fighting an intense urge to vomit. Fernando, my makeup guy, hovered next to me with a plastic bowl.

Calm down, I kept telling myself. No one will know I'm nervous. They're all watching Troy, anyway. I gasped and Fernando lunged forward, holding the bowl beneath my chin. False alarm. I waved him away, trying to ignore the concerned stares of my fellow actors. The audience was supposed to be my prey to conquer, the stage my territory to claim. As shameful as a lioness that quivers in fear of a wildebeest so, too, was my shame as I rocked back and forth. So very un-Wallingford of me.

I swallowed against the building bile. The actor who played the Prince of Verona prepared for his entrance. He stretched his legs, cleared his throat, then patted me on the head. "Poor little thing," he whispered.

That's right. Poor little thing. Seventeen-year-old Mimi Wallingford great-granddaughter of Adelaide Wallingford, shaking like a leaf, surging with anxiety, wishing that she could be anywhere but there. Wishing that her life could be completely different.

Does everyone wish that? Perhaps not. Maybe you think that I shouldn't complain about my life. Perhaps you are someone who spends time in front of the mirror, dreaming of the spotlight and applause. That's a fine dream, as long as it belongs to you. But I'd been acting in Shakespeare's plays since age three. As soon as I was out of diapers, my mother slapped a pair of wings on me and thrust me into a production of *A Midsummer Night's Dream*. I played some kind of woodland fairy creature and Mom tells me I was adorable. Thus began my career, an endless chain of rehearsals and performances that swallowed up any chance of a normal childhood—no public school, no neighborhood buddies, no Girl Scout meetings, those kinds of things. I always learned my lines and did my best but the acting thing wasn't *my* dream.

As I waited for my entrance, I reminded myself that *Romeo and Juliet* was scheduled to close the next night. Then I'd leave for Los Angeles to spend two months with my aunt Mary, a surgeon. Sunshine and beach towels were sure to ease my crazy state of mind and give me some time to think about my future.

"Blah." Troy Summer made a vomit sound in my ear. He bent over to adjust his tights. "I hate these freakin' things," he complained, pulling the spandex. He reached under his tunic and rearranged his "package." He caught me watching and smiled. "Try not to have vomit breath during our kissing scene," he teased. Then he strode onto the stage like the arrogant dolt that he was, completely forgetting that in his first scene Romeo is supposed to be depressed and lovesick.

Troy appeared as neither as he raised his arms above his head and waved to the front row. An explosion of hysterical screams rocked the house.

Another wave of nausea hit me, and Fernando held the bowl under my chin again. "I'm okay," I lied, pushing it away. I tried Dr. Harmony's centering technique, focusing on the single phrase *om ya*. Fernando took out a powder puff and dabbed my upper lip.

"Shiny," he whispered. He pulled out a lip liner and fussed. "Stop licking your lips. You make Fernando crazy."

"It tastes like rancid margarine," I complained. We kept our voices hushed.

"So? This is the cost of beauty. Juliet must be beautiful. Beautiful women have nice, full lips. Tonight your lips are thin and droopy, like spaghetti."

Onstage, Troy said, "Love is a smoke raised with the fume of sighs." Squeal, shriek, giggle.

I kept to my chair, doing my best to face my fear. Trying for the zillionth time to understand why this was happening. Why, after a lifetime of acting, did the stage suddenly terrify me?

The actors playing Nurse and Lady Capulet took their places, each casting nervous glances my way. The time had come. I clenched my jaw. Lights dimmed as stagehands rushed out to change the set to the interior of Capulet House. Lights rose and Nurse and Lady Capulet made their entrances.

"Nurse, where's my daughter? Call her forth to me."

Fernando stepped aside and made the sign of the cross

11

on his chest. I took a deep breath and stood, smoothing my long gown. I took a step, sliding my slippered foot across the floor toward the precipice.

"Where's this girl?" Nurse called out.

One step, then another. Left foot, right foot. I could see the edge of the audience. Seats groaned as people shifted. A few coughs broke the silence. They waited for beautiful, full-lipped Juliet. Tragic, lovesick Juliet. Phobic, nauseated Juliet.

"What, Juliet!" Nurse cried. My cue.

I stepped into the light. Nurse looked at me and raised her gray eyebrows. It was my turn to speak.

I opened my painted mouth but my line did not issue forth. Rather, a stream of vomit ran down my dress and puddled at my feet.

"What's in a name?"

AFTER A PERFORMANCE, the women's dressing room is usually a frenzy of activity, so crowded I have to use my bony elbows to get space at the counter. But on that night I stood alone at the mirror, surrounded by an invisible danger zone into which no one dared set foot. Women tiptoed past me as if the merest upset might cause me to explode like a vomitous volcano. Eyes burned into my back. No one said anything to me about getting sick on stage and I appreciated that. I tried to appear calm while wiping away Fernando's makeup with a towelette. A deception, of course. Tears waited impatiently behind my eyes for a moment of solitude to free them.

Heels clicked at the end of the hall. The room fell silent as the heels made their approach, gradually increasing in volume and speed like a bomber's engine on takeoff. Anger and disappointment rang in each beat of each heel. A touch of shame as well.

"Everyone out," my mother announced upon entering.

They fled, young and old, novice and seasoned professional. They grabbed coats and shoes and cleared that room before the bomb dropped.

"I'm sorry," I mumbled. Truly I was. I had scarred the family's reputation, but I was also sorry because public humiliation was high on my list of things not to experience—especially if it involved disagreeable body sounds and/or spewing.

My mother patted my arm. "Thank God for Doris. What would we have done without Doris?"

Doris, the actor playing Nurse, knows a thing or two about ad-libbing. Here's what she did. She stepped right in with a line Shakespeare had not written. "What now, little lamb?" she said, taking off her apron to wipe my mouth. "What now, my poor dove?" she cooed, clutching my arm to keep me from running off stage. "All the commotion hath disturb'd my lady's stomach?" Doris dropped her apron to the floor and wiped up the puddle with a swirl of her foot. The audience members who had come just to see Troy Summer up close and live had no idea that the vomit wasn't part of the show.

Fernando supplied mouthwash and the wardrobe master took my costume to be cleaned, giving me a replacement. The play continued and I managed to hold it together, even when Troy took an extra long time with his death scene. *Hello? Just drink the poison already!*

So there I stood, in my invisible danger zone. I wanted to go home and crawl into bed. I wanted to swallow Juliet's sleeping potion and sleep forever.

My mother took a towel from the counter and wiped off

a stool before sitting. She tucked her turquoise skirt under her long legs. "We'll tell everyone it was food poisoning," she decided. "Clams are never good this time of year. We'll tell everyone that you ate bad clams."

I swept the towelette across my eyelids, dislodging mascara globs. Clams might work. I wasn't keen on discussing my real condition with the public. Tomorrow night this would all be over, the curtain would fall, and I would take a nice break in Los Angeles. I would drink fresh-squeezed orange juice and bask in sunlight while New Yorkers shoveled snow off their stoops.

"Reginald Dwill called this afternoon," my mother announced. I put down the towelette and leaned against the counter, steadying myself for what was sure to be bad news. "He's very intrigued by the success of our show. He wants to film it for DVD. Isn't that exciting? I don't have to tell you how prestigious it would be to have him direct you. We're meeting with Troy's agent tonight but you've got to prove to Reginald that you're in control." My mother froze her smile, waiting for my enthusiastic reply.

"But I'm going to Los Angeles, remember? You said I could stay with Aunt Mary. I'm all packed."

"That was before Reginald called. The future of this theater takes precedence, as does your career."

My career.

How long do you think the average career lasts? My great-grandmother was eighty-two when she died, having just finished a performance. She was buried in her favorite Lady MacBeth costume so she could continue her career in the next life. That's not normal, is it? I'm glad my great-grandmother loved her job but don't most people change careers at least once in their lifetime? Somehow I needed to convince my mother that fourteen straight years of acting, since age three, was a good solid run and that there was no shame in wanting to move on.

Most of the time I felt like an actor in my own life, walking a path that my family had designed, saying my lines, and following my blocking instructions. But the path I wanted to take, one of my own making, hadn't been paved yet. I was still waiting for the building permit.

I turned away from the dressing room mirror. "How am I supposed to shoot a DVD with all this anxiety? It's getting worse."

"You will have to control it."

"But I can't."

"You *can!*" She smoothed her skirt. "You'd better. I'm close to paying off some substantial debts and Reginald's DVD will bring in new investors. I can't do *everything* on my own." There it was, in case you didn't catch it—the Guilt.

Truthfully, I felt as sorry for my mother as I felt for myself. She had once been an actress, and it was no secret that she had married my father to further her career, becoming a Wallingford by marriage. But being famous doesn't automatically make you rich, and our household income came mostly from the Wallingford Theatre. When my father died, the business of running the theater fell into my mother's hands— an overwhelming job that forced her to stop doing what she loved. Her metamorphosis from starlet to businesswoman was rough. She certainly beat me in the stressed-out category. And while she worried about the theater's future, she worried about mine as well, focusing all her unfulfilled desires on *My Career.*

"You need broader exposure. You need to reach an audience beyond New York. A DVD will open more doors." She folded her manicured hands in her lap as I wiped gloss from my lips. "Mimi, sweetheart, I'm going out with Reginald tonight but I want you to go straight home and get a good night's sleep. There will be special guests in the audience tomorrow and your performance must be your absolute best."

"Special guests?"

"Yes. I've invited the admissions committee from the Theatre Institute."

The Theatre Institute—my mother and father's alma mater, the crème de la crème of New York acting degrees.

"This is the final step in the application process," she said.

"Application? I didn't fill out an application."

"I filled one out for you. And I called Dr. Harmony and he's going to come over after breakfast tomorrow and work with you so that you'll be very relaxed and focused for tomorrow night's performance." She reached out and took my hand. "You must do your absolute best, Mimi. Tomorrow could be the most important night of your life. Theatre Institute training is exactly what you need to reach your full potential. And I think some intensive study will help you to overcome your . . . ." She stopped. She couldn't say *stage fright,* as if I had picked up a sexually transmitted disease or something. As if. I was seventeen years old and had never been on a real date. Dateless = Virgin.

I had already given a great deal of thought to college. That was one of my reasons for planning the Los Angeles trip. An acceptance letter had arrived from UCLA and my aunt was going to take me on a tour of the campus. Admittedly I was hiding this plan from my mother but she had left me no choice. When the catalogs had arrived the previous fall, she had dumped them straight into the recycling bin. I had fished them out, secretly studying the photos of happy coeds. I'd been schooled by tutors my entire life, usually between rehearsals. I wanted to carry a backpack and eat in a cafeteria and sleep in a dorm without an ounce of pancake makeup or the glare of a spotlight. College would be my chance to get away. My chance to drive a car. Make some friends. Meet some guys.

"Your father and I loved our years at the Theatre Institute," my mother said. "I can even use my influence to make sure you get cast in the lead roles of the school productions. And you can live at home, just like I did."

Holy crap!

A swirling abyss opened at my feet. "What are you talking about?" I took a deep breath. "Mom, I've been thinking about some other colleges . . ."

My mother's eyes pooled with tears. Genuine tears? Remember that she had once been an actress. "I only want the best for you, darling. When I'm gone, you've got to be able to support yourself, just like I did after your father died."

"But Mom, I'm still thinking about pre-med."

"That again?" She raised her eyebrows. "You can't even

look at an accident scene. You're too sensitive. Just forget this whole fantasy about being a doctor and accept your God-given talent. You're an artiste. You can't ignore the call of the theater any more than Shakespeare could ignore the call of the page." She stood and kissed my cheek. "The driver is waiting. Go straight home."

"But my flight to L.A.?"

"I've already canceled your ticket." She took her exit, startling the women who had been eavesdropping outside the dressing room door. "Ladies," she said through a clenched smile. They parted down the middle like one of Fernando's hairdos. As I fought back tears and removed the last of the makeup, Veronica Wallingford's heels clicked into the distance.

Three bombs dropped at once: a DVD, drama school, and no trip to Los Angeles. Sorry about extending the metaphor, but shell-shocked is the best way to describe how I felt at that moment.

As they walked past the door, the stage crew made plans to meet for drinks. I sat down to tie my boots when Troy Summer sauntered in. "Seen Clarissa?"

I shook my head. Clarissa was my understudy and Troy's girl-of-the-week.

"I told her to meet me here." He sat down on one of the stools. "Thank God this is almost over. I'm totally sick of Shakespeare. Can't understand a single word."

He was sick of Shakespeare? I lived Shakespeare. I dreamed Shakespeare. I ate, drank, and peed the guy. Sure,

Shakespeare was a genius, but ever hear of overkill? If I could go somewhere and never again hear a single, solitary Shakespearean word, I'd be a happy camper.

"I only did this because my agent thinks Romeo is the perfect role for a sex symbol," Troy said.

What an ego. Why was he talking to me anyway? I acted like my boots were the most important things in the world. I had tried my best to avoid Troy ever since our first stage kiss—a kiss I relived on a daily basis, like a bad taste I couldn't help regurgitating.

Here's what happened. On day one of rehearsals, Troy sauntered into the performance hall with his sunglasses and browned-butter tan and I couldn't take my eyes off of him. Neither could anyone else in the cast. He knew his effect and seemed to feed off our admiration and desire, charming everyone with his music video moves. He paid attention to me, more than to the other girls. He let me sip his mineral water and take bites from his PowerBars. He even asked the director if we could have extra rehearsal time to work on our lines. I didn't mind. Not one bit.

I had a full-blown crush. I admit it. I'd find myself staring at his faded jeans, which were worn to a velvety softness and moved with his thighs like a second skin. Even during the coldest winter days he wore T-shirts with surfing logos that stretched across his broad chest. I liked the reddish blond hair that speckled his arms and the way his long, pale lashes could only be seen up close. I bought all three of his CDs and a copy of *Troy's Got Trouble*, the cable sitcom that had launched his career.

Then came the moment for our kissing scene and I hadn't slept at all the night before. I had practiced on my bathroom mirror, deciding that I should close my eyes because if I kept them open, I'd probably go cross-eyed. With the entire cast watching, Troy Summer leaned over the fake balcony railing and pressed his lips to mine. They didn't feel cold, like the bathroom mirror. I didn't move. I didn't know what to do. Was I supposed to open my mouth or just move my head from side to side like in an old movie? When he finally pulled back, I opened my eyes to find him smiling. No, he was smirking.

He knew. He knew it had been my very first kiss, ever.

"You need to work on that," he whispered in my ear. "I'd be happy to give you some lessons."

"That was perfect," the director called out. "A perfect virginal kiss."

I just wanted to die, but death never comes at a convenient moment. Blood rushed to my face and I told the director I needed a bathroom break. When Troy caught up with me later, he asked if I wanted to go grab some dinner or . . . something else.

When the teen idol heartthrob of your generation offers to give you kissing lessons, you can take it one of two ways—you can either be thrilled by the opportunity or devastated by the humiliation of it all.

"Thanks, but no thanks," I said, gathering my pride and hurrying away. He took Dominique, the director's assistant, out to dinner that night. The following week, Lauren, the stage manager, nestled in the crook of his arm during breaks. Turning down the kissing lessons had been the right decision.

I would have been just another notch. So I started ignoring him except when we were onstage together. We still had to speak words of love and we still had to kiss, but I kept the kisses quick and tight-lipped.

But on that night one year ago, Troy and I were alone in the dressing room. Other girls would have killed to be in my boots but all I could think of was making an escape. Hadn't I made it perfectly clear that I wasn't interested in being one of his groupies? I didn't want kissing lessons from the biggest jerk on the planet, like he'd be doing me a favor. What made him think he was such an expert anyway? Practice does not make perfect all the time. For all I knew, he could totally suck at kissing.

"*Romeo and Juliet*'s a stupid story when you think about it," he said. "What guy would poison himself over a girl he had known only for a few days? Romeo must have been retarded or something."

That's why you're perfect for the part.

He fiddled with a lipstick tube. "They're talking about a DVD."

"I know." My voice sounded heavy and unfriendly.

"What about the stage fright thing? You puked all over yourself."

Thanks so much for the reminder. My pride, though shriveled and damp, still had a few sparks left. "I *puked* because I ate bad clams."

"Yeah, right." He swept a golden lock from his forehead. "No one's going to believe that spin."

I pulled my coat from the rack. "I don't care."

"I'm leaving tomorrow, right after the curtain call. I'm shooting a music video in the Virgin Islands." I might have been overly sensitive but I'm pretty sure he hesitated on the word *virgin*. "Want to hear my new song?" He noticed the mirror and leaned forward to inspect his teeth.

"Not really." I buttoned my coat.

"Tell me what you think." He must have graduated from the Veronica Wallingford School of Listening because he cleared his throat and started drumming his fingers on the counter as he sang. "Girl, you got me throwin', Girl, you got me sowin', Down the seeds of love, Down the seeds of love. Girl, you got me rowin', Girl, you got me stowin', On the sea of love, On the sea of love."

My mouth hung open as Troy pulsed his shoulders to his music, pointing a finger at me every time he said "Girl." Simply asinine. Oh God, there was more.

"Girl, oh, oh, oh, oh, oh, oh, girl." He stopped pulsing and stared at me. "So, what do you think? Be honest."

"It's kind of . . . stupid."

"It's totally stupid." He ran his fingers through his thick hair. "Some moron wrote it. I keep trying to persuade the producers to let me record my own songs but they say my stuff is too 'alternative.' They totally underestimate the girls who buy my CDs. The music doesn't always have to be fluffy, you know?"

Clarissa the understudy entered. "Babe," she said, wrapping her arms around Troy's waist. Then she shot me a wicked look. "I heard you're going to the Theatre Institute." News traveled fast.

"It's not for certain." I fumbled with my gloves and dropped them.

"Of course it's for certain. You're a *Wallingford*." She said my name as if describing something she had coughed up.

"It's not for certain. I don't know if I want to go." I put on my gloves.

"Don't want to go? Are you nuts? I'd kill to go to the Theatre Institute." She stepped toward me, her eyeballs blazing with envy. "But I don't have connections. I just have talent. Guess I'm screwed."

The tears that had been waiting pushed around the edges of my eyes as the truth of her words stung.

"Hey, you're really stressed out," Troy said to me as I tried not to blubber. "You should get out of New York for a while. Some of the cast are coming with me to the Virgin Islands. They're going to be extras." Why was he telling me this? I put on my hat. "Why don't you come with us? You can be Bikini Girl Number Four."

I looked at Troy, golden, beautiful, idolized Troy, and I didn't like what I saw. He felt sorry for me. He gave me the same kind of look that I gave my neighbor's cat the time it had a piece of poop stuck on its back leg.

"Thanks, but no thanks."

I grabbed my backpack and left the dressing room. A mob churned outside the backstage door so I walked quickly down the hall to the lobby, empty of employees and patrons. My driver waited outside the glass door.

Me, Bikini Girl Number Four in a Troy Summer music video. That would kill my mother. Exposure, certainly, but not the kind she desired. For the briefest of moments I felt I just might do it. I might rebel. I felt sand between my toes and the sun shining on my butt cheeks. I tasted coconut milk as the chorus of "Girl, oh, oh, oh, oh, oh, oh, girl," pounded in my head.

But then I did what I often did before leaving the Wallingford Theatre. I turned and looked up at my great-grandmother's portrait. Adelaide returned my gaze, sobering me with her green eyes and miffed expression. *"Thinking about a rebellion, are you?"* I imagined her asking. *"Tell me, Mimi, what would you do if you left the theater? What talents do you have besides acting?"*

I had no answer.

"You have no idea how tough the real world is. I know because I came to this country without a penny. I took the Wallingford name out of the factory and the low-rent district and I put it in lights for all to see."

"I know," I murmured.

"I did all that, and I'll have no great-granddaughter of mine sullying the name by wiggling her bare derriere in a music video."

She probably would have gone on all night if I had let her. I left the lobby with the weight of Adelaide's legacy pressing down on my shoulders.

Rebellion smothered.

What was I thinking anyway? I didn't even own a bikini.

Three

"Now is the winter of our discontent."

S NOW CONTINUED TO fall. The limo's wipers squeaked out a rhythm that reminded me of Troy's horrid song. I was furious at myself for crying in front of Clarissa and Troy. My unhappiness was none of their business. They had probably laughed about it on their way to one of Troy's parties—laughed at the girl who had it all but couldn't handle it all.

Steady snowfall had turned our brownstone into a frosted gingerbread house. I thanked the driver and stepped cautiously onto the slick sidewalk. Larry, our neighbor, was also returning home. A large, silver cross swung from his neck as he tried to keep from slipping. "Hello, Mimi," he greeted, holding an umbrella above my head. He offered a fat arm as well. "Good performance?"

"I barfed all over the stage."

He laughed. He thought I was joking.

"No, really. I puked up my dinner in front of everyone."

"Holy St. Francis," he said, shaking his head. Then he

gave me a kindly pat on the back. "Look at the bright side. That's a performance no one will soon forget."

I collected the day's mail and took the stairs to the second floor. Silence and cold air greeted me as I stepped into our apartment. A lingering aroma of lemon Pledge meant that the cleaning lady had been there earlier. Neither my mother nor I spent much time at home so it lacked our own personal smells. We didn't have any pets or plants, unless you counted a pathetic cactus that refused to die. The place was tomblike in its lifelessness.

I locked the door, turned up the heat, and dumped the mail, my gloves, and my backpack onto the kitchen table. My stomach growled as I opened the refrigerator. We used a catering service—a woman who cooked our meals for the week and put them in tidy paper containers. My mother insisted on low-calorie, low-fat entrees, which was why my father used to spend so much time at the diner on the corner, savoring sausages and gravy-drenched mashed potatoes— contributing, no doubt, to his heart disease. I pulled out a box labeled Sun-dried Tomato Pilaf, and popped it into the microwave.

The night had been a complete disaster. During past performances of *Romeo and Juliet*, I had managed to keep the stage fright backstage. Sure, my Juliet may have appeared more nervous than most Juliets, a bit more wild-eyed, nothing more than that. But that night what I feared might happen had. What would the next night bring? Loss of bowels?

While the microwave hummed I pulled off my hat and

started muttering to myself, a perfectly normal thing to do when there's no one else to talk to. Solitary muttering allows you to say all those things you don't have the courage to say to all those people who are driving you nuts. I told Clarissa she had no right to judge me. I told Troy he was a jerk for making me think I actually "liked" him. I told my mother to stop controlling my life. I told my father I would never forgive him for dying so young and leaving us with that cruddy theater. And I told William Shakespeare that *Romeo and Juliet* totally sucks because everybody just dies and none of the characters get what they want. What kind of ending is that, anyway? I'd totally write a different ending.

I sat at the kitchen table and took a few bites of pilaf. The center was still cold but I didn't care. When you're riddled with anxiety, food gives you no pleasure. A brown, padded envelope stuck out of the mail pile. It was addressed to me with a return address from World Family Clinic, Los Angeles. My aunt's clinic.

At that time, my mother despised my aunt Mary. They had had a big falling-out after my father died. Mom went through the house and threw away all the photos of Mary that she could find. I found a forgotten photo, buried beneath some mismatched cuff links. The photo had been taken after Mary graduated from medical school and had gone off to Africa. In it she's wearing a white smock and stethoscope and is surrounded by children with purplish black skin.

One day, my mother found the photo in my room. "For God's sake, why do you have that?"

I had spent a great deal of time staring at the photo, wondering how it felt to live in a place where people had so little. "Why don't we ever see Aunt Mary anymore?"

"She's selfish. She abandoned your father."

"But she helps the poor."

"There are plenty of poor in New York City. Why couldn't she be a doctor here? We needed her help with the theater when your father fell ill. Wallingford is her name, too." Despite a series of strokes, my father had continued to serve as executive director of the Wallingford. My mother was convinced that work-related stress finally killed him. She told everyone that if Mary had stepped in, he would still be alive. A blood clot had actually killed my father, formed from frosted doughnuts, fried catfish, and greasy diner sausages.

A fast food addiction wasn't the only thing that good old Dad had been hiding. Turns out we were in debt, big time. He had taken out a number of loans to keep the theater afloat, all the while we wore expensive clothes and hosted fabulous parties. No one suspected that we hovered on the brink of poverty, not even my mother.

After Dad's funeral, Mary went off to New Zealand for two years, then to Costa Rica. She always called to check up on me, always asked about the plays, the theater, even about Mom. She told me that American doctors can work anywhere in the world. *Anywhere.* That sounded exciting. I began to imagine myself in that white smock and stethoscope. When she moved to Los Angeles a few years ago to open her own clinic, I realized the possibilities were endless.

I pushed the pilaf aside and opened the padded envelope, pulling out a letter and a small something wrapped in tissue paper. Inside the tissue lay a silver chain, from which hung a tiny glass vial filled with silver powder. I read the letter.

> *Dearest Mimi,*
>
> *I was so unnerved by your last e-mail that I spent the night searching through all my old psychology textbooks, trying to find something that might help with your stage fright. I agree with Dr. Harmony about centering techniques, but it sounds like things are getting worse. I think a change of scene is what you need. I can hardly wait to see you next week. Don't forget your bathing suit!*
>
> *Love, Aunt Mary*
>
> *P.S. While rummaging through my old boxes, I found this necklace. I bought it at an antiques shop in Stratford-on-Avon before I went off to college. The owner said it was very rare but I suspect it's just a tourist trinket. Fun idea, though. Maybe it will bring you good luck during these last days of performing. Can't hurt to give it a try.*

A little card was paper-clipped to the back of the letter. It read:

SHAKESPEAREAN CHARM

In 1890, Mr. Burtrand, a merchant and collector of William Shakespeare's writing implements, decided to auction off his collection. Unfortunately, on the eve before the auction, a fire overtook his house, destroying everything.

Being a merchant of clever mind, Mr. Burtrand scooped up the ashes of the burned implements and poured them into small bottles. He claimed that he had captured the genius that had traveled from Shakespeare's hand through his favorite quills.

This is one of those very bottles. Whether the ashes come from the quill that wrote *Hamlet*, *Twelfth Night*, or *Romeo and Juliet*, they are certain to influence your destiny.

I examined the tiny vial. Probably ashes from someone's fireplace. But the fact that it came from Aunt Mary cheered me up a bit.

However, the good feeling was short-lived. As I shuffled through the rest of the mail, my mother's words filled my head. *You need to reach an audience beyond New York.* I shuffled faster. *Theatre Institute training is exactly what you need to reach your full potential.* I threw the bills across the room and slammed my palms on the table. Damn!

I tossed the remaining pilaf into the garbage. I just wanted to go to bed and disappear into a dreamworld where I was an orphan. Orphans always complain about their status but it sounded lovely to me. While collecting the scattered mail, one of the envelopes stuck to my boot. I tried to shake it free but it wouldn't budge. Focusing all my anger on that envelope, I stomped on it and ground it into the floor until it ripped open. Then I reached down and removed it from my heel. I had seen this envelope many times. It came every so often from Stronghead Financial Planners, addressed to Veronica Wallingford. The words *trust fund* peeked out from the torn paper. I pulled out the statement.

Looking back, I realize that I was completely ignorant about money matters. I knew that there were times when we had money and times when we didn't have money. I knew that as a professional actor I received a paycheck and that it went directly into a trust fund. I knew that I would get that trust fund when I turned eighteen. I never questioned this arrangement.

The next words I noticed were *beneficiary: Michelle Adelaide Wallingford*. My trust fund. The fund where all my money went. What a discovery! I found the balance column. $532. Excuse me? From my calculations, that figure was missing quite a few zeros. I moved my finger to the debit column and held my breath. A withdrawal with quite a few zeros glared back at me.

A withdrawal? I hadn't taken any money from my trust fund.

I carried the statement to my bedroom and closed the door. The cleaning lady had tidied my bookshelves and had stacked my pillows. I dropped the shocking evidence onto my bed, expecting it to burn a hole through the quilt. My mother was spending my money. Was that legal? Orphans don't have mothers who steal from them.

After changing into my nightgown and brushing my teeth, I turned off my bedroom light and sat on the windowsill, pressing my cheek against the snow-speckled glass. The cold felt oddly soothing. The old lady in the apartment across the street was watching television. Her feet poked out of the end of a crocheted blanket. Her black-and-white cat sat on the windowsill, his usual perch. In the morning he always watched the birds and squirrels that hung out in the maple tree. That night he pressed his face against the glass, just as I did.

Did he feel trapped as well? Captive in a life he had not chosen for himself? If he could, would he jump out that window? Would he risk it all and cross the street, running toward the beckoning limbs of the maple?

As I cupped the Shakespearean charm, the black-and-white cat mouthed a meow, then lay down to sleep, giving in to his imprisonment.

What we desire and what we do—as different as a Shakespearean sonnet and a Troy Summer song.

Four

*"Of all base passions,
fear is the most accursed."*

THE NEXT EVENING I sat in the limo as it made its way to the theater for the final performance of Shakespeare's beloved tragedy. Usually my feelings of panic didn't set in until I stepped onto the sidewalk. But that night, as soon as we pulled away from the apartment building, my armpits began to produce sweat at an athlete's pace. My heartbeat kicked up two notches and dread wormed its way through my limbs.

Ever had a panic attack? You know how some people tell you to look at the bright side of things, to look at a cup as half full instead of half empty? There is no bright side to a panic attack. And I was about to have one.

The fact that I hadn't slept the night before didn't help. I hadn't been able to get that trust fund statement out of my head. I had tried to call Stronghead Financial Planners but, it being Sunday, all I got was a recorded message. If I really wanted an answer to where my money had gone, I'd have to ask the person sitting next to me in the limo.

"Your future may very well rest on your performance tonight," my mother said.

Hello? I'm a wreck over here. How about some compassion?

I clenched my jaw and tried to block out her voice by reciting my centering mantra. "Om ya, om ya, om ya."

"There is no better school than the Theatre Institute." She brushed something from my coat sleeve. "In order for you to grow as an actress, you must get the very best training or you might end up on one of those horrid soap operas like your second cousin Greg."

I narrowed my eyes until she blurred, her worried face melting into her fur collar.

"Why are you looking at me like that?" she asked.

"Like what?"

"You know very well what I'm talking about. That look that you're doing, right now. That look."

Go away. Leave me alone. You're making me crazy.

"Mimi. Answer when I speak to you."

Here we go. I couldn't stop myself. I no longer cared that she was stressed out and unfulfilled. I was ready to fight her guilt trip with one of my own. "Why are you withdrawing money from my trust fund?" She played it cool. She wiped some lipstick from the corner of her mouth, then opened her purse and began to sort through its contents. "Why are you taking money from my trust fund?" I demanded, turning my voice up another notch.

"How dare you shriek at me." She flicked open a compact. "I'm not *taking* your money. I'm *borrowing* it."

"But it's my money."

"And I'm your parent. The money is under my trustee-ship until you turn eighteen. It's all perfectly legal and nothing for you to worry about."

"What did you do with it?"

"The theater couldn't manage the salaries last quarter. But thanks to Troy and his hungry fans, we're close to coming out of the red." So, Troy and I were financing the theater. "All the money will be returned to your account, eventually."

"Eventually?" That didn't sound good.

Then she tried to turn things on me. "How do you know about this? Have you been opening my mail? That is not respectful, Mimi."

Neither is borrowing someone's money without asking. Sweat broke out behind my knees. "We never talked about this. I worked hard for that money."

"*You* worked hard?" My mother looked like I had slapped her. "Don't forget, young lady, that single parenting is the toughest job on the planet. But I don't expect you to appreciate my sacrifices. You're too young." She reached into her purse and took out a tissue, which she pressed to the corner of her eye. "We shouldn't be arguing. You must focus on your future. Focus on your dream."

"It's not my dream," I mumbled. "It's your dream. There's a big difference."

"You're being ridiculous, Mimi. Then just focus on your performance. It's closing night."

But it wasn't really closing night, not for me. Without my trust fund, I couldn't afford UCLA or even Backwoods Technical College. I had to face facts. I would act at the

Wallingford until my teeth fell out and my bones turned brittle from osteoporosis. Until my skin turned so wrinkled and papery that the next generation of Fernandos would have more to complain about than my spaghetti-thin lips. Stage after stage, audience after audience, review after review. I'd be buried in a Queen Gertrude costume, just in case God's a fan of *Hamlet*.

As we turned the corner and the theater came into view, dread pressed on my chest. Girls were lined up, huddling together against the cold. My mother started in again. "The admissions committee and Reginald Dwill will be seated with me in the sixth row center. Don't disappoint us."

Suddenly I couldn't get a full breath of air. I clutched my knees and closed my eyes as my heart sped out of control. My mother's voice grew distant, her words decomposing into mumbo jumbo. The leather seat pressed against me, the doors of the limo closed in. The air turned into smog. I was suffocating, drowning. Where could I go to escape this sensation? What had happened to all the air?

"Mimi!" My mother stood on the sidewalk, peering at me through the open passenger door. "Mimi, why are you just sitting there?"

I couldn't move. I wanted to move. I wanted to run down the street, run as far away from the theater as possible. But I sat, sweat running along my spine and down my butt crack. If my heart beat any faster, it would burst through my coat.

My mother poked her head in. "Mimi, why are you breathing like that? Oh God, don't tell me you're going to be sick again?"

It's almost impossible to communicate in the middle of a panic attack. When the fight-or-flight response takes over, words are useless, thoughts are single-minded. All I knew was that I couldn't go in there. I would completely lose control. I would vomit all over the stage and forget all my lines and totally screw up my future. I would get stuck on a soap opera with second cousin Greg, where, at the very least, I'd get to *play* a doctor.

Clarissa and a few actresses walked by. "What's going on?" Clarissa asked, peering over my mother's shoulder. "Oh, is she freaking out again? Does that mean I get to go on?"

"She is not freaking out." My mother shooed them away, then stuck her head back in. "You can't be doing this. Not tonight."

I imagined myself running across the street, racing down endless sidewalks, my feet taking me far away from the Wallingford Theatre. Somewhere else. Anywhere else. My head spun and I leaned forward, gagging.

"You're doing this on purpose," she accused. "Just to hurt me. After all my hard work, after inviting the admissions committee here. This is all just an act, isn't it, Mimi? You don't really have stage fright, do you? Well, this is the best acting you've done yet."

I shook my head.

"Don't lie to me. I know melodrama when I see it. I'm the queen of melodrama." She got back into the limo and shut the door as the driver waited politely on the sidewalk. She took my shoulders. "Most people go through life without the kind of opportunities that you've been given. And life goes by very quickly, Mimi, believe me." Her voice, though stern, grew a bit softer but she continued to squeeze. "You don't think I remember what it was like to be seventeen? You don't think I remember all those feelings and desires? All the uncertainty about the future? I'm trying to save you all that uncertainty. Face it, Mimi. This is the only thing you know how to do. Your future is here, right now, and it will be glorious. You just have to pull it together. If not for yourself, if not for me, then do this for your father."

Desperate for relief from the panic, I was willing to grasp at anything that seemed rational. Her voice was strong and steady and she wrapped her arms around me like a life ring. She was right. Acting was the only thing I knew how to do. I'd probably flunk biology as soon as they made me dissect something. I couldn't even watch when a nurse drew my blood. I couldn't even take the skin off chicken breasts. Who was I kidding? Pre-med?

Somehow I willed my legs to climb out of the limo and walk to the dressing room, where my gold and lavender gown waited, fresh from the dry cleaner. Somehow I managed to sit still as Fernando curled my hair and camouflaged my dark circles. He gave my shaking hands a tender squeeze but didn't say anything. Clarissa circled me like a vulture.

"You don't look good," she whispered. "I don't think you can do it tonight. Why not let me go on instead?"

"Go away," I hissed. Fernando raised his eyebrows.

Clarissa leaned in close. "I hope you blow it," she said. "I hope you blow it, *Wallingford*." She slunk away.

Fernando dabbed my face with powder. "You're so

sweaty," he said. "Stop making all that sweat. Juliet is sup-posed to glow, not drip."

The curtain rose as I made my way to the wing where the little chair waited for me. But I felt way too anxious to sit. I paced as the narrator delivered the opening lines.

"Two households, both alike in dignity, in fair Verona where we lay our scene."

Troy came and stood next to me, massaging his temples. "I partied all night with the band," he mumbled. "I feel like crap. I think I'm the one who's gonna puke tonight." Nurse and Lady Capulet stood across from us. The Prince did knee bends.

My mother hurried over to check my condition. "What's that?" she asked, pointing at my necklace.

"Aunt Mary gave it to me." Totally the wrong thing to say.

She pursed her lips. "It's not a period piece. You can't wear it. It's not part of the costume."

I tried to tuck it into my bodice but the chain was too short. "I'm wearing it."

"The wardrobe master will insist that you remove it."

"I'm not taking it off."

"Could you keep it down?" Troy complained, still rub-bing his temples. "I'm trying to focus over here. God, I can't wait to get the hell out of Shakespeare land."

My mother put her hands on her slender hips. "Give it to me," she whispered. "Everything has to be perfect tonight."

"No."

She made a *humph* sound, then hurried off, only to return moments later with Garth, the wardrobe master.

"That's got to go," Garth informed me.

I wanted to swat them both away like flies. *Leave me alone. Everyone just leave me alone.*

"You're violating the wardrobe code," Garth said.

"I don't care."

"Shut up," Troy moaned.

"If you don't take it off, I will take it off for you," my mother threatened.

Suddenly, that moment stood for everything wrong in my life. That necklace belonged to me and no one else. I didn't get to choose my food, or my college, or even my career, but I was damn well going to choose my own jewelry. "You just try to get it!" Both Nurse and Lady Capulet shushed me.

My mother reached for the charm but I pushed her hand away. Determined, she reached again. I stepped back, bumping into Troy.

"What's your problem?" he asked. "Just take off the stupid necklace."

"I won't."

"You're acting like a child," my mother said. She darted behind me and grabbed the chain at the back of my neck. She tried to get it over my head but it got caught in my hair. She kept pulling and the chain tightened across my larynx.

"Can't breathe," I uttered, struggling to loosen her grip. She was going to kill me, just like a Shakespearean tragedy.

"You're choking her," Troy realized, pushing my mother aside. He tried to loosen the chain as I gasped for air. "Oh crap!" He struggled as my throat started to burn. "I can't get it free." He grabbed the glass vial and pulled. The chain snapped.

And so did I.

"I hate you!" I yelled at my mother with my very first breath. "You had no right to take my money!"

"I had every right."

"No you didn't. I'll find a lawyer." I couldn't believe what was coming out of my mouth. "That money was for college. I made plans with Aunt Mary."

"Damn your aunt Mary!"

The director ran backstage. "Dear God, we can hear you in the audience. Keep your voices down."

"I won't! I'm sick of everyone telling me what to do all the time!" The other actors backed away, except for Troy, who was still holding the chain. "I'm going to Los Angeles just like I planned. And I'm not coming back."

"You wouldn't dare leave. You couldn't survive without me." My mother's voice had risen to a screech.

"Oh really? I think that you couldn't survive without *me*." I was screeching as well. "At least, not without my money."

"She's out of control," the director said, shaking his head. "Someone go and get Clarissa. She'll have to go on tonight."

"Oh no she won't," my mother said. "No one takes Mimi's place. This is a very important performance."

The panic attack revived itself, full force. My head started to spin. The floor felt soft. Too many faces stared at me. I had to get out of there. I had to get some air. I turned and ran down the hall. My mother continued to argue with the director.

Panic shot down my limbs. *I can't go out on that stage.*
I can't go out on that stage. No way was I going back. But
where, exactly, did I think I *was* going? I didn't have a plane
ticket. I didn't even have enough money for a bus ticket.
I need air. I need air. I tripped over an extension cord. Troy
grabbed my arm.

"Mimi?" He had followed me down the hall.

"Leave me alone."

"I just wanted to give this back and apologize for breaking it." He held out the chain. I couldn't catch my breath. I
grabbed the Shakespearean charm so hurriedly that the delicate glass shattered in my hand.

"Mimi!" my mother yelled from the far end of the hall.
"Come back here!"

"I can't!" I screamed. "I can't do this anymore." I stumbled toward the exit. My heart pounded in my throat.

"Are you really going to L.A.?" Troy asked as I grabbed
the doorknob.

"Maybe. I don't know." I tried to hold it together, but I
knew that as soon as I opened that door and was all by myself,
I'd lose it. The tears would come and I'd cry forever. "I just
want to be somewhere else."

"Well," he said, "you're dressed for Verona. Maybe you
should go there. I hear it's a nice place." He was trying to
ease the tension with humor. But I couldn't laugh. Laughter
and tears are too closely related and I was still trying to hold
it together.

"Verona is as good a place as any," I said.

I opened the backstage door and a blast of winter wind

hit me straight on. Startled, I tried to shield my face. The wind blew the ashes from my palm. They swirled and danced like sparkling flakes in a snow globe. What had been just a small pinch of ash began to form a silver cloud, growing larger and larger, swirling faster and faster. The ashes went into my nose and mouth. They must have gone into Troy's mouth, too, because we both started coughing. The ashes burned my throat and stung my eyes. I needed fresh air. I stepped into the alley.

Someone rushed by, knocking me off balance. I fell to the ground, landing in something wet.

Five

*"Two households, both alike in dignity,
in fair Verona where we lay our scene . . ."*

THE ASH CLOUD cleared and I stared in horror at the puddle of gunk into which I had fallen—thick and putrid, it smelled like the cow farms that we'd pass when we drove through Vermont. It coated my hands like chocolate frosting. Eggshells and potato peelings floated on the surface. I leaped to my feet, shuddering to imagine what other ingredients I might find. Mud splotches covered the front of my costume. The hem had soaked up the stinky sludge as well. Talk about bad karma—but I guess that's what happens when you tell your mother that you hate her.

Despite my tumble into garbage, my panic attack subsided. I took a long, deep breath, relieved to see that neither my mother nor Troy had followed me into the alley. I wiped my hands on the front of my dress. No way was I going back inside to wash them. I'd stop at the nearest Starbucks, a half block in any direction, and use their bathroom. One of the nice things about New York City is that everyone has seen everything, so I knew I wouldn't have to deal with people

staring or pointing fingers. Mud-stained Renaissance clothing is mild compared with what some of the street perform-
ers wear. As soon as I got home, I'd change clothes, pack my
bags, call Aunt Mary, and beg her to book me a new flight.

Shaking some mud from my hem, I started up the alley,
but I didn't make it more than a few steps because I twisted
my ankle on a cobblestone. In the fourteen years that I had
been entering and exiting the Wallingford Theatre, there
had never been cobblestones in the alley. And what was all
that light beckoning from the alley's entrance? One of those
spotlights, I guessed, that advertises a grand opening.

"Capulet scum!" a voice cried. A woman leaned out an
upper-story window in the building across the alley. At that
time, a classical dance troupe rented the upstairs studio.
"Damn you Capulets to hell!" The woman shook her fist at
me, then tossed out some slop from a bucket, creating
another puddle of gunk that missed me by mere inches.

Enough already. I just wanted to get home. "That's disgusting," I told her. "What's your problem?" She shook her
fist again, then retreated. In my experience, dancers are
notoriously temperamental, especially those of the classical
persuasion. She had probably auditioned for *Romeo and Juliet*
and was holding a grudge against me. Had she dreamed of
Juliet's role for as long as I had dreamed of people calling me
doctor? I stepped over the new puddle. Dancers are notorious
binge eaters as well; maybe that's what the slop was all about.
But I wasn't interested in pondering eating disorders.

My ankle was a bit sore as I hobbled up the alley toward

the blinding light. Certainly the symbolism of that moment was not lost on me. The dead move toward the light, seeking God and everlasting peace. A panic attack can leave its victim feeling like the living dead. But moths move toward the light as well, only to get fried. *Zap!* What fate awaited me?

At the end of the alley I squinted, shielding my eyes as they adjusted. The spotlight perched high overhead and penetrated my costume with its heat. As my pupils constricted, I found that it was not a spotlight at all. It was the sun. And that is the moment I will never forget.

I warned you in the beginning that you might not believe the story I was about to tell, so you've probably anticipated this moment. You may also have read the book's jacket copy so you know that at some point I am going to take an unexpected trip. I did not have the luxury of a book jacket, however, to prepare me, so I felt totally bewildered. The sky, not aglow with city lights or heavy with snow clouds, sparkled baby blue like the bottom of a painted swimming pool. Cottonball clouds floated, cast here and there by a light breeze. And the air was thick with humidity.

What had, an hour earlier, been a familiar city street, was transformed. Before me lay a market square. A stone tower stood across the way and a cluster of stalls overflowed with flowers and produce. A central fountain, shaped like a cake stand with a sculpted lady on top, spouted water. Chickens scurried about, pigeons flew past, and two piglets slept in a basket. A crowd had gathered at the far end. It looked like a Renaissance fair, the way everyone was dressed. For a moment

I thought that a film crew had set up shop, except that even Steven Spielberg couldn't move entire buildings, and two city blocks' worth had simply disappeared.

My instinct was to get somewhere that made sense, so I turned back. Fickle, you might be saying to yourself, but at that moment I would have welcomed the Wallingford Theatre, would have kissed its dingy carpet if it meant that I hadn't lost my mind. The dancer had returned to the alley window so I decided to try the main entrance. But I couldn't find the building I knew so well. No marquee with twinkling yellow lights, no glass lobby doors, no ticket booth. No pimply-faced guy.

A wooden sign with a painting of a high-heeled boot hung above a simple wooden door. I flung the door open, hoping with all my heart to find the Coat Check Crones gossiping and smoking. Instead, I stepped into a cobbler's shop, poorly lit by a few candles. "We're not open yet," a man muttered. He hammered on a piece of leather.

"Hold on, Rodney." Another man stepped forward, wringing his hands. "We'd consider opening early for a lady, if she's got the means to pay." He looked at my soiled dress and pursed his lips. "Perhaps you're looking for the dress shop, two doors down."

I backed up, stumbling into the square. A group of children ran past. More people made their way toward the growing crowd. I suddenly felt numb. I now know it was shock. Shock serves a purpose by turning off your brain for a moment so it doesn't self-destruct. Shock creates a barrier so that you can gradually let the experience in, like slowly wading into frigid water.

"Mimi!" a man called. I spun around but didn't see any familiar faces. Was I hearing things? No, there it was again. "Mimi!"

"I'm over here!" I replied, waving my hands in the air. Which direction had the voice come from?

"The prince is speaking," people told each other as they hurried by. Men dressed in tights and short pants climbed the fountain, stretching their necks for a better view. Women in long dresses pushed into the square. I kept spinning, searching desperately for my caller. The sea of bodies forced me toward the center of the square.

"I'm over here!" I called again.

"Quiet! You must listen to the prince," a man scolded. The crowd stilled and a voice burst forth from somewhere ahead. I couldn't see the speaker but he spoke familiar words.

"Rebellious subjects, enemies to peace, listen to the sentence of your prince!" I found myself squished between an enormously fat woman and a guy who smelled like onions. I could just make out a hat with a red feather that bobbed as the prince spoke. "Three times now, the Capulets and Montagues have fought in our streets, spilling their own blood as well as the blood of innocent bystanders. I will stand for no more. If either house disrupts the peace again, the punishment shall be death! That is the word of your prince."

The Capulets and the Montagues? Okay, this was getting stranger by the minute.

The crowd began to murmur, many nodding their heads in agreement. The fat woman glared at me. "Did you hear that, Capulet?" She was missing a few teeth. "Tell your menfolk that they'll hang by their necks if they keep fighting."

Another woman purposefully bumped into me as she walked by, spitting at my feet. "Capulet scum," she hissed.

I didn't know if I should burst into tears or start giggling hysterically, so I did both. I stood there like a crazy person, in my mud-splattered dress. This was just like the opening of the play, when the prince makes his proclamation. Just like the play that I was trying to escape. How could this be happening?

"Move on, move on," a group of men ordered as they swept across the square. They wore matching red capes and red felt hats. "Move on, orders of the prince." The crowd obeyed and the spitting woman moved away as well. "Back to your business, everyone. You there!"

Turns out, I was the "you there."

One of the men strode toward me, a unibrow dripping over his dark eyes. "I don't recognize you."

What was I supposed to say? I had nothing to say. I couldn't have been more confused if I had landed on Mars. Then I remembered the ashes that I had inhaled. What if they hadn't been fireplace ashes after all, but had been magic mushroom ashes, or some other kind of ashes that bring on hallucinations? Okay, that was possible. That sounded good. I had never done drugs before and I hadn't ever intended on doing drugs, but it was possible that I was in the middle of some sort of acid trip.

The man grabbed my arm and squeezed real hard. "You're wearing Capulet colors. It's against the law to pose as a noble. You want that pretty little neck of yours hanging from a noose?"

My mind spun as I stared into his angry eyes. How could a hallucination hurt? And why was he yelling at me, spattering my face with spittle? Another panic attack ignited in the soles of my feet, ready to shoot up through my core. *I will not lose control. I can deal with this. I can deal with the fact that I have no idea what's going on.* He tightened his grip like a deadly blood-pressure cuff.

"I've got a right mind to take you to jail, unless you want to give me a little something in return." He grabbed me around the waist and pulled me against his hip. The hilt of his sword dug into my ribs.

"Please stop, you're hurting me," I whimpered.

"There is no need for violence," a kindly voice said. An old man in a brown robe stepped forward. A large silver cross hung around his neck. "We should give this woman a chance to explain." He placed a speckled hand on the soldier's arm, melting the tension. I pulled away. Then the speckled hand patted my shoulder. "You are frightened, my child. Take a moment to catch your breath."

Frightened? More like scared out of my mind! A crowd of onlookers gathered around.

"Well?" the soldier asked impatiently. "Who are you?" He leaned close, enveloping me with his halitosis. "Lavender and gold are Capulet colors and like I said, it's against the law to pose as a noble. I have to arrest you if you're not a Capulet."

I couldn't find my voice.

The old man patted my shoulder again. "Have you come for the party?" he asked. His hair was cut in a strange ring encircling his head. "Capulet cousins have been arriving all week long for tonight's party. Is that why we do not recognize you? Perhaps you have traveled far. Is that why your dress is soiled?"

"Yes," I managed. Dear God, what was I saying? But for the first time in my life, telling someone that my name was Mimi Wallingford great-granddaughter of Adelaide Wallingford was not going to help me. I just wanted that soldier to go away. "I'm a Capulet cousin."

"Ah, there, you see, we have an answer." The old man clapped his hands together.

The soldier adjusted his red hat. "Then you'd better get to Capulet House. There's no telling what might happen to you on the streets." It was a blatant threat and his sinister expression terrified me.

The old man watched the soldier saunter away. "Holy St. Francis," he mumbled. "Everyone is so hot-tempered these days." He picked up the hem of his long robe and smiled. "I must be off, as should you. Heed the soldier's advice and get to Capulet House right away. And if you need spiritual guidance of any sort during your visit, you can find me at the Church of St. Francis, the most beautiful church in Verona."

Verona?

"Just ask for Friar Laurence." He hurried off, his sandals kicking up bits of dirt.

Friar Laurence was a character from *Romeo and Juliet*.

The onlookers continued to glare at me. I wanted to hide. To curl up into a little ball someplace dark. So I ran back into the alley from which I had come. Back up the rabbit hole. Please, oh please, back to reality. But I found no stage door. Stumbling, I followed the alley, winding here and there and down a little hill until it widened into a lane. I passed under a series of archways, then rounded a sharp corner where the lane came to an abrupt end. I reached up to swat a fly from my face and found myself gazing at a horizon dotted with tall trees and rolling hills. Not a single skyscraper or yellow taxi or pedestrian anywhere to be seen. Directly in front of me stood a crumbling stone wall. Rows of fruit trees lay to my left. Goats grazed in a field to my right. The shock wore off. I plunged into the icy waters of reality.

New York City was gone.

Six

*"An honest tale speeds best,
being plainly told."*

I COULD HAVE FREAKED out, *again*. Certainly, that would not have been out of character these days. But I didn't. It didn't have anything to do with courage. I think I was simply too exhausted to freak out. I sat down on the wall and took a centering breath, like Dr. Harmony had taught me. Then I remembered the ashes and waved my hand through the air, expecting psychedelic colors to bleed from my fingertips. But no colors bled. I didn't feel drunk or spacey. Just confused.

It seemed that I was in a bit of a predicament. Insanity occurred to me. I really, really didn't want to be insane. My mind could have snapped from all the pressure—a classic nervous breakdown. Actors have nervous breakdowns all the time. My mind could have created this place as a coping mechanism because I couldn't handle my real world anymore. But if I were truly insane, I wouldn't be worried about it, would I? If I were insane I'd have no problem with the fact that one minute I'd been standing outside the Wallingford

Theatre in New York City and the next minute I was half a world away in Verona, Italy, where characters from *Romeo and Juliet* walked the streets—speaking English, no less. That would seem perfectly reasonable to an insane person and it didn't seem perfectly reasonable to me.

So, not insane.

I don't know how long I sat there—long enough for my arms to start to sunburn. Deep in thought, I didn't notice the little boy until he tugged at my skirt.

"My lady?" His eyes were wide with curiosity. He tilted his head and scrunched his freckled nose. "My lady, are you injured?"

It's so much easier to admit confusion to a child. I had an overwhelming urge to hug his little frame, to feel the warmth of another human being. "I don't know where I am." A few goats had followed the boy from the field. One started nibbling at my hem.

The boy frowned. "You're sitting on the old city wall, that's where you are." He came closer. "Did you bump your head on something? Once I bumped my head and it made me forget for a little while."

When I fell into that puddle, had I bumped my head? Dorothy bumped her head and woke up in Munchkinland. It made perfect sense that I had woken up in Romeo and Juliet land, having lived the story for the last six months. I felt my scalp but found only the regular bumps. Maybe I had inhaled too much of that ash and it had knocked me out? Could this simply be a dream? Could I be lying in the alley next to the theater at that very moment, with Fernando leaning over me, worried about me smudging my mascara? Clarissa had probably gone back to the dressing room, ecstatic that she was finally going to get her chance. I didn't care. Let Clarissa entertain the stupid admissions committee. I'd take a break in dreamland while she did her thing onstage. My mother could yell at me about stage fright, but she couldn't blame me for being unconscious.

A dream, then.

"I might have bumped my head. I don't remember," I told the little boy. "I'm kind of messed up right now."

"I guess your dress is a bit messy." The goat tugged at my dress. "Get away," the boy said, pushing the creature's bony rump. It ambled off, taking half my hem with it. "I'm sorry about your dress. How'd a lady like you get it so dirty?"

I held out my mud-splotched skirt. "I fell in a mud puddle. And last night I vomited all over the front of it." I laughed weakly. "I hate this dress. Your goat's welcome to eat the whole thing."

"Are you hungry?" the boy asked, pulling something from his pocket. "This one got a bit flattened but I know where we can get more. Come on, I'll show you." He took my hand and tugged. "Come on. After I got that bump on my head, my mother made me eat. She said food would help me feel better. Come on." He tugged again.

Such a nice little boy. Maybe he had come to guide me through my dream. If I followed him I would probably figure out what the dream was about. Dreams took girls to wonderful places like Oz and Wonderland. I let him pull me through the grass until we came to a tree, heavy with apricots. He reached up and plucked one, then bit into it. Juice dribbled down his soft chin. "Go on. Try one." A black and white goat affectionately rubbed its head against the boy's back.

I picked an apricot and cupped it in my hands. It seemed so normal. "I don't know what I'm doing here," I confessed.

"You're eating apricots, that's what you're doing." He stuck the rest of his apricot into his mouth, then spit out the pit. "They're delicious."

The apricot had absorbed the sun's rays and its juicy center burst on my tongue. I hadn't realized how hungry I was, and it felt as though I were actually eating. The boy climbed to the thickest branch and began to throw apricots to his goats. I wandered deeper into the field, munching as I went.

The summer grass tickled my ankles and apricot juice clung to my fingers as I stared at the outskirts of my dream-world Italian city. Too bad we can't choose our dreams because I most certainly would have chosen someplace else, as sick as I was of the Capulets and Montagues. But thankfully, my subconscious wasn't forcing me to speak Italian, or even Shakespeare's lingo. In fact, there is no goat herder or apricot orchard in *Romeo and Juliet*. At least my subconscious had changed the story.

The boy took a bell from his pocket and jangled it. The goats lifted their heads and began to amble toward him. "I have to be off now. I've got another job to get to." He started to walk away, jingling the bell a few more times. But after only a few steps, he turned and ran back to me. "You shouldn't stay out here by yourself. There's a Montague over there." He pointed to a large tree, then scampered off.

A Montague over there?

Curious, I walked slowly toward a gnarled willow. Grapevines coiled around its trunk. Sure enough, on the other side, a young man sat, his head resting on his bent knees. He sighed a few times. "Oh Rosaline." He sighed again, wrapping his arms around his black tights. He was dressed just like the Montagues in our play.

A shiver of excitement ran up my spine. I didn't have to ask his name.

Seven

"One pain is lessen'd by another's anguish."

Lost in thought, Romeo Montague didn't notice me standing next to him. Not even when my apricot pit plunked into the grass. He mumbled words like *woe* and *agony*. There sat the true Romeo of Shakespeare's story—the depressed-out-of-his-mind Romeo. You see, Romeo is supposed to begin the play in a deep state of melancholy. He could be the poster boy for the antidepressant pill of the week. But Troy never quite got the fact that a depressed person wouldn't strut onto the stage. A depressed person wouldn't wink at the audience. Troy, who had probably never spent a depressed moment in his sunshin-y life. Troy, who probably had no idea what it was like to be attracted to someone but have that someone ignore him or outright ridicule him with offers of kissing lessons.

"Rosaline," Romeo murmured. That is the reason, or I should say, *she* is the reason for his despair. Romeo tightened his arms around his legs. His puffy shorts were dyed the color of an apricot and his white shirt had come untucked. A breeze

59

blew the willow's graceful branches so that their long shadows seemed to caress him—as if the tree felt his pain. I felt his pain. It flowed from every pore in his body, tumbling forth with each breath.

Would it be rude to interrupt him? Possibly, but how could I walk away from an opportunity to talk to one of the most famous teenagers ever? Even if he were only a figment of my imagination it sure beat waking up and going back onto that stage. I cleared my throat.

"Leave me alone, Benvolio." He spoke softly, then buried his face deeper.

"Hello," I said.

He leaped to his feet, and I took a step back. We looked at each other with equal surprise. Then he bowed. "Forgive me, my lady. I did not hear your approach." We stood in silence as he composed himself, running his hands through his short brown hair and wiping his cheeks dry with his billowy sleeve. His gaze was almost unbearable, the sorrow penetrating.

"I'm Mimi."

"I'm Romeo." He bowed again but did not straighten all the way. It took effort for him to stand. His shoulders slumped like the branches of an overabundant fruit tree. To ease his burden, I sat down in some matted grass. He sat next to me. I wasn't sure where to begin. It wasn't like I had prepared an interview sheet. Fortunately, he took up the conversation for me. "I mean to say that I *was* Romeo. I don't feel like him anymore. I fear that I have lost myself."

"I'm lost, too," I said excitedly. We had something in common. "I don't feel like myself either."

He scooted closer to me. He smelled sweaty, but in a nice way. My dream Romeo looked boyish and cute, with smooth skin and only a light dusting of fuzz on his upper lip. A late bloomer. "Is love the reason you are lost?"

Where to begin? I was lost on so many levels. "I've never been . . . in love."

"Nor I, until last Thursday, when I first saw Rosaline. I told her that I adored her. I offered my heart." He sighed and gazed into the distance. "She said she would not have me so I told her that I possess chests overflowing with gold coins. Still, she would not have me." He clenched his fists. "She has vowed to live chaste. Why would a woman turn away from love?"

I knew it wasn't personal. According to Shakespeare's play, Rosaline would not have any man. She had chosen a chaste life, to enter into God's service. Strange, but even though I was aware that I was in a dream, I wanted to help Romeo feel better. I wanted to tell him that soon he would see Juliet at a party and he would fall in love with her and never think of another woman again.

And then he would be too dead to think of any woman. Maybe I shouldn't tell him that.

"Forgive me, but I can think of nothing else. All day she torments me. All night her beauty haunts me. Lady Mimi, do women suffer for love as much as men?" His sorrow pierced me all over like straight pins. "Tell me what you know of love."

"I don't know anything about love," I replied. Romeo sighed and rested his head on his knees. I had disappointed him, but what wisdom did I possess? Me, the dateless wonder? Sure, there had been that *crush* thing, but I'd gotten over it. Sure, Troy had made fun of me and maybe I hadn't gotten over that part, but I didn't like him anymore. I didn't even think about him. What a waste of time that would have been. "You'll fall in love again" was all I could think to say.

"My opinion exactly," said another voice.

Now it was my turn to leap to my feet, bumping my back against the willow's trunk in the process. So caught up in Romeo's plight, I hadn't noticed the other man coming toward us. Unlike Romeo, this guy carried a sword, though it was tucked away in a scabbard. He wore similar black tights and puffy orange shorts. He hadn't bothered to tie his linen shirt so his chest glistened like some cover model for a romance novel.

"Romeo, are you out of your mind? Talking to a Capulet and a woman nonetheless." I caught the disgust that flashed across his face when he said *Capulet*. I felt as if I'd been spit upon, which made no sense since I wasn't really a Capulet. But I felt it, all the same.

"Huh?" Romeo peered up at me. "A Capulet?"

The man shook his head. Black curls fell across his forehead. "So lovesick you didn't even notice her colors? Truly, you worry me, cousin." He turned his attention to me. "My lady, I advise you to continue on your way. It is my duty to look after my younger cousin and your presence endangers him." He pushed aside a short black cape, exposing a brown shoulder in the process. My gaze traveled up his long neck and over his stubbled jaw, stopping on lips that Fernando would have killed to gloss. Something took flight in my stomach. This was how those giggling girls in the front row felt when Troy walked onstage.

"Romeo, your father has sent me to find you."

"Leave me alone, Benvolio."

"What? Leave you here to moan and groan on such a lovely day? Do you see this, my lady? Fifteen years of age, nearly a man, and he's devoted his heart to a nun. Cousin, I urge you to examine other beauties." Benvolio raised an eyebrow at me and my face went hot. His was the part that Troy should have played—the flirt. I stared at his classic face, at the aquiline nose and high cheekbones that the Italian masters had preferred to sculpt. The blood of the Caesars coursed through him. Embarrassing, lusting after a character from a dream. Totally pathetic.

He crouched next to Romeo and placed a gloved hand on Romeo's shoulder. "Be ruled by me, cousin. Forget about Rosaline."

"Forget about her?" Romeo's voice rose in desperation. "Then teach me how I should forget to think!"

"You are hopeless." Benvolio stood and grasped his sword's hilt. "You should go," he said to me. "Romeo is in no condition to defend himself if the Capulet Guard come." His urging was gentle, yet firm. "You must get yourself to Capulet House."

I was endangering Romeo, I knew that. But shouldn't I be able to control my own dream? I could just send the guard away. Yet the soldier, Friar Laurence, and Benvolio had each insisted that I go to Capulet House. Seemed to be the direction my dream desired. "I don't know how to get to Capulet House."

"You are not of Verona?"

"No. I'm from Manhattan. I've come for the party."

"Well, that explains why you were sitting with a Montague. Do you not know the situation around here?" I played dumb. Truth be told, I liked his attention and I could have leaned against that tree until my imaginary legs gave out, if it meant talking to him. "The houses of Montague and Capulet are at war, my lady. Whether you are from Verona or some distant land, your Capulet blood makes us enemies." He looked around, then folded his arms. "I will guide you to Capulet House but you must not walk beside me, not as long as you wear Capulet colors."

"I understand."

"Come along, Romeo. Your father has not seen you in two days and it looks as if you have not eaten or bathed in as many."

"I shall remain here for a while longer," Romeo said. "I must figure out how to change Rosaline's heart."

"Suit yourself." Benvolio rolled his eyes.

"Good-bye, Romeo," I said.

"Good-bye, Lady Mimi. Someday you will know love. I hope it is as deep and as true as mine."

Benvolio groaned. "I shall return for you, Romeo, and when I do, we shall seek wine, women, and dance. Anything to snap you from your trance." He focused his chocolate eyes on me. "Shall we go, Mimi of Manhattan?"

I followed Benvolio into the city. Followed his dark tights and long body. He turned to check my progress now and then. People watched as he passed by. He bowed to a few, waved to others. The men hissed "Montague" under their breaths but the women stared lustily.

"My lady!" A guy in a leather vest strode toward me, his bulky quads stretching the fabric of his golden tights. He carried a sword and appeared to have no neck. "Have you come for the party?"

I stopped walking. "Yes. I'm from out of town."

"Have you no guard?" the guy asked.

Benvolio leaned against a wall, pretending to be interested in the state of his fingernails. He watched me from the corner of his eye.

"Thanks, but I don't need a guard," I said.

"All Capulet women must have guards, by order of Lord Capulet himself." His porous face turned red as he scowled. He spoke loud enough for Benvolio to hear. "You are not safe on the streets with those low-life Montagues lurking about." Benvolio coolly ignored the challenge. "You will come with me."

"I'm doing just fine on my own," I told him, not wanting to leave my hunky escort. It was like choosing between a creamy cappuccino and a deep-fried slab of hamburger. I knew which one I would prefer with my morning walk.

But the guy was insistent. "I am under orders. I shall escort you to Capulet House."

I turned my back to Benvolio and said quietly, between clenched teeth, "Thanks, but no thanks. I'm fine on my own."

I tried to slip away but he blocked my progress with his beefy frame.

"If you do not come willingly, then I shall be forced to carry you."

"Carry me? Look, buddy, go find another Capulet woman to harass. I don't need your help." In a single swoop, I found myself in midair, then slung over a broad shoulder. "Hey!" I shouted.

"My apologies, my lady, but I shall lose drinking privileges if I disobey orders." He started up the road.

Benvolio slipped into a bakery as we passed by. I had planned on telling him that he shouldn't take Romeo to the Capulet party because it would only end very badly, but I decided not to call out to him. No telling what the guard would do. When I looked back, Benvolio had returned to the street. Our eyes met and it felt as if I had stuck my finger into an electric socket.

Eight

"The lady doth protest too much, methinks."

B EING CARRIED LIKE a sack of potatoes was fun at age five. I would pretend to fall asleep on the couch, and my father would scoop me up and whisk me off to bed. But it was a miserable mode of transportation at seventeen because my hip bones and boobs kept getting pinched. My head pounded with each step.

"Put me down. I can walk." My *driver* ignored me, jogging past countless people who also ignored my protests. "Someone tell this gorilla to put me down." The gorilla tightened his grip on my thigh.

What's a girl to do when she finds herself upside down? I pushed my elbows into the guard's lower back and tried to hold my head upright, taking in my dreamworld as we charged down winding street after winding street. We passed velveteen rich people and tattered poor people, merchants calling out their wares, and customers arguing over prices. A fat woman herded swine and a group of skinny boys chased a dog. My neck started to spasm so I gave the gorilla another thump on the back, just for good measure.

The ride continued, swerving left, then right. This was my warped version of the yellow brick road. I hummed a few lines and pictured Dorothy's kick-step choreography. *Follow, follow, follow, follow, follow the yellow brick road.*

Finally the trip ended and the hulk deposited me in front of a huge door, upon which he pounded. I swayed as blood rushed from my head. A little panel in the door opened and a bloodshot eye peered out. "Who goes there?"

"Gregory. I found one of our women wandering the street."

The door opened immediately and a knotted hand reached out and clutched my arm. "Oh dear, we had best get her inside before her ladyship hears about this. Can't have Capulet women wandering the streets."

Gregory stomped off, muttering about a "damn thirst." The knotted hand belonged to an ancient man. He pulled me inside, then locked the door with a brass key and hung the key on a hook. He clutched my arm with his bony fingers, guiding me down a hallway. Gold-framed portraits hung on either side of the hall. The largest caught my eye. It was an oil painting of a woman covered in jewels. The painter had positioned her irises so that they stared directly at the onlooker. Her thin lips were curved into an expression that is best described as miffed.

"Who's that?" I asked.

The old man squinted at the portrait. "She was the

matron of this prestigious family, her most esteemed and virtuous Adelaide Medici Capulet. Are you certain that you are Capulet?"

"Yes." I had hesitated. He tapped his boot and pursed his lips.

"Then why did you not recognize this portrait?"

I should have recognized it. She looked exactly like my own Adelaide, after a session with a sixteenth-century stylist. "Silly me, of course I recognize it."

He stood on tiptoe, examining my face. "Yes, I do see a family resemblance. You and Juliet have the same chin."

How strange, I realized, that I hadn't cast myself as the leading role in my own dream. Sure, I was sick of the part and I hadn't done it justice on stage with my stage fright and all, but shouldn't we all be the stars of our own dreams? The face that launches a thousand ships, the hero who kills the dragon, or the girl who finds true love on a balcony.

But I had cast myself as a Capulet cousin—a lesser role.

And that was my state of mind one year ago. You see, my deeper truth was far more toxic than stage fright or resentment of my mother. Somewhere along the path of my childhood, in my dutiful fulfillment of the Wallingford role, I had lost myself. I had been taught that the family always came first. Somewhere along the way, I had come to believe that I was secondary.

The old man picked a black seed from his teeth. "Her ladyship's in a wretched mood. You are the thirty-third guest to arrive today. Been arriving all week, they have. Problem is, we've run out of guest beds. I must find out where to put you." He guided me to a bench. "Stay here." Then he scurried off.

During his absence, the hallway came alive with traffic. Cleaning women ran to and fro, carrying buckets of water and scrub brushes. Men in aprons hauled barrels and crates. A boy passed by with an enormous round of cheese balanced on his head. Everyone was talking about the party.

The Capulet party takes place in the first act of Shakespeare's play, a lavish shindig arranged to introduce Juliet to her suitor, a man named Paris. It was my favorite scene in the play because we wore masks, which helped ease my stage fright, and we danced, which I loved, even if it had to be with Troy. Sometimes he held me closer than necessary, so close that our thighs touched. Sometimes he spread his palm wide against my lower spine. I shivered thinking about it.

Even in a dreamworld I couldn't deny my feelings. I still liked the big braggart. I still sighed each and every time he walked into the room and I still wondered what it might be like to hold our stage kiss just a bit longer. But I didn't want to feel that way. I didn't want to love someone who didn't love me back. At least Troy wasn't *in* my dream. That was a good sign.

The old man returned. "Her ladyship wants to see you. Follow me." We made our way up a grand marble staircase. "Have you traveled far?" he inquired.

"Yes. I'm from Manhattan."

"Don't know it. Where are your traveling cases?"

I looked around, wondering if my subconscious would provide some. "I don't seem to have any."

"Were you robbed?"

That sounded believable. "Yes. Robbed."

"God forbid!" We had reached the top of the staircase. "Those Montagues were behind the robbery. I'd wager a day's pay on it." We stopped outside a narrow door. "Your name, please?"

"Mimi."

He knocked three times, then opened the door, motioning to me to enter. I stepped into a room thick with the smell of floral perfume. "Introducing Mimi of Manhattan," the old man announced. "Just arrived for the party and newly robbed." He bowed and exited, closing the door.

Crates of flowers lined the far wall where a group of women were busy weaving garlands. I stayed by the door, unsure of what to do. Voices whispered from behind a screen to my right. "Your ladyship, I must collect the debt," a man insisted.

"You know I cannot pay you today. You must persuade your superiors to extend my credit just a few more weeks," a woman insisted.

"My lady, perhaps your husband . . ."

"My husband has no mind for money." She raised her voice for an instant, then lowered it again. "I run this house. My husband might as well be dead for all the help he gives me. He wanted to wait and see if Juliet would agree to the marriage. Can you imagine? Asking a child? Thankfully, I convinced him that we must proceed." She paused. "Just a few more weeks. Once my daughter's marriage is secured, I will receive a substantial payment from her husband, more than enough to cover our debts."

"Plus interest, your ladyship?"

"Yes. Now be gone. I have to prepare for the party."

A man emerged from behind the screen. He tucked a bundle of papers under his arm, nodded at me, then left the room. A tall woman stepped out and clapped her hands. "Hurry, hurry, ladies. We must get those garlands hung." She raised her eyebrows, creasing a superhigh forehead— an effect created by a plucked hairline. "Who are you?"

"Mimi, from Manhattan."

Her stare was hypnotic. You might not know this but Lady Capulet is the villain in Shakespeare's tragedy. She doesn't have a big speaking part in the play but she's at work behind the scenes. It's her hatred that fuels the war between the two households. It's her hatred that ultimately kills the young lovers, in my opinion. But I'm not very objective when it comes to mothers.

"What happened to you?"

"I was robbed."

She narrowed her eyes. "Is that why your gown is torn and muddied? Did the robbers molest you? Is your virginity still intact?"

My virginity was not a subject I wanted to focus on. Look, it's not that I was embarrassed by my virginity. Given the choice, I would choose to wait until someone loved me and I loved him back and we made a commitment to each other and all that good stuff. Then I'd have a decision to make about my virginity. But I hadn't even come close to having to make a decision. You see the difference?

"They didn't molest me," I answered nervously. She made me feel uneasy, standing so close, her bony frame towering over me. "But they took my traveling cases."

"Those clay-brained Montagues shall be punished for robbing you. I shall speak to my husband when he returns. I think hand-severing and eye-gouging are in order."

Gouging Benvolio's beautiful eyes? "Oh, that's not necessary."

"Not necessary?" She frowned. "Even though you come from Manhattan, you are required to loathe the Montagues to the same degree that every other member of this family loathes them. We shall have our revenge against the Montagues. Mark my words. We shall have our revenge."

I nodded. I didn't want to argue with her. It would be so nice if I could keep this a happy dream.

She curled her upper lip as she inspected my costume. "I cannot allow you to be seen in that dress. Every Capulet woman holds the family's reputation on her shoulders. Those shoulders should always be clean and stylish." She drummed her fingertips together. "I have ordered all the women to nap before the party, but I have been informed that we are out of beds. Therefore, you shall nap in Juliet's room."

Nine

"Look like the innocent flower,
but be the serpent under 't."

L ADY CAPULET GLIDED down the hallway. My subconscious had formed her well. A bit of the Wicked Witch of the West in her long, pointy face. A bit of Cruella de Ville in her bleached hair with roots so dark it looked like someone had dumped coal on her head. And a bit of my own mother in the topic of conversation—the family name.

"Above all, the Capulet reputation must be kept intact," she said with pronounced seriousness. "Our appearances, our manners, and our goals must be cohesive. The Capulet name must stand above all others as it always has. We are Capulets. We are Verona."

We are Wallingfords. We are theater.

Lady Capulet walked with long, exaggerated strides and I followed like a bridesmaid keeping time to a painfully slow rendition of Troy Summer's hit ballad "Girl, You Are My World." Drifts of powder had accumulated along the nape of her neck. I couldn't remember having experienced such minute details in a dream before. Like the way the coldness of the stone floor made my feet ache, even though I wore slippers. Or the way my frayed hem tickled my ankles. Who dreams, like that? And who dreams in real time, because it certainly seemed that way? I felt hungry and I needed to pee, which couldn't be good because when you need to pee in a dream, you either wake up or you wet the bed. I didn't want to do either. I wanted to stay in my dreamworld, at least until Clarissa finished the performance. Maybe longer. If I fell into a coma, say for a week, maybe Reginald Dwill would find someone else for his DVD.

Lady Capulet pointed to a tapestry as we glided past. "Have you ever seen such a magnificent Capulet crest? My daughter's work. So loyal and obedient is my daughter, Juliet. She is so dear to me."

So dear that you sold her to the highest bidder.

She wrenched her neck and cast me a suspicious look. "Where is your mother? Why did she not come with you?"

Oh no. I didn't want Veronica Wallingford turning up in this dream—turning it, most assuredly, into a nightmare. "She's dead."

Lady Capulet pursed her painted lips. "Pray tell, did she die of plague? We lost so many in the last outbreak."

"Yes." That sounded good. "Plague."

Lady Capulet pressed her fingertips together. "When your mother lived, did you obey her in the manner that a beloved daughter should?" She raised an eyebrow and, honest to God, a shiver ran down my spine. When a fly passed by, I half expected a forked tongue to dart out of her mouth.

"Oh, I obeyed. Believe me, I obeyed," I said. "But now she's gone so I must take care of myself."

Lady Capulet grimaced. "Young ladies are incapable of taking care of themselves. Young ladies must be directed. There is only one thing to be done. Since your mother is dead, I shall take her place. While you are here I shall act as your new mother." She placed an ice-cold hand on my shoulder.

Oh, no thank you. Because you scare the crap out of me. You really do.

"I don't think I need . . ."

"Do not presume to tell me what you need. I have decided to become your guardian in matters both moral and physical. Once I make a decision, it stands."

Here was my chance to finally break free of parental handcuffs, even if it was just a fantasy. But lo and behold, another mother from hell to *direct* me. It appeared that my subconscious wasn't going to let me off the hook so easily.

Lady Capulet stepped aside to reveal a narrow door, upon which she knocked. A rotund, middle-aged woman with large pores opened the door. "Nurse, this is Mimi of Manhattan, Juliet's distant cousin. She is just arrived. The devil's offspring have robbed her of her traveling cases."

"The Montagues?" Nurse asked.

Lady Capulet scowled so hard her eyebrows became one. "Of course the Montagues! Who else would dare attack a Capulet woman but those wretched whoresons? The eternal fires of hell await them where they will be flayed like suckling pigs on the morn and eaten by cannibals at dusk." She smoothed her embroidered bodice, relaxing her face. "Tell me, Nurse, how is my Juliet?"

"Quite well, my lady. She naps like the innocent spring bud that she is."

Lady Capulet nodded. "How beautifully put. Like a spring bud waiting to blossom into womanhood. Now then, I must find Mimi an appropriate dress for tonight's festivities. See to it that she naps." Lady Capulet turned and glided back down the hallway. Both Nurse and I sighed with relief.

Nurse ushered me into a dimly lit room that contained a bed, a large wooden chest, a painted table with matching stools, and a high-backed chair. She shut the door. "Spring bud," she muttered. "That'll be the day. More like winter mud or summer crud." She fluffed a pillow, then wagged a finger at me. "See here, Capulet cousin. I've got enough on me hands, what with that beastie over there." She pointed to the bed, where someone lay beneath a pile of blankets. Juliet, I assumed. But a beastie?

"Me old heart can't take no more tricks or tricksters. Beastie over there is bad enough. Don't get me wrong. I love her like me own child, but she sucks the life from me, she does." She stood close and looked me over. She smelled like a mildewy shower curtain. The source, I guessed, was her dingy apron.

"Did those Montagues molest you?" she asked, pointing her red, bulbous nose up at me. "Did they hold you down and have their manly way with you?"

I might let Benvolio have his manly way with me, if my dream could find him again. I stepped away, searching for sweeter air. What was up with all the odors? I couldn't remember ever smelling stuff in a dream before.

The pile of blankets moved and a pair of bare feet popped out. Nurse shuffled over to the side of the bed. "You're supposed to be sleeping, you are."

"I am," came a muffled reply.

"I am, she says." Nurse adjusted her apron, then spoke again to the pile of blankets. "How can you be asleep if you just said, 'I am.'"

"Exactly so. I must be talking in my sleep." The feet retreated back under the covers.

"Sassy little whelp," Nurse muttered. "Well, get on in," she told me, pointing to the bed. "Lady Capulet wants you to nap as well. But watch yourself. Your bedmate's been known to bite." Nurse handed me a pillow.

The lump moved over. I kicked off my slippers, picked up the edge of the bottom blanket, and crawled in. A hand pulled the pile over my head, trapping me in a toasty cocoon. "Shhh," Juliet whispered in my ear. I couldn't see her but she scooted over until her shoulder pressed against mine. Nurse shuffled about, then both she and the chair groaned as she sat down.

"O, what a miserable life," Nurse complained. "Nurse-maid to a terrible, thankless beastie."

Juliet giggled and plunged her feet back out, exposing mine as well.

"Don't think I don't know you're not asleep, because I know you're not asleep, young lady." Nurse's words began to slow. "And it'll be meself that has to listen to her ladyship when she finds that you've got bags under your eyes from not taking your nap. Not me fault . . ." Her voice faded, followed by loud snoring.

Juliet giggled again and threw back the blankets. I found myself face-to-face with the character I had played for the last six months.

Ten

"How stands your disposition to be married?"

JULIET CAPULET HAD about the worst case of bedhead I had ever seen. Masses of kinky brown hair shot up in the air in a chaotic defiance of gravity.

"I am not sleepy," she informed me.

"Me neither." How could I be? I was already asleep.

Juliet slid out of bed and tiptoed over to Nurse. As the exhausted woman breathed deeply, Juliet tied Nurse's apron strings to the chair's back rungs. She had to stop for a moment, to stifle a giggle. Nurse shifted her hips but kept sleeping. Juliet tied a front knot across Nurse's roly-poly belly.

Juliet tiptoed back to the bed and pulled off a blanket. "Nurse is such a bother," she whispered to me. "Bosses me around all day. Do this, do that. Come hither, go thither." Her voice was somewhat boyish, the way mine sounds when I have a cold. We sat cross-legged on the floor, beneath a shuttered window. "I'm Juliet."

"I'm Mimi."

Cracks in the wooden shutters let in bits of daylight.

Juliet stared at me with large brown eyes, like I was some kind of alien. She had a round face with a clump of freckles on the ridge of her nose. Not scattered like most freckles, just kind of dumped in one place. She wasn't at all like Fernando's Juliet—full-lipped and perfect. Nor was she like Hollywood's Juliet—graceful and angelic. She looked *real*, the way a girl is supposed to look. A real girl, cute and full of energy, like she'd be more comfortable in soccer gear than in her long nightgown that dripped with lace and bows. But what I most noticed was how young she was.

She reached up and took a little knife from the windowsill. She started poking the wall with the blade, flaking off pieces of plaster. "Are you going to the party?"

"If your mother can find me a dress," I told her.

"My parents are giving this bothersome party because they want me to get married." She stabbed the wall extra hard. "I am not yet fourteen and they want me to get married. Mother had a baby by fifteen." She scrunched her nose.

"At fifteen?" I asked, horrified, remembering the Oprah show about the girls in Africa whose insides got torn apart because they gave birth too young. I shuddered.

Nurse snored loudly, her chin resting on her overflowing cleavage.

Juliet leaned close. "Mother says that Paris will seek my hand tonight. He is a member of the prince's family and twice my age. I am to marry an old man!" She flicked another piece of plaster. Multiple holes covered the wall, from previous attacks. "She said that marrying her only daughter into the prince's family is an excellent route for the Capulet name. But what she really wants is his money."

"Have you told your mother you don't want to get married?" I asked.

Juliet frowned. "What good would that do? She does not care what I want. She only cares about the Capulet name."

How painfully familiar.

Two daughters, both alike in dignity, forced down paths of their mothers' choosing. I had never realized the similarity between Juliet's and my plight. It made perfect sense that my subconscious had selected this story for my dreamworld.

"My mother's the same way," I confided. "She only cares . . . cared about me becoming an actor. She owned a theater in Manhattan. She wanted me to follow in her footsteps."

Juliet stopped stabbing and widened her eyes. "You are an actor? On the stage?" I nodded. "A troupe was here last month. They performed some of the Greek tragedies. It looked like so much fun. They get to travel the world. I am not allowed to leave the house except to attend church or family gatherings." She leaned closer. "Your husband allows you to act?"

"I don't have a husband."

Juliet narrowed her eyes. "Did your husband die?"

I shook my head. "I've never been married. You don't have to get married in Manhattan if you don't want to."

For a moment she sat speechless, letting the knife fall to the floor. "Amazing! I want to go there. Will you take me there?"

"Uh, I really don't want to go back there. How about we go somewhere else? How about Paris or London?" Why not? It was a dream, after all.

"You do not wish to go home?" She smiled. "Then we shall run away together."

Nurse farted and momentarily woke herself up. Juliet and I froze until she had nodded back to sleep. I giggled because, by far, it was the loudest fart I had ever heard.

Juliet stood and began to pace, her crazy hair bobbing to and fro. "What am I talking about? My mother will never let me run away. She would send her guards after me even to the far corners of the world." She stomped her foot. "And tonight I have to go to that wretched party and meet the old windbag who wants to marry me. He spied me last month when I attended a cousin's wedding and claims he fell in love with me at first sight. He said I am as beautiful as one of his roses. He is obsessed with flowers. Spends all his time in his garden. He told my father that there could be no lovelier addition to his flower collection than me. He will probably stick me in a vase." She shuddered. "I must find a way to make him *not* in love with me so he will withdraw his proposal."

I considered myself the expert on making guys *not* in love. All those plays, all those leading men, and not one, except Troy, had ever asked me on a date—if you count kissing lessons a date. Aunt Mary said that my family name made me unapproachable and my mother, who intimidated everyone, served as a major roadblock. Aunt Mary said my lack of dates had nothing to do with who I was inside. I didn't believe her. If somebody really wanted to date me, they would have found a way. Even if it meant dealing with my mother. Even if it meant climbing an enemy's balcony.

"Will you help me to get rid of Paris?" Juliet asked.

Getting rid of Paris sounded like a lot of fun. He's such a butthead in the play. "Sure, but how?"

"I am not certain. I only know that I do not wish to be his pretty little flower."

"Then why not become an ugly weed?" I suggested.

Her mischievous expression returned. "Brilliant!" she exclaimed, clapping her hands in glee. Nurse remained in a stupor as Juliet opened a door onto a small balcony. *The* balcony. Light spilled in and a warm breeze drifted through the room. I discarded the blanket and stood next to her as she leaned over a railing. "Boy," she called, trying to restrain her voice. The boy from the apricot orchard sat on a crate in the street below. He scrambled to his feet.

"Yes," he answered, giving me a little wave.

"Do you know the man named Paris who lives in the villa at the edge of town? The one with all the flowers?" The boy nodded. "I should like you to go to him. Tell him that you overheard some women in the market. Tell him that you thought he might be interested in what you overheard because it concerned Juliet Capulet. Then pretend that you are too embarrassed to continue because it concerns a delicate matter. He will urge you to speak." She snickered and looked over her shoulder. Nurse snored on. Juliet tiptoed back into the room, removed a coin from the wooden chest, then tiptoed back to the balcony.

"What shall I tell him, my lady?" the boy asked.

"Tell him that the women were discussing a boil, the likes of which has never before been seen. And that this boil resides on Juliet's bottom." She paused for a minute, strumming her fingers as she thought. "Tell him that it is a *recurring* boil that bursts forth with every *full moon*." She snickered again. "Tell him that Juliet is in such pain that she cannot dance, so the party has been canceled. Did you get all that?"

The boy nodded. "Juliet has a boil on her bottom, the likes of which has never before been seen. It bursts forth with every full moon."

"Yes, but don't forget that Juliet cannot dance so the party has been canceled."

"Right. Canceled."

"Remember that you overheard this at the market." Juliet tossed the coin. The boy caught it and ran off. "He is a good, loyal boy," she told me. "He will tell no one that I sent him. We shall see what Paris thinks of girls with boily bottoms."

I decided then and there that I really liked her. She was the crazy little sister I never had. A rebel at heart. She was my alter ego.

The bedroom door opened and Lady Capulet entered. The room's temperature instantly dropped a few degrees. "Why are you two not napping? Move away from that breeze," she hissed. "You shall both come down with fevers."

Juliet closed the balcony door as two servants entered the bedroom, each carrying a gown. "Put those on the bed," her ladyship directed. Then she leaned over Nurse and called her name. Nurse awoke with a jolt and kicked out her legs so hard that she kicked Lady Capulet in the shins.

"Get up, get up," Lady Capulet ordered, waving her hands as Nurse struggled to free herself from the tied apron strings. "What ever is the matter with you? Are you having some sort of fit? Go on, get out of here. I wish to speak with my daughter and our guest."

Juliet smirked as Nurse slammed the chair against the wall a few times, finally freeing herself. "Beastie," Nurse mumbled as she and the servants fled.

"Daughter," Lady Capulet said. "I bring wonderful news. We have concluded negotiations with Paris and it is agreed by all parties that the wedding shall take place as soon as possible—perhaps by week's end."

Juliet's mouth hung open in disbelief. But she didn't say a word. Perhaps she had learned, as had I, that some arguments could never be won. Lady Capulet kissed her daughter's forehead. "Prepare yourself to meet your future husband." She tried to pat down Juliet's hair but it stubbornly refused to oblige. "I shall send the hairdresser."

Juliet did not move for a very long time after her mother had left. Her arms hung limp and she stared at the floor.

"Juliet?" I asked, touching her shoulder.

"I am to marry a man I have not even met." She started to breathe quickly.

"There's still hope. Remember the boil."

"I feel strange," she said. "I feel like the room is getting smaller. I feel so trapped." She flung the balcony door open, gasping for air.

"Calm down," I told her, as I had so often told myself. "It will be okay." But would it? If my dream followed the traditional story line, then Juliet was doomed to commit suicide in a few days' time. In that case she *was* trapped—trapped in a Shakespearean tragedy. However, this was my dream, so I wouldn't let that happen.

"My heart's beating so quickly. Why must they force me to marry?" She clung to the rail. Her hands began to shake and her jaw began to tremble. Tears rolled down her flushed cheeks. She opened her mouth, taking in shallow breaths.

Wow. It was like watching myself. "You're having a panic attack," I realized, clutching her hands.

"Panic? Yes, I do feel a sense of panic. I cannot catch my breath."

"Listen to my voice. We have to slow your breathing or you'll hyperventilate." I started to chant my centering mantra, over and over. "Do it with me," I insisted and she did. *Om ya, om ya, om ya*, until her breathing slowed and we both sank to the balcony's stone floor.

She cried for a bit and I kept hold of her hands. Shakespeare may have created this predicament but I was the one who could change it. I wasn't going to let this girl kill herself. Even if it meant that I had to stay in this dream for a very long time. I was determined not to wake up until Juliet got her happy ending. One of us deserved a happy ending.

"I do not wish to get married," she pleaded, squeezing my fingers.

"We'll come up with a plan," I assured her. "I don't know what it is yet, but I'm going to help you get out of this engagement."

Eleven

"Why, then the world's mine oyster."

THERE WAS NO way to get around it. I had to pee.

Juliet had burrowed beneath her blankets once again, insisting it was the best place for her to think. "If I lived in Manhattan, I would never have to get married. Are you certain that you do not wish to go back to Manhattan?"

"Totally certain. I'm sure there are other places we can go." I looked under the bed for a chamber pot but found only dustballs and a slumbering brown mouse. What the heck did they do in the sixteenth century? I remembered reading that in the Middle Ages, people stuck their butts out holes in castle walls. No way was I doing that. Dream or no dream, I had my pride.

"Juliet?"

"Escape will be impossible with my mother's henchmen following us. Even a nunnery could not protect me." She punched the blanket with her foot.

"Juliet?" I squirmed like a first-grader. "Where's the bathroom?"

"I refuse to share a bed with that old man!"

"Juliet, I need to *urinate*."

"You need to piddle? The closestool is behind the screen, in the corner."

I hadn't noticed the screen, painted the same off-white as the walls. It concealed a stool with a hole cut in the center and a ceramic pot held beneath, like a toddler's training potty, only larger. I could deal with that.

As the pee filled the pot, doubts trickled into my mind. The sensation felt warm and relieving—like the real thing. What if I was actually peeing? Oh my God, did that mean that I had just wet myself in the real world? How totally embarrassing, especially if Troy had witnessed the act. He had already seen me vomit. Just great. I couldn't blame wetting my pants on bad clams.

Wait a minute. Falling in a dream feels real, but the dreamer isn't actually falling. So it's possible I wasn't actually peeing.

But doubt lingered. Dreamers don't wonder if they're actually dreaming or not. When asleep, they accept the dream as reality. Yet there I sat, a nagging doubt tapping me on the head.

"Oh Mimi, even if I had money, which I do not, and even if I had a horse and carriage, which I have not, two women cannot travel alone. We'd be noticed immediately."

"Then we'll dress as boys," I suggested, grateful to have a distraction from my confusing thoughts.

"As boys?"

"Why not? It's a classic theme. Even Shakespeare uses it."

"Shakespeare?"

The room filled with voices. I straightened my dress and emerged from behind the screen. Two serving women placed bowls of water on the bedroom table while two others pulled Juliet from bed—a bit roughly, I noticed. Juliet pouted and squirmed while they washed her face with small towels and brushed her hair. Two more women began to remove her nightgown.

"No thanks," I insisted as one approached me with a washcloth. "I can do it myself."

"I never get to dress myself," Juliet pouted, standing in a sort of tank top and slip. "Never!" she yelled in a woman's face. "I suppose that the Capulets of Manhattan are allowed to dress themselves."

Not this Capulet. At some point in my development, probably when my breasts refused to fill anything larger than an A cup, my mother decided that I should look exactly like Audrey Hepburn. "She's a classic," she had told me, filling my closet with trench coats and sleeveless dresses. "And she's dead so you can't upset her if you look exactly like her." My crisp style garnered me a few mentions on the best-dressed list but I didn't care. It wasn't *my* style.

"I don't get to dress myself either," I commiserated.

Juliet tapped her foot irritably as an attendant pulled a long white shirt over her head. "That hurts. Stop tugging on my hair. I shall scream if you keep tugging like that." All of a sudden I felt bad for Fernando, recalling all the times I had whined while he had simply done his job. I slipped off my filthy costume and took the shirt handed to me. The servants widened their eyes at the sight of my bra and panties, but said nothing. Juliet was too busy squirming and complaining to notice. "You are all wretched and I hate every one of you," she told them.

With the shirts in place, we slipped on long underskirts. Then the attendants held up our dresses. Juliet's was green, mine was blue, both with square necklines and ribbons for cinching the waist. "At least Father doesn't make us wear Capulet colors to all parties," Juliet said, grimacing as the cinching proceeded. I let the attendants help with my dress, since it was such a complicated procedure. The sleeves were huge puffy things that had to be attached at the armholes with laces. This took forever and my arms got tired as I held them aloft. Why would my arms get tired in a dream? And why did I feel so hungry? Nagging doubt returned but still, I ignored it. A party awaited, with music and dancing and guys to dance with. I had attended tons of charity events over the years but never unchaperoned. I was going to cut loose tonight, maybe try some wine, maybe even do some slow dancing with that gorgeous Benvolio. In Shakespeare's story, he sneaks into the party with Romeo in tow.

Oh, that's right. Romeo was going to be there, too. That would definitely complicate things, as we all know. A happy ending was still my goal so I'd just have to do my best to keep Romeo and Juliet apart.

"How dare they!" Lady Capulet screamed, popping into the room like a champagne cork. Her hair hung loose and her sleeves had not yet been attached. She held a piece of paper in one hand and a bouquet of roses in the other, which she shook so vigorously that red petals flew about. "Those monstrous, motley-minded Montagues are at it again." She flapped the paper in the air. "They told Paris that my daughter has a boil on her bottom!"

Juliet gasped, playing it cool. I, on the other hand, would have crumbled under that woman's interrogation. One gaze from her and I'd give up name, rank, and serial number. "Mother, such unkind words."

Lady Capulet raised her eyebrows. "You don't, do you? Have a boil, that is."

"Mother!" Juliet stomped her foot, crunching the fingers of the poor attendant who was trying to tie her shoes. "How would a Montague know what is or what is not on my bottom?"

"How indeed!" Lady Capulet thrust the paper at me. "Paris sent this. Read it aloud, Mimi. I am too distraught."

I took the little note card. A capital *P* sat in the upper corner, embossed in gold. The writing swirled in delicate loops and curlicues. Aroma of rose drifted off the page.

My dearest Lady Capulet,

> *How saddened I am to hear of your daughter's unfortunate condition. Boils can be dreadfully unpleasant, especially if they sprout on such a delicate derriere as I can only imagine your daughter possesses. I would be happy to recommend a skilled surgeon if lancing becomes necessary. In no way does this lessen my*

esteem for your daughter. Even the most beautiful rose
can succumb to a case of blackspot now and then.

I am disappointed that the party is canceled.
Please send word as soon as Juliet is recovered so that
we can move forward with marriage arrangements.
Consider these flowers as a token of my admiration.

Yours most respectfully, Paris Calchetto IV

"He thinks my daughter is spotted. Spotted! And that
the party is canceled." Lady Capulet tore the note from my
hands and crumpled it. "I will send word immediately that
the boil is a vicious lie and that the party is not canceled.
Damn those malignant Montagues." She threw the bouquet
on the table. "Use the rose perfume. Paris prefers roses. And
where is the hairdresser? Your hair will ruin us all."

As soon as her mother had left, Juliet kicked over one of
the stools. Then she pushed through the flock of attendants.
"Everyone be gone!" A woman handed me a pair of leather
booties with wooden heels, then followed the others from the
bedroom. "Rose perfume," Juliet complained, throwing the
bouquet across the room. "I shall not smell like one of his
roses. I shall smell the opposite of a rose." Juliet had clearly
bounced back from her panic attack. She didn't seem to suffer from depression, unlike poor Romeo. She had simply
freaked out, and who could blame her? Her situation totally
stank. But Juliet Capulet was not the kind of person willing
to give in to despair. Her spunky nature wouldn't allow it.

She opened the chest, took out a coin, then stomped onto the balcony, her wooden heels clacking like castanets. "Boy!" she called. Dusk had come but the air still held summer's warmth. Despite the growing darkness, the boy had returned to his crate. He eagerly leaped to his bare feet.

"I did what you asked, my lady."

"Yes, excellent work. Now I want you to go to the market and purchase some onions—the ones with green stems."

"The market is closed, my lady. But my mother has onions in her garden. How many would you like?"

"Three. Three should do it." Juliet tossed him the coin and he ran off, just like last time. "Paris may be willing to forgive a boil, but we shall see what he thinks of onion breath." She wrapped her arm around my waist in a conspiratorial hug. I ate up her rebellion like a starving French peasant.

"Ladies!" a voice sang, startling us both. A man wearing a floppy scarlet hat entered Juliet's bedroom. In fact, his entire outfit blazed scarlet, from his tight-fitting doublet to his even tighter leggings. Two servants followed, carrying a bench. Nurse entered as well, tottering under an enormous basket filled with ribbons and combs.

"Oh, no," Juliet whispered. "My mother's hairdresser."

The scarlet man bowed gracefully, swirling his hand through the air like a cook whisking egg whites. He smiled patronizingly. "My dear little poppy. You should not scowl like that. Your scowls make Vincento crazy."

Juliet scowled harder, thrusting out her bottom lip like a bulldog. Vincento shook his head with disapproval when he sized me up. "Two heads of unruly hair that Vincento must tame. Nurse, fetch some wine. Vincento must arouse his muse."

Nurse set down the basket and departed with a huff, muttering that if anyone needed wine and arousing, it was she.

Vincento motioned for Juliet and me to sit on the bench. He grabbed a comb that looked like a barbecue fork. "I shall create my latest invention—the Leaning Tower of Hair."

Crap! How many hours had I spent having my hair and makeup done? I wondered. What was keeping me from walking down the hall rather than sitting on that bench? Why should I torture myself? I could go anywhere I wanted in this dream. I could pull my hair back with one of those ribbons and say, "See ya later" to Juliet. "I'm outta here."

But I didn't want to leave her. I had promised I would help. Even if she was just an unconscious vision, I felt connected to her. I'm well aware of how strange that sounds, but it's the truth.

Nurse came in and slammed a carafe of red wine on the table. "It's half empty," Vincento complained.

"I know nothing," Nurse said, wiping her mouth with the back of her puffy hand. She hurried from the room. Vincento guzzled the remaining wine, then began to work his magic. Using two wooden structures, odd bits of wig, and our own hair, he combed and braided and wove until towerlike appendages sprouted atop our heads. The weight made me tilt slightly to the left. Vincento complimented himself as he circled us, patting the ridiculous towers as if they were poodles.

But it didn't end there. Vincento's work continued as

dusk turned to darkness and cicadas started harmonizing outside the window. He applied thick white makeup to our faces, necks, and hands. Had he been trained by the circus? When he had finished with me, I went and sat in Nurse's chair.

I didn't intend to fall asleep but that's what happened while waiting for Juliet. Visions of Troy floated through my head. He didn't pull back from our kiss. He didn't smirk at my virginal lips. In my dream we just kept kissing and kissing and kissing.

Imagine my confusion when I woke up from the Kissing Dream to find that I was still in the Verona Dream. Like a reflection of a mirror in a mirror in a mirror. I woke up! How could I have just woken up? And that is when the nagging doubt erupted like an aggravated boil. "Hello?" nagging doubt screamed. "Haven't you figured it out yet?"

I pinched my arm. It hurt. I pinched again, so hard that my fingernail broke the skin. I bled. I felt my pulse. My heart beat wildly.

I was awake.

"Magnificent," Vincento said, bowing to Juliet. "You are ready. Go to the party and let everyone bask in your beauty. Tomorrow, Vincento's Leaning Tower will be all the rage."

As soon as he and his servants had left, Juliet stood over me. "Are you ill?" she asked, puzzled by my queasy expression.

I didn't move. Juliet's pupils dilated. A pulse beat at the side of her neck. If I pricked her, she would also bleed. Juliet Capulet in the flesh. My God. I was awake! I had been awake the entire time. The upside-down ride on the guard's shoulder had hurt because it had really happened. The nurse had smelled bad because she actually smelled bad. The pee had felt warm because pee comes out that way. Holy cow! I was awake.

How amazing is that?

Juliet rushed to her mirror. While I thought we looked like drag queens, she had a sixteenth-century reaction. "Oh no!" she cried. "We are irresistible." She rushed to the balcony, her tower swaying with each footstep. "Boy!" she called, reaching her hands into the darkness. An onion flew through the air, then a second and a third. She caught each one, then tore off the green stalks and tucked them under her dress sash. She cupped the bulbs in her hands. "Like precious pearls, plucked from an oyster," she whispered. "Mother will kill me if she finds out."

And my mother would kill me if I missed my performance.

Which is what I was doing since I was . . . AWAKE!

Forget her. Forget the theater. Forget everything. Certainly I could have returned to Nurse's chair to fret about the how, where, and why of my situation. Forget that. Something magical had happened to me.

I stood, trying to keep my balance with the stupid hairdo. Happiness flowed through my body. What an adventure. What a fabulous, amazing thing to actually be standing next to Juliet Capulet, no matter how weird we looked. And I was about to go to a party where no one would know my real name.

Juliet stood so close that our towers knocked together.

She started to giggle, a sound that fed my euphoria. Juliet Capulet, famous love-struck heroine, was about to eat a handful of raw onions so a man would find her disgusting. I felt more mischievous than I ever had, like we were about to pull a Halloween prank. But what we were really about to do was to mess up some parental plans.

Now why hadn't Mr. Shakespeare thought of that?

"Come on," I said, tucking the bulbs beneath my sash. "Let's go make a man fall out of love."

Twelve

"O' she doth teach the torches to burn bright!"

Equipped with a hunger for rebellion, green onion stalks, and three onion bulbs, we made our way to the party hall. It probably won't surprise you to learn that things didn't go as planned. I'm eager to tell you what happened, but I'd like to set the stage first because the Capulets' hall deserves attention.

It lay in the center of Capulet House, fed at one end by a corridor from which a constant stream of white-frocked servants flowed. At the other end, two immense doors opened to an inner courtyard that was ornamented with Greco-Roman columns and marble nudes. A huge tapestry, bearing the Capulet crest, hung on the western wall. A quartet of musicians played beneath, wearing brown hats that looked like overturned soup bowls. I recognized their instruments because we used them in the Wallingford production—a flute, a mandolin, a drum, and a clavichord. A balcony jutted from the eastern wall, from which Lord and Lady Capulet surveyed the festivities like chaperones at a school dance. The arched ceiling held dozens of chandeliers, their candles twinkling like the night sky.

I peeked over the shoulder of a woman nestled beneath a peacock-feathered hat. Servants squeezed between mingling party guests, offering treats from silver platters. Guests wearing black masks like Renaissance superheroes danced in the center of the hall.

A servant handed us our masks and we tied them on, careful not to topple the Leaning Towers. Laughter and conversation drifted around the edges of the hall as did a courtyard breeze, stirring up the fog of hot, perfumed bodies.

How far away New York City seemed. How far away my troubles seemed as I plucked a stuffed egg from a passing tray. I gobbled up the creamy treat, rich with soft cheese and yolk, flavors not found in those paper containers of low-fat meals back home in our refrigerator. I plucked a marzipan-covered apricot from another tray and tapped my feet in time to the lively music. This was going to be fun.

As we crossed the great hall, all eyes turned our way. With this particular entrance I felt no stage fright—only anticipation. Would Benvolio be here? Just thinking about him set a blush across my powdered cheeks.

Teetering under the weight of our hairdos like two Weebles, Juliet and I squeezed through the crowd. As ridiculous as I looked, it didn't take long for me to realize that ridiculous was *in*. Women had coiled their hair like horns and men wore absurdly huge codpieces shaped like all sorts of creatures. A codpiece, by the way, was a fashionable item in those days, worn over a man's privates like a fancy athletic cup. In the same way that modern women try to make their breasts look bigger with padded bras . . . well, you get the picture.

Juliet ignored all questions about her new hairdo as she led me through a maze of bodies. Our destination, I realized, was the balcony where her parents stood, dressed in matching outfits like those couples who square-dance together. His golden cape, her golden dress, his ruby doublet, her ruby gloves. But a man stepped forward and purposefully blocked our path. His golden codpiece was shaped like a cobra, arched and poised to strike. "Whom do we have here?" he asked curtly.

Juliet rolled her eyes then tried to push past him, but he wouldn't budge. "Tybalt, I don't have time for your games."

Now here's an interesting character from Shakespeare's play. Tybalt is Juliet's cousin, nephew to Lady Capulet. Actors love this role because he is the quintessential bad guy—serious, hot-tempered, and deadly. Toward the end of the play, Romeo kills him in a sword fight.

Tybalt held himself as stiffly as a military officer and narrowed his eyes at me. "I'm Mimi," I told him. "Juliet's cousin. Yours as well, I suppose."

"My aunt told me of the robbery. Describe the Montagues who robbed you and I shall personally chop them into pieces and feed them to my bulldog. I live for the moment when I can slice Montague flesh." He spoke matter-of-factly about slicing flesh. A real sociopath. He stepped around Juliet and pressed his codpiece against my leg. "Dance with me."

"Uh, sorry. Juliet and I are busy."

"Busy?" he said, curling his upper lip. "You refuse me?" He poked me again with his gold-covered wiener. How totally rude. I hoped that Romeo would kill him right away so he would stop bothering me.

Thankfully, another woman called out Tybalt's name and Juliet and I made our escape. "I detest him," Juliet told me as we started up the balcony stairs. "He tried to kiss me once. Forced himself on me." She stopped halfway up the stairs. "There's Paris," she whispered, pulling the onion stalks from her sash.

A gangly man stood between Juliet's parents. He wasn't attractive at all. Sort of soft in the features and basically chinless. And way too skinny. His long neck poked out of his collar like a Popsicle stick.

Juliet ducked behind my skirt to hide from the Capulets' prying eyes. She shoved some green stalks into her mouth and started chewing as fast as she could. "Juliet," her father called. She swallowed, shoved in more greens, and pointed at my sash. I pulled out the onion bulbs.

"Juliet," her mother insistently sang.

She couldn't chew any faster or she'd choke. I pressed my fingernail into one of the onions, freeing some of its juice. "I'll dab this behind your ears," I told her. She smiled and nodded. Even with her cheeks inflated like a chipmunk's she managed to shove in an onion bulb.

"Do my neck, too," she mumbled.

"Juliet!" Lady Capulet squawked.

With her mother about to swoop, Juliet devoured the second onion but one still remained. I looked around frantically, then shoved it into my tower of hair. "Let us see how he likes this flower's stench," she said before stepping onto the balcony.

"My dearest lady," Paris greeted. "I am honored that we should finally meet." He kissed the palm of her hand. His tongue darted over his lips, tasting the onion, no doubt.

"You are enchanting this evening," Lord Capulet told his daughter, rapidly blinking tiny eyes that looked like finger pricks in risen dough. He sniffed the air curiously. "How strange a smell."

Before he could detect the source, I stepped forward. "Hello. I'm Mimi, of the Manhattan Capulets. Thanks so much for inviting me to your party. I've never tasted such delicious stuffed eggs before. And those must be the finest musicians in all of Italy."

Lord Capulet beamed. "You have a keen palate as well as a discerning ear. Marks of good breeding. Manhattan, you say?"

"Juliet, would you do me the honor of a dance?" Paris asked, bending his long neck to one side. Juliet curtsied and presented him with an exaggerated grin. Green stringy bits dangled from her front teeth. Lady Capulet gasped and wildly pointed to her own teeth. Juliet ignored her.

"I should love to dance," Juliet replied, leaning as close to Paris as possible and exhaling extra hard on *dance*.

Paris took a step back as Lady Capulet pulled her daughter aside. "What have you been eating?" she demanded in a tone best described as a whispered shriek.

"Whatever do you mean, Mother?" Juliet asked, her

onion breath enveloping the balcony. She turned and took Paris's arm. "Let us dance the night away." Paris scrunched his nose and led his wife-to-be down the stairs. He could barely hide his repulsion. I wiggled my toes excitedly. Success was at hand.

For the briefest of moments I stood next to Juliet's parents. Lord Capulet, still sniffing the air, checked his own underarms and was about to check his wife's but she pushed him away. I had no desire to hang out with those two. I peered over the railing. A servant headed past the stairs with a tray of miniature tarts. The realization that I was wide awake struck me again as my mouth watered. Maybe I should have taken the time to consider my situation. Maybe I should have found a dark corner where I could have thought things through. Where exactly was I, if not in a dreamworld? How had I gotten there? What was to become of me?

But again, I ignored all those questions. You see, when faced with magic, it's easier to accept than you might imagine. I had been waiting for something in my life to change. I had been whining about my life for so long I could barely stand to be with myself. I let the moment envelop me. No worries about stepping onto a stage. No worries about what the future would bring. Only that moment mattered as I stood in some kind of alternate reality, and all I really wanted at that moment was one of those tarts.

With a growling stomach, I lifted my dress's heavy hem and took the stairs as quickly as possible. "Excuse me," I said, pushing through guests, trying to catch the servant. But as hard as I tried, the tray remained just out of reach.

"Excuse me. Sorry," I repeated, having stepped on someone's boot.

"The fault was mine for having placed my foot in the path of a hungry woman."

A masked face stared back at me. Black curly hair cascaded down a dark brown neck and my body temperature shot up ten degrees. "Lady of the Orchard," Benvolio said. How could he possibly recognize me with this freaky hair and mask? But he had. He took a huge risk in speaking to me in public. How did he know I wouldn't turn him in? I might have yelled out, "Montague! A Montague has sneaked into our party!" and Tybalt would have rushed right over and impaled him with his golden codpiece. But of course, I did no such thing.

"Your beauty makes the torches burn brighter," he said.

In Shakespeare's play Romeo delivers that line to Juliet. Maybe Benvolio had stolen the line but I didn't care. I felt kind of woozy, but in a good way. Benvolio reached over my shoulder and whisked two tarts from a passing tray, presenting me with one. "Thanks," I said. He popped the other into his mouth, focusing his sultry gaze entirely on me. It's difficult to eat when someone's staring at you in a lusty way. I nibbled on the pecan-filled crust as if I had no appetite at all. I didn't want bits of food between my teeth.

"I have a dilemma, Mimi from Manhattan. You are a Capulet and yet, I cannot bring myself to hate you."

"I don't hate you either."

He smiled. "Then will you dance with me?"

"Um, okay." You'd think after performing Shakespeare

most of my life, I'd be able to express myself a bit more eloquently.

As he led me toward the other dancers, I shoved the rest of the tart in my mouth. I was starving! I grabbed another tart along the way. Benvolio wasn't wearing one of those stupid codpieces, which made me like him even more. On the dance floor, I ended up standing next to Juliet. Paris had scrunched up his face as if in pain.

The ladies formed a center circle, the men formed an outer circle. The steps were easy—four left, dainty jump jump, four right, dainty jump jump. Benvolio guided me and my nerves melted under his confident touch. Paris coughed as Juliet continued to bombard him with her breath. She leaned close to tell him about her boil. "It's inflamed," she said. "Near to bursting." She giggled, obviously pleased when he actually plugged his nose and came up with an excuse to stop dancing.

Benvolio grabbed my waist and lifted me off the ground, which totally took me by surprise. I giggled like a pathetic airhead. I hoped the next dance would be slower, so I could press against his chest the way I had pressed against Troy's in the Wallingford production. As we smiled at each other, I tried to remember what I knew about Benvolio. He didn't die in the play, so that was a good thing. He was loyal to Romeo and often proved to be the voice of reason. As if reading my mind he said, "I wish Romeo would come and dance. But he insists on moping in the garden."

"Oh, that's too bad." Honestly, I didn't care about Romeo at that moment. The Wallingford burden had been lifted from my shoulders. I was someone else. That moment belonged to me and my Italian hunk. So caught up in my euphoria, I didn't notice what was transpiring on the balcony until Lady Capulet's voice pierced the room.

"What have you done?" she screamed at Juliet.

The music stopped. Paris was nowhere to be seen.

"Keep playing," Lord Capulet ordered the musicians. They started up again.

Straining to see what was going on, I caused a traffic jam in the dance circle. Lady Capulet's face contorted with rage and she began to pull Juliet down the stairs. Juliet grimaced as her mother yanked her arm. She was in huge trouble. She'd probably get grounded. I needed to explain.

I started toward her. "I cannot follow you," Benvolio told me, taking my hand. "I must not go anywhere near Lady Capulet."

"I've got to see if Juliet's okay."

"I understand." He smiled sweetly, then kissed my hand. "Until we meet again."

My entire body felt that single kiss. Reluctantly, I slid my fingers from his. "Yes. Until then."

Struggling to get through the crowd, I lost sight of Juliet and her mother but figured that they would head to her bedroom. The uncomfortable wooden heels clunked as I stumbled up the marble stairs, twisting my ankle twice. Nurse stood outside Juliet's door, still in her stained apron, pacing fretfully. Juliet's sobs penetrated the walls. "Oh dear," Nurse said, wringing her hands. "She's in dire trouble, she is. Don't go in there. Her ladyship's temper is not fit for delicate ears."

"Mother, please!" I heard.

I went in anyway.

Lady Capulet held Juliet by the shoulders. The Leaning Tower had tumbled over and Juliet's black mask lay on the floor. "How dare you do such a thing?" her mother shrieked. "You have embarrassed the entire family."

I said nothing. I didn't know what to do. I stood in the doorway, trembling.

"Mother . . ." Juliet choked back tears.

"Don't speak to me, ungrateful child." She slapped Juliet's cheek—a sharp sound like the snap of a whip. Juliet gasped and ran to the corner, but Lady Capulet followed. "You will obey your parents. We know what is best for you. *I* know what is best for you." She slapped her again and Juliet fell to the floor.

I wanted to rush forward and hug Juliet. I wanted to slap Lady Capulet myself. My mother had never slapped me— never. But she had called me ungrateful. And she had told me she knew what was best for me countless times. All my resentments bubbled to the surface. *Yell back*, I wanted to shout. *Tell her you don't want to marry him. Tell her to leave you alone. Tell her you hate acting.*

Lady Capulet stood over Juliet, who lay in a heap of velvet and fallen hair. "I shall have to lower my price, if he will still have you. Your father shall beat you for this insolence. Do you hear me?"

Juliet said nothing and, honest to God, Lady Capulet raised her foot, about to kick her daughter.

"Wait," I cried out. If this were Manhattan I'd tell that

woman to lay off. I'd tell her that I would report her to the authorities for child abuse. I'd take Juliet to Los Angeles with me. "It wasn't her idea."

Lady Capulet turned on me like a vicious dog, all teeth and spittle. "What do you know of this?"

"Mother," Juliet begged. "Please, she knows nothing of this."

"Aha!" Lady Capulet said, plucking the last onion from my tower. "I should have known. I thought there was something suspicious about your sudden arrival. How much did the Montagues pay you?"

"What?"

"How much did they pay you to shame my family?" Then she slapped me as well. And it hurt. Even with a thick coat of oil-based makeup to cushion the blow, it hurt.

I don't know if you've ever been hit by another person. I hope not. It's a vile experience because, along with the shock and pain, you feel shamed by the act itself, when it's the hitter who should feel the shame. But Lady Capulet showed no remorse.

Tears stung my eyes and I pressed my hand against my throbbing cheek. "You had no right to do that."

"Mother," Juliet begged again. "It was all my fault. My fault."

This wasn't fun anymore. What happened to all the fun I was supposed to be having? What happened to the great adventure? "Come on, Juliet," I said. "Let's just get out of here."

"Silence!" Lady Capulet grabbed hold of my arm and

109

forced me into the hallway. Anger fueled her surprising strength. I tried to fight her off but couldn't. She locked Juliet's door. I tripped and stumbled as she forced me down the hall. I managed to get a few steps ahead when we reached the marble stairway, fearful that she might push me to my death. Can you die in an alternate reality? She pushed me past the portraits and landscape paintings, past happy party guests, and out the front door of Capulet House, where she planted one final push. I fell into the darkness, landing on cobblestones.

"You are henceforth unwelcome in this house, Mimi of Manhattan, if that is truly your name," she announced. Three Capulet guards pointed swords in my direction. "You are hereby exiled from Capulet land and from Verona as well. I give you one day to be gone. If I catch sight of you after that, your life is mine."

I'm still not sure if it was courage or fear that brought me to my feet. A group of guests mingled in the doorway, snickering and staring through their masks. Darkness crept around me, as did a few drunken men. I suddenly realized my vulnerability.

"What do we have here?" one of them asked, grabbing my waist. I squirmed from his grasp, starting back toward the house but three more guards drew swords. "Come on, love. Give us a kiss."

I had promised Juliet that I would help her. "Juliet!" I called out. My hand throbbed. I had cut it on a sharp cobblestone.

Another drunk tried to grab me. I supposed that girls

disappeared as much in the sixteenth century as in the twenty-first. Gone missing because they had been in the wrong place at the wrong time. I had no choice. I had to leave Juliet. Drunken laughter faded as I ran. Guided by pale moonlight, I found an alley and slipped into its shadows.

Now was definitely the time for contemplation. My train of thought went something like this.

I had already established that this was not insanity or a dream. Clearly I was not the victim of time travel. Romeo and Juliet are fictional characters. While Shakespeare had set his play in an actual historical place and time, and while feuding families had plagued the Italian city-states, the Capulets and Montagues are fictional. So I had not stepped into some sort of wormhole. I had not gone back in time.

Shaking, and breathing way too fast, I thought back to those last moments in Manhattan. Standing by the back-stage exit, I had said something to Troy about wanting to be somewhere else. He had said that I was dressed for Verona and I had said, "Verona is as good a place as any." Then the charm had broken and those ashes . . .

Whether your ashes come from the quill that wrote Hamlet, Twelfth Night, *or* Romeo and Juliet, *they are certain to influence your destiny.*

The charm?

Look, I'm not stupid. I know it took me a long time to figure it out, but put yourself in my shoes, without a smidgen of hindsight. How was I to know?

This was kind of like that movie where the two teenagers get pulled into a black-and-white television show. Who in their right mind could believe such a thing? Yet there I stood in my Renaissance platform shoes, my head pounding beneath a towering head of hair, my leg bruised by a golden codpiece, and my hand bleeding from a sharp cobblestone. I had stepped into Romeo and Juliet's world—their fictional world. It's very strange to think that someone can be transported from the real world into a story. It's unbelievable. We're talking about magic here. Crazy old world magic.

Obviously, the story I had walked into was based on William Shakespeare's *Romeo and Juliet*. But not exactly. No one was speaking Elizabethan English. The people I had met sounded more like me than like Shakespeare. But the framework of his story was all around me.

Then I remembered the Prince of Verona. When I had first arrived, he had been giving a speech in the town square somewhat like the speech he gives in the play. Shortly after the prince's speech, Romeo is supposed to enter the town square and complain to his friends about Rosaline. But that had not happened. I had found him sitting beneath the willow tree. By speaking directly to Romeo, I had changed Shakespeare's story. I had conspired with Juliet, danced with Benvolio, and angered Lady Capulet. I was the reason the story had changed direction. Could I be the reason it sounded different? The ashes had sent me somewhere else just as I had wanted, far away from the Wallingford Theatre. Could this be *my* story, not Shakepeare's?

The alley's dampness seeped through my clothing. Surely an equally important question was, How could I get out of there? And how would I survive in the meantime? Where would I spend the night? What would become of me if Lady Capulet found me? Would Juliet's father truly beat her?

"I told you that I would not meet anyone. No one can take Rosaline's place." Romeo's soft voice floated down the alley.

"You refused to take notice of other girls. You sat in the garden all night."

Romeo and Benvolio walked past the alley. Maybe they would help me? I didn't know who else to turn to.

"Try to cheer up," Benvolio urged his cousin. "How about that strange little song we learned today? That should ease your melancholy." As they strolled off, Benvolio began to sing a tune—a tune I recognized.

"Girl, oh oh oh oh oh oh, girl."

"Wait!" I cried, running after them.

Thirteen

"Holy St. Francis! What a change is here."

"WHERE'D YOU HEAR that song?" I called.

"Mimi?" Benvolio held a small torch above his head. "Mimi, what are you doing outside Capulet House again?" He lowered the torch and gently took my wrist, turning my palm upward. "You are injured. How did this happen?"

Romeo stepped forward and traced his finger along my cheek. "You have been crying," he said softly. "Why do you cry, Lady Mimi? Why are you unhappy?" His tender voice coaxed my tears and I began to blubber in a most embarrassing way.

I tried to explain but I'm not sure I managed a complete sentence, between the outright sobs and runny-nose sniffling. I don't know what was more upsetting to me at that moment—the idea that I had been transported into an alternate reality, or the fact that Lady Capulet had mauled me. At least I felt safe with the Montague cousins.

"Easy," Romeo said, sweetly patting my arm. "Did you just say that you were thrown from Capulet House?"

"And exiled." I wiped my nose on my sleeve.

"Who exiled you?" Benvolio asked.

"Lady Capulet."

He lowered his voice. "You must tell us what she said. Her exact words."

I took a deep breath. "One day, she said. I have one day to get out of Verona or my life is hers."

Benvolio raised the torch and looked around. "Then you must return home. Immediately."

"Yes," Romeo agreed. "Immediately."

"Home? I don't know how to get home." My face contorted as I fought back another bout of sobbing. "I don't have any more ashes." Then I remembered Troy's song. "That song you were just singing. *Girl, oh, oh, oh, oh, oh, oh, girl.* Where did you hear it?"

"I found a man in the square, earlier today," Benvolio said. "A Capulet guard had attacked him. He wore Montague colors so I helped him."

Could it be? "Is he all right?" I asked.

"He's injured but he will survive. I took him to Friar Laurence to treat the wound. The friar gave him herbs to take away the pain and to put him to sleep, but last I checked he had not yet woken. He sang that particular song in his sleep, over and over. Do you know this man? Is he a Montague?"

"Yes." I couldn't believe it. Troy had been transported as well. His was the voice I had heard in the town square. "He's a Montague, from Manhattan."

"The two of you traveled together?" Benvolio narrowed his eyes. "He is your lover?"

"No. Definitely not. I didn't even know he was here until just now."

"He followed you then. He desires you?"

"He must be in love," Romeo said.

"He's not in love with me. He has lots of girlfriends. We're just acquaintances." My mind raced. Troy was here. Maybe he'd have some ideas about getting home. I had to talk to him right away.

Marching feet approached. Romeo and Benvolio pushed me back into the alley. Benvolio blew out his torch and put his hand over my mouth. "Steady," he whispered. Five Capulet guards passed by. We sighed with relief when the last one cleared the alley's entrance. I pushed aside my tower of hair, which had fallen across my forehead. "Your hairstyle will draw attention," Benvolio said. "If we are to walk across the city, then you must blend in." Feeling in the dim moonlight, he began to unwind my hair, pulling out pins and ribbons and dropping them to the ground. Romeo kept a lookout at the alley's entrance as Benvolio removed the wooden frame. What a relief. My hair tumbled free as he worked his fingers through the knots. You know how nice it feels when someone combs your hair? I could have stood in that alley forever, pressing against Benvolio's comforting fingers. "We had best get you to a safe place. All clear?"

"All clear," Romeo replied.

I followed Romeo and Benvolio down the street, away from Capulet House and that crazy woman, but also away from Juliet. Poor girl, locked in that room. "We will take you to Friar Laurence's. He can mend your hand and give you safekeeping," Benvolio said. "And reunite you with your *acquaintance*."

I sensed a touch of jealousy in his voice. Had I more experience at that point in my life, I would have wondered about this jealousy. I would have realized that it was way too early in our "relationship" for jealousy. But you don't know how to spot a possessive man when you've absolutely zero experience with men. But still, I felt safe with him.

The moon rose above the city roofs. Our walk turned out to be a long one, due not to distance but to the fact that Romeo moved like a zombie. He sighed at least a hundred times. His depression made my own look about as serious as a yawn. The journey should have given me plenty of time to ponder my situation, except that Romeo kept interrupting my thoughts. "Why doesn't she love me? I cannot live without her. Griefs of my own lie heavy in my breast," he cried, seizing his chest.

I tried really hard not to judge him, recalling the adage about not judging someone until you've walked in his shoes. People judged me all the time—Clarissa, for example, who thought my life was so perfect and blessed. Every person has a right to be unhappy, to suffer in peace without someone else telling her that she is acting like a spoiled brat. Without a certain someone telling her *constantly* that her life is the stuff that everyone else dreams about. Happiness is not a one-size-fits-all kind of thing. No way was I going to judge Romeo. If he wanted to act like the living dead, then good for him. But a little whining goes a long way. I should know. I'm the Queen of Whining.

"Woe is me," he sighed.

You might think I'm being hard on Romeo. Some of you might have imagined him in a different light. But the truth is, if you go back and read the play, he's a real downer. And way too melodramatic about the whole love thing. I mean, he claims he can't live without Rosaline and then that very night he decides he's in love with Juliet and he can't live without her. But the onion incident had changed the story. Even though Romeo still suffered from a broken heart, the onions had actually saved his life. No Juliet, no suicide. I had changed things for the better. If only I could figure out how to make things better for *me*. I didn't want to live in a sixteenth-century fable forever, especially not with a crazy Capulet after my head.

We walked up the steps of a quaint stone church. "Get those friggin' leeches away from me!" a familiar voice yelled from a second-story window. Inside the sanctuary, Benvolio and Romeo dipped their fingers into a basin of holy water, making the sign of the cross the way Catholics do. It was a simple church, humble by Renaissance standards. A marble statue of St. Francis overlooked the altar where candle nubs burned. At this late hour the benches were empty. We climbed a flight of narrow stone stairs at the back of the church. With no light, I kept close to Benvolio. I could feel his warmth in the damp stairway. When I tripped, he reached back and took my hand. It felt calloused and strong. I remembered that same hand touching my waist at the Capulets' party. Funny how a touch can linger long after the act.

"I said, no leeches!"

Lamplight tumbled from an open door at the top of the stairs. I wanted to rush in but Benvolio held me back. "Is that your acquaintance?" he whispered, his breath tickling my neck like velvet fingers. I peered around his shoulder. Troy lay on a cot, inside the room. I felt overjoyed at seeing him. Even though I had spent the last few months avoiding him and trying to convince myself that I hated him, I wanted to run up and throw my arms around his tanned neck. I wasn't alone after all, in this strange place and time. But Benvolio wouldn't let me pass. "Wait," he whispered. "We should not interrupt the friar's work."

Friar Laurence stood over Troy, holding a bowl and a pair of tweezers. His silver cross reflected light onto Troy's face. "I must apply these to the wound again," the friar said calmly and steadily, as if speaking to a child. "They must be applied at regular intervals."

Troy raised his head from a grungy pillow. "No way. You touch me again and I'll sue!"

"My son, there is no reason to be distraught. The leeches will cleanse your wound." The friar scratched one of his enormous ears with the tweezers. I once read that human ears continue to grow throughout life. The friar's were in overdrive.

"Distraught?" Troy's arm lashed out at the bowl. "I'm pissed. You hear me? Totally pissed! Get those leeches away from me."

The friar was not easily bullied. "I have taken an oath to God to heal the sick. God, in His wisdom, has placed you in my care."

"My insurance doesn't cover freaky friars or leeches." Troy sat up and swung his legs over the cot. A strip of cloth was wrapped around his gray tights, just above his left knee. A dark red stain had spread across the strip. "When my agent finds out you've kept me here, instead of taking me to a hospital, he'll cram a lawsuit up your butt so fast you'll be the one who's . . . *distraught*."

The friar shook his head. "My son, your anger blinds you." He placed the bowl of leeches on a bedside table. "But you have the freedom to choose your own method of healing. If you do not want the leeches, then I shall put them aside." He took a long drink from a blue jug.

"Great! Just get them away from me." Troy rubbed the side of his head. "How'd I get here? What idiot brought me here?" I took a step back, hiding in the hallway's darkness. I was the idiot. They had been my ashes, after all.

"He seems dangerous," Romeo whispered.

"I agree," Benvolio whispered back, adjusting his sword. "Remain here, Mimi, while I speak to him." Benvolio and Romeo entered the room. "I see that you have awoken."

Troy struggled to his feet, keeping his weight on his good leg. Seeing them face to face, I realized that Troy and Benvolio were polar opposites. Benvolio, the winter warrior, dark as night, calm as the morning sea. Troy, the summer prince, golden as the sun, temperamental as the California surf. They glared distrustingly at each other.

"Who are you?" Troy asked.

"I am Benvolio Montague. This is Romeo Montague, my young cousin."

Troy grimaced. "Are you guys some kind of Shakespeare fanatics, like those *Star Trek* freaks who walk around dressed like Klingons? Is this one of those Renaissance fairs?"

"This is the man I told you about," the friar explained, indicating Benvolio. "He found you injured and brought you here."

"Oh yeah? Why didn't you take me to a hospital? What's up with those costumes?"

"I brought you here because you are a fellow Montague," Benvolio explained, placing his hands on his slender hips. "And you had been stabbed by a Capulet guard. Had I left you in the square, he would have returned and made mincemeat of you."

Romeo bowed to Troy then leaned against the wall and sighed.

Troy snorted. "Capulet guard? Fellow Montague? What is this, *Candid Camera* or something? Am I being punk'd?" Then he groaned and fell back onto the cot. "My leg is killing me." He winced as he untied the bandage.

"You were stabbed, my son," Friar Laurence explained.

I leaned forward to see what Troy was gawking at. His wound ran from his knee to his upper thigh. Black stitches crisscrossed it like something from *Frankenstein*. Locks of blond hair fell over Troy's burning eyes. "What have you done to me? I'm supposed to be shooting a beach video tomorrow. I can't wear shorts looking like this. And what's with this bandage?" He waved it. "It looks like an old dish towel. I'll probably get gangrene." Then his face went slack. "What do you want with me?"

"Want with you?" the friar asked.

Romeo slunk to the windowsill and peered into the darkness. "Woe is me," he moaned.

"My child," Friar called softly. "What ails you?"

"He's lovesick," Benvolio explained, helping himself to the blue jug. "He has given me a headache with all his moaning about Rosaline. I'd wager he has given Mimi a headache as well."

"Mimi?" Troy dropped the bandage.

I took a deep breath and stepped into the room.

Fourteen

"Though this be madness,
yet there is method in 't."

"Mimi? What happened to you? What's that white stuff all over your face?" Troy didn't wait for my reply. He turned and pointed a finger at Benvolio. "What's she doing here? You've got no right bringing her here. Look, my label will pay whatever ransom you want—just let her go."

He thought we had been kidnapped. "Uh, Troy . . . ," I said.

He hobbled forward, grimacing with each step, and roughly took my arm. "Don't say a word, Mimi," he whispered. "These guys are nutjobs. Look at them. They're dressed like Renaissance fair nerds and that guy pretending to be the friar says it's 1594. They stabbed me in the leg. There's no telling what else they're capable of, so let me handle this." He was using that parental voice I knew so well.

Fine. Go ahead and make a fool of yourself. My feet were killing me anyway. I sat down on a stool and took off the wooden shoes.

"How much do you want?" Troy repeated.

"While I do not understand your question, I do understand your tone, sir, and I find it insulting." Benvolio wrapped his fingers, slowly and menacingly, around his sword's hilt. Romeo pressed his face against the window's glass, still staring into the darkness.

Troy raised his hands in a motion of surrender. "Okay, okay, let me try that again. What do you want from me?"

"Gratitude would be appropriate, for saving your life."

"Saving my life? Oh, from the Capulet guard. Right." Sarcasm oozed from Troy's mouth. "Sure, thanks a lot."

"Troy, we need to talk," I said. If I could get him alone for a few minutes, I could explain everything. "I know what's going on."

He waved to me to be quiet, as if I were annoying background noise. "Look, whatever your name is . . ."

"Benvolio Montague."

"Right. Look, *Benvolio*, why don't we go outside and get a taxi? My label has a New York office. We can go there and get you a money order or something." He smiled, thinking himself clever. "Come on, what do you say?"

Benvolio raised an eyebrow. "I am beginning to believe that you are insane." He sat on the windowsill next to Romeo, his long leg swaying like a metronome. Romeo whispered Rosaline's name. I walked barefoot across the plank floor and stood in front of Troy, my back to the others.

"Remember how I grabbed my necklace from you and then I opened the door and those ashes flew all over the place?" I spoke as quietly as I could. "Remember when I said I might go somewhere and you said that maybe I should go to Verona?" Troy frowned. "Well, that's exactly what happened. They haven't kidnapped us. My Shakespearean charm brought us here. It's magic."

"Oh, that's very interesting," the friar whispered, having stuck his overgrown ears where they didn't belong. "A charm? Pray tell, did I meet you in the square early this morning?"

"Yes," I told him.

"What are you talking about?" Troy demanded. "What do you mean you met him? I don't remember any ashes."

"You don't remember the ashes? How can you not remember the ashes? We choked on them."

"I am afraid that is a side effect of the herbal tea I fed you," the friar explained, squeezing his rotund self between us. "The tea deadened your pain and put you to sleep so I could perform surgery on your thigh. Your memory will be foggy for a short while, but it will return."

"You drugged me?" Troy's eyes widened. "DRUGGED ME?"

"Excuse us," I said to the friar, pushing a crazed Troy into the corner. "Listen to me."

He wasn't ready to listen. "That guy's a madman. A sadistic butcher. Did you see my leg? I've got to get to a hospital." He turned and faced our *captors*. "Look, just name your price and let us go."

"There is no price, my son. Go, if that is your wish." Friar Laurence tilted his head toward the open door, then took another drink from his blue jug.

Troy raised his eyebrows. Then he grabbed my hand and started hobbling as fast as he could, which wasn't very fast.

"Wait," I said. "You don't understand. They're not holding us for ransom."

"Come on," he urged.

"Mimi?" Benvolio called, sliding off the windowsill. I wrenched my hand free of Troy's and stared into eyes as hot as espresso. "Are you leaving with him? Are you going back to Manhattan?"

"Mimi!" Troy yelled. His voice cracked with impatience.

Was I going back? I didn't quite know how to answer that question. Back to Reginald Dwill's stupid DVD. Back to vomiting onstage. Back to the Theatre Institute with its 100 percent acting classes. Back to tutors and cardboard food and identifying with a cat who spends its days and nights pressed against a window, yearning.

Benvolio looked like he was yearning—for me. He took both my hands and pressed them to his chest, right over his heart. Corny, I know, but the gesture made my legs feel weak. "Will you leave so soon?" he asked softly.

"Mimi!" Troy stood in the doorway.

Benvolio gently kissed the cut on my hand. It had stopped bleeding.

What would it be like to kiss a man from the sixteenth century? Not the close-mouthed kiss that Troy and I knew so well, but the kind of kiss I longed for—a kiss that makes your eyeballs roll backward. A kiss that doesn't leave room for breathing. Would Benvolio nibble on my lower lip? Would his tongue taste like the contents of the blue jug? At that moment, I forgot all about Lady Capulet's threat.

I don't want to go back. I want to stay here with you and

126

become Mrs. Montague. I want to go to parties and sleep next to your naked body and never have to act again.

"Mimi! Are you insane? MOVE IT!"

Benvolio dropped my hands and moved swiftly to the door. "Do not speak to her in that manner." He slammed his fist into Troy's jaw. Troy tumbled into the hallway.

"Stop it," I cried, snapping out of my lovesick trance. Benvolio stepped aside as I helped Troy to his feet. "I need to talk to him," I told Benvolio. "I'll be right back."

"Take a light, my child." The friar handed me a candle. "And wear your shoes. There are rat droppings about."

I slipped back into the shoes. Holding the candle, I led Troy down the winding stairs. He rambled the entire way, stringing sentences together as if he'd had too much coffee. "Have you lost your friggin' mind, playing along with them? Did they drug you, too? Can you believe those costumes? They must have dressed like characters from our play so they could sneak backstage. Then they must have gassed us or something. I don't know. I wish I could remember. What kind of twisted pervert comes up with a scheme like this? That fat guy stuck leeches on me. Leeches! We'll get a taxi then call the police." We reached the bottom step and started past the altar. "And what's up with you letting that creep touch you? You aren't one of those girls who sympathizes with her kidnapper, are you? Because they stabbed me, Mimi. Stabbed me! And I guarantee he'd like to stab you as well, but not with a sword, if you get my drift."

I wasn't going to argue with him. He wouldn't believe a word until he saw the city with his own eyes. After all, look how long it had taken me to figure things out—and I have more than half a brain. I pushed open the church's heavy wooden door and we stepped into darkness.

Darn it! It was too dark to see anything. The moon had disappeared behind heavy clouds.

"Smells like sewage," Troy said with disgust as he limped down the church stairs. "What part of New York is this? There must be a treatment plant around here."

I couldn't see more than a few yards ahead. I didn't bother to answer Troy because he wasn't ready to believe. And until the effects of the herbal tea wore off, he wouldn't remember anything about the broken charm or the ashes.

"Why aren't there any streetlights? I can't see a single street sign. How is a taxi supposed to see us without any street-lights?" He grabbed the candle from my hand. "Still can't see anything." He held it at knee level. "Some kind of dirt road. They must have driven us outside the city."

I didn't like the idea of wandering those streets at night. If the Capulet guards came along, I'd be in big trouble. "Troy, let's just go back inside and wait until the sun rises."

"Look, you obviously don't understand the severity of this situation." He held the candle at arm's length and started down the road. "This isn't a game, Mimi. This isn't a moment of insanity or a dream. Those freaks back there are capable of a lot more than stabbing me in the leg so start looking around for a phone or something."

"I can't stay out here, Troy."

"Why not?" He stopped walking and even though I couldn't clearly see his face, I could feel his eyes burn through me. "You want to go back to lover boy?" He stepped closer. "He'll hurt you, Mimi. Get that through your thick head. He'll hurt you." He started up the street again, the candle's flame bouncing with every hobbling footstep. "The gas they used to knock us out is still clouding your brain. Come on."

"I can't. I have to go back. It's safer for me back at the church."

"Fine! Go back!" The candlelight grew smaller and smaller, then disappeared around the side of a building, leaving me alone.

Something scurried across my shoe. Lady Capulet had mentioned a plague. Didn't rats spread plague? Getting stabbed in the leg or slapped in the face had to be like a Disney cruise compared with a case of bubonic plague. I stumbled in Troy's direction. He had stopped walking so I bumped right into him.

Dawn's rays started to trickle into the city. As Troy and I watched, light spread across windows, curled around sleeping pigs, and seeped through steaming manure piles. Like a well-rehearsed play, nature's alarm clock woke the city. Windows opened and hands tossed garbage and pots of urine into the gutters. Doors opened and storekeepers began to set up shop. Troy's mouth opened and, standing speechless, he looked like the village idiot. I shivered, remembering the rat, and shook my foot in case any bubonic germs clung to it.

"Where are we?" he asked.

"I'll tell you, but you have to promise not to say anything until I've finished."

Fifteen

"A horse, a horse. My kingdom for a horse!"

W E HUDDLED NEXT to a baker's window. The scent of
warm bread mingled with the stench from a nearby
gutter. There we stood as a world we had each memorized,
yet didn't really know at all, wove its way around us.

I explained as best I could. Even though a Capulet guard
might have stomped down the street at any minute, I did not
rush my explanation. Truth lay in all the crazy details, beginning with the arrival of Aunt Mary's letter and the charm.
Troy listened, turning his back to the street as if to block out
all distractions. His gaze never strayed from my face as I
described the ash cloud, the woman in the alley, and my first
encounter with Friar Laurence. I talked about the shepherd
boy and about meeting Romeo, about Juliet's predicament
and Lady Capulet's terrible temper. "I thought this was a
dream but it isn't," I concluded. "It's really happening." Troy
didn't say a word. "It's magic, Troy. Those ashes transported
us into the story. But by being in it, we've changed it."

A tower of wooden crates stood behind an old cart, just to the side of the bakery. Troy removed the top crate and sat on it, stretching his good leg. I sat next to him, resting my head against the bakery wall. Aside from my little nap in Nurse's chair, I hadn't slept since the night before the final performance. The night I had discovered that my mother was stealing from me—a discovery that had not led to a restful night's sleep. That had been Saturday night and by my calculations this was Monday morning. No wonder I could barely keep my eyes open. A deep, gaping-mouthed yawn possessed me, as did another and another.

"I wish I could," Troy murmured, "but I don't remember a necklace. Stupid friar and his *herbal tea*."

"He was just trying to help you," I said, yawning again.

"Whatever. I could use some coffee. Do you see a Starbucks anywhere?"

He still didn't quite get it. "Troy, this is 1594, remember? There are no Starbucks. I don't even know if they have coffee."

"Great," he complained. "That's just great."

"Give me one," a familiar voice demanded. I stifled another yawn and craned my neck so I could see over the cart. Tybalt, Juliet's vile cousin, was bullying a girl who held a basket of bread. He tossed a coin in the air, then grabbed a flat brown loaf, forcing the intimidated girl to chase after the coin.

My heart fluttered. "We've got to get out of here," I whispered to Troy. Certainly I was worried about my own neck, having gotten myself exiled by messing with Juliet's engagement party. But Troy's neck was also in jeopardy because he was dressed in Montague orange and black.

Troy peered over the cart. "That guy looks familiar."

"He's totally dangerous. Come on." Troy didn't bother to argue this time. The fact that I had dug my fingernails into his arm might have helped persuade him. The fact that Tybalt looked like a salesman for one of those home body-building systems didn't hurt either.

We could have made a clean getaway, except that when Troy struggled onto his bad leg, the tower of crates tumbled over. Before I could duck, Tybalt turned. "You there!"

I grabbed Troy's hand and started running in the opposite direction of Friar Laurence's church. What else could I do with Tybalt blocking the other direction? Despite his hobbling gate, Troy managed to keep up. "You there!" Tybalt called again. Just before we darted into an alley, I glanced back. Tybalt had discarded the bread and had unsheathed his sword. He and his golden cobra, poised for battle, were on the move!

"I know that guy," Troy said as we hurried to the other end of the alley. "How do I know that guy?"

"That's Tybalt." I told him, scared out of my mind. He'd kill us. No doubt about it. Well, he'd kill Troy and probably drag me back to Lady Capulet for a round of eye-gouging and limb-hacking. We ran from the alley and followed a series of twisting streets until we came to a square. It appeared we had lost Tybalt so we stopped to catch our breath beside a fountain. "Hey, I remember this place," I said. It was the cake pedestal fountain with the sculpted lady on top. "This is where it all started."

Troy stood beneath the sign with the painted boot. "I think I came out of this shop," he told me. "Yes, I remember coming out of this shop but I don't remember how I got into that shop. Maybe this is the way out. Maybe there's some sort of door or time portal, like in *Star Trek*." Sounded as probable as anything else so we went inside. While I pretended to want a new pair of shoes, Troy inspected the cobbler's walls. When the cobbler knelt to measure my arches, Troy darted into the back room. He returned, shaking his head.

"Thank you," I told the cobbler, slipping the wooden shoes back on my feet. "I'll have to think about it."

Back outside, Troy splashed fountain water on his face and neck. Then he sat on the fountain's rim. "Tell me about those ashes again."

So I did.

"They came from Shakespeare's quill? So what if we just get another Shakespearean quill? Hey, buddy," he called out to a man. "Is there a quill shop around here?"

"Next door to the cobbler's shop," the man said over his shoulder as he walked by.

Sure enough, right next door. So we entered the shop and were greeted by a thin man with yellow skin and teeth. "Just got some quills in from Egypt," he told us. "Have you ever seen such exquisite feathers?"

"Do you have any Shakespearean quills?" Troy asked.

"Shakespearean? I do not know what you mean."

"You know, William Shakespeare, the playwright." Troy tapped his foot. "Come on, you know. Do you have any of his quills?" I figured this was a lost cause. Shakespeare wrote the story, he wasn't a character in it.

"I am not familiar with William Shakespeare. Can I interest you in an ostrich quill?"

"Are there any other quill shops in town?" Troy asked.

The man scowled. "I am the only quill dealer in Verona. But if my quills are not good enough for you, then you shall have to go to Venice."

"Thanks anyway," I said, opening the shop door. "Let's get back to the friar's. It's safer there." We stepped outside, only to catch Tybalt's attention.

"Stop!" he screamed from across the square.

And so the chase continued. We stumbled down another alley and onto a road that ran alongside a river. It was a wide open space, providing zero places to hide. To the right the road narrowed under an archway and turned back into the city. To the left it crossed a bridge. Tybalt rushed into the alley and shouted at us. "Come on," I urged, turning right in the hopes of making a full circle back to the friar's church. Back to Romeo and Benvolio, who would continue to help me, I hoped. But could I persuade them to help Troy as well?

But just like a cheesy Hollywood movie, a couple of peasants chose that moment to push their cart, filled with kindling, down the narrowest part of the road. As they passed under the archway, with only a few inches to spare on either side, the cart got stuck in a rut. I kid you not. I skidded to a stop in those stupid shoes, scanning the road for another exit, but with a building on one side and the river on the other we had to get past the cart. Trapped. How were we going to get out of this?

"Excuse me," I begged, dropping to the ground. Maybe I could crawl underneath.

"Let us by," Troy insisted. As I squeezed under the cart, he tried to climb over. Just as I got about halfway through, someone grabbed my dress sash and yanked.

"Where do you think you are going, Montague whore?" Tybalt stood at the other end of my sash. His party mask was tucked into his belt. He pulled me to my feet.

"Hey, let go of her," Troy said, sliding off the cart.

"What have we here?" Tybalt pushed me aside, focusing his venomous gaze on Troy. "We meet again, Montague scum," he hissed, aiming his sword at Troy's chest. What was he talking about?

Troy raised his palms. "See, I don't have a weapon. And I'm not a Montague. There's been some sort of mistake."

"There is no mistake." Tybalt pointed the blade at me. "Her ladyship told me that you cavort with Montagues. I see this is true. That dress is stolen property. Return it at once."

"I'll return it as soon as I can," I assured him. "As a matter of fact, I was just on my way to change my clothes. If you'll just let us go, I'll . . ."

"Now. Give it to me now."

"Now?" What was I supposed to do? Walk around in my underwear? "Please, Tybalt, this is all a terrible misunderstanding."

The peasants nervously backed away from their cart. Tybalt lunged forward and grabbed my sash again, pulling me so close I could see the rims of his bloodshot, after-party eyes. "You will return it to her ladyship and face punishment." His gaze was hypnotic and I couldn't turn away, locked into a paralyzing stare down.

That's when Troy hobbled forward and punched the distracted Tybalt in the face. Quite a punch, too, because it knocked Tybalt against the wall. Since he was still gripping my sash, it ripped clean off. "They fight!" the peasants cried, abandoning their cart. Before Tybalt could regain his balance, Troy punched him again. As Tybalt fell to the ground, the sword was knocked from his hand.

"I remember you. You're the guy who stabbed me," Troy yelled. "Who do you think you are? Don't you know that I'm a celebrity?"

Tybalt sat up and ran his hand under his bleeding nose, his eyes welling with hatred. With a grunt, he leaped to his feet and ran full force at Troy, ramming him in the gut. Both lost their balance and tumbled down the riverbank, landing just at the water's edge. Tybalt began to scramble back up the bank but Troy grabbed his foot. "Why'd you stab me?" he cried. "Do you hate my music or something?" How dense could a person get? In Troy Summer's mind, the world revolved around him. Even an alternate world.

Tybalt kicked Troy's hand free and clambered up the slope. Before he reached the side of the road, I grabbed his sword. It was as heavy as a cast-iron frying pan and I could barely fit my fingers around the hilt. What was I supposed to do with it? I tried to look confident as Tybalt took a few steps toward me. Who was I kidding? I wasn't going to stab anyone.

"Don't let him have it," Troy yelled, reaching the road.

I tried to bluff. "Stay away or . . . or . . ."

Tybalt smiled and grabbed the sword from me as simple as that. I felt like a total failure, but it wasn't like I had ever been trained to use one of those things.

As Tybalt turned on Troy, two men in short red capes ran under the archway, led by the peasants. The prince's men. "Hold there!" They started to climb over the cart. Tybalt cursed and took off.

"Troy," I said, rushing to his side. "Montague and Capulet are not supposed to fight. They'll arrest us. We've got to get out of here."

"Stop!" one of the soldiers cried.

Strangely enough, we followed Tybalt back up the alley, the three of us in equal peril. But before we parted ways at the bakery, Tybalt did what every great villain is meant to do—he issued a nasty threat. "I could have killed you both." He returned his sword to its scabbard. "Be warned, I shall not show mercy the next time we meet. And there will be a next time. Mark my words."

Sixteen

"The game is up."

BENVOLIO WAS WAITING on the steps of Friar Laurence's church. "Mimi," he said, rushing to my side. "You should not have gone into the streets without a protector."

"I protected her, thank you very much," Troy said, wincing as he limped up the stone steps. He *had* protected me, at the very least from having to walk around in my underwear. Who knows what Tybalt would have done to a half-naked girl? Maybe Troy had even saved my life.

Benvolio placed a hand on my back and guided me into the church, not bothering to hold the door open for Troy. "You must stay inside," he insisted. "Word has spread throughout the city that you are exiled and that Lady Capulet has offered a reward for your arrest. Yet I think I may have a solution."

"What is it?" I asked. Troy pushed the door open and flung himself on one of the benches.

Benvolio continued. "Because you are a Capulet woman, the Capulet family has jurisdiction over you. But if you were to marry a Montague, then your Montague husband would become your master. You would have a legal right to stay in Verona."

"Marry?" Troy blurted.

"Master?" I choked on the word.

"Yes." Benvolio took my hand and tenderly kissed my fingertips one at a time. Goose bumps popped up all over my arm. "I hope that you will consider this option. In the meantime, I must go and train the Montague guards. It is my duty. But I will return tonight and we can discuss this matter further." Discuss the matter? It's not like I was going to marry a guy I hardly knew—especially a guy who might not actually exist. No matter how much I liked it when he kissed my fingers.

"Where's Romeo?" I asked.

"He has returned to Montague House to shut himself into his room. I fear that Rosaline will be the death of him." Benvolio frowned. "Adieu, sweet Mimi. Remember, stay here until I return. Only danger awaits you outside this sanctuary." He pointed a finger at Troy. "Look after her."

"What do you think I've been doing?" They stared at each other with narrowed eyes and clenched jaws. I half expected them to pound their chests.

After Benvolio left I pushed my full weight against the door, trying to shut out the horrible, dangerous Romeo and Juliet world. Then I slid to the floor and yanked off the wooden shoes.

I expected Troy to tease me about Benvolio's marriage proposal. Had it been an actual proposal or just a suggestion? But

Troy sat deep in thought. St. Francis stared at me from the end of the aisle. A carved bird perched on his stone hand. Mounds of wax drippings covered the altar. Sunlight streamed through the stained-glass windows, casting blues and greens on blisters that had formed on my big toes. The sanctuary smelled like dust and sweat. My sweat. I needed a bath.

"I remember." Troy's voice startled me. "I remember that I couldn't see through all those ashes. They stung my eyes. I tried to follow you outside but the stage door had closed and I couldn't find the knob." He paused, as if downloading the images. "When the ashes cleared, I was standing in that cobbler's shop. I ran through the shop and onto the street but everything had changed. I wandered around trying to find the Wallingford. Then I saw you."

"Yes! You called my name."

"That's right." His words came quicker. "But there were so many people, I couldn't get to you. And then Tybalt pushed me down and stabbed me. He kicked me in the head. I must have passed out." He rubbed the side of his head again.

"That's when Benvolio found you."

"Right. Benvolio." His tone soured. "You've got to be careful with that guy. I know his type."

"What type is that?"

"The controlling type."

"Oh, really?" Like I even cared about his opinion. "Well, I don't find him one bit controlling. I think he's charming." I folded my arms and smirked.

"Whatever," Troy said, frowning. "Look, we've got to figure out how to get home. I'm supposed to be in the Virgin

Islands today. I'm under contract. My producer's going to be pissed." Which brought up the question—where did everyone think we had gone? Both of us missing at the exact same time. Had my mother called the FBI? Probably. I could just see the headlines: Bad-Boy Pop Star Runs Off with Virginal Wallingford Heiress.

Troy ran his hand along the church bench. "I'm sitting in Friar Laurence's church. No one is going to believe it."

Maybe a hundred years from now teleporting into stories will be commonplace. Only a century ago it would have been a stretch to believe that human beings would actually walk on the moon. Or that one day we would bounce music off satellites or play three-dimensional computer-generated games. If you still think I'm making all this up, you should read Troy's autobiography, *Summer Love: Days of Sand, Surf, and Song,* which is due in bookstores next year. He dedicated the last two chapters to this adventure.

"Friar Laurence's church," he repeated, shaking his head in wonder. "So if this is Shakespeare's story, how come everyone's not talking like the play? Perchance, forsooth, 'tis and 'twas, all that crap?"

"Because I didn't wish myself into Shakespeare's play. I'm as tired of Shakespeare as you are, Troy. I wished myself *somewhere else.* I was desperate to get away from the Wallingford and, thanks to your comment, Verona was on my mind."

"Amazing. I'm going to talk to my agent about pitching this as a movie. Wouldn't this make a great movie?"

"Depends on the ending," I said worriedly. "How are we going to get back without the charm?"

He shrugged. "Maybe we just need to get to the end of the story. You know, when Romeo and Juliet die. Or maybe we just need to say the last lines. I bet that's all there is to it." He stood and delivered the last lines from Shakespeare's beloved tragedy. "For never was there a story of more woe, than this of Juliet and her Romeo." We waited. I closed my eyes, then opened them.

I was not surprised to see morning sun streaming through stained-glass windows. I opened the heavy church door just enough to poke my head out. Nothing had changed. Troy repeated the lines again and again. Still nothing.

Was I relieved? Somewhat. I wanted to see Benvolio again. I wanted to dance with him and maybe even get a kiss. This place was built on fantasy and at some point I would need to go back to the real world. I still had a life to live. A real life. But until then, Benvolio beckoned.

Troy's face fell. "Don't tell me we have to go through the entire story in order to end it. I'm sick to death of this play and now I have to live it? What act are we in?"

"Troy, this is not the play."

"What act are we in?"

"We're not in an act or a scene," I told him. He scowled at me. No use arguing. He'd figure things out later. "Last night was the Capulet party."

"Okay, so this is the morning after Romeo meets Juliet. Tybalt obviously hasn't been killed yet, but that should happen soon. Then we shouldn't have much longer to wait for the big suicide scene and, voila . . ." He clapped his hands. "We're outta here."

He was clueless.

"Holy St. Francis," Friar Laurence said as he waddled past the altar. "Where have you two been?"

"Sightseeing," Troy replied, stepping away from the friar when he tried to inspect his leg.

"Your wound will need a new dressing. I'll tend to it when I return."

"Over my dead body. Unless you can convince me that you've read a medical textbook by someone other than the local witch doctor or the Spanish Inquisitor, you're not getting near this leg."

"Where are you going?" I asked the friar.

"I have been summoned to Capulet House. There is to be a wedding tomorrow and I'm to officiate."

"A wedding?" I asked.

"Yes. Between Lady Juliet and Paris Calchetto IV. Not a love match, I'm afraid to say. And she's so young, poor little flower." The friar stroked his cross. "I understand that there was some confusion at the party last night and that Paris almost called the wedding off. But Lady Capulet was able to sway him."

The onions and boil-y bottom hadn't worked. Lady Capulet would get her way, after all.

"Friar, you don't have to pretend with us," Troy assured him. "We know all about Romeo and Juliet. We know that you're going to marry them in secret." Troy was under the assumption that Juliet and Romeo had met, had confided their love to the friar, and that everything was proceeding as originally written. I cleared my throat but the friar spoke.

"Marry Romeo and Juliet?" Friar Laurence gasped. "Why ever would I do such a thing? They are mortal enemies."

"Look, we know that they're in love and that they want to get married." Troy returned to the bench, carefully positioning his wounded leg.

"Troy," I said. "They're not in love. They haven't met yet."

"But they were supposed to meet at the party."

"I know, but they didn't."

"How do you know?" he asked.

"Because I was there and they never met." He narrowed his eyes, waiting for me to explain. "A bunch of stuff happened and Juliet got sent to her room before she even saw Romeo." I swallowed nervously.

Troy sighed with frustration. "Let me get this straight. We're stuck in the story of Romeo and Juliet and we can't get home without a magic charm made from Shakespeare's quill, which doesn't exist in this world. However, we might be able to get home when the story ends, but if Romeo and Juliet don't meet, then we don't have a story. More important, we don't have *an ending*."

Friar Laurence *tsk tsk*ed. He placed his speckled hand on Troy's forehead. "Bless you, my son, but a fever has muddled your mind." He sniffed. "Smells like the wound is festering."

"Festering?" Troy cried.

Friar Laurence rubbed his bald spot. "Good gracious, this is a dilemma. Her ladyship will certainly have me exiled if I don't come right away. I shall tend to your leg when I return. Go upstairs, children, and get some rest. Help yourselves to whatever you find." He opened the church door and hurried on his way.

"Festering?" Troy repeated with alarm. "Fever? Oh my God, I'm going to get gangrene. Mimi, we've got to get home right away. I've got to get to a hospital."

What if he did get gangrene? What would we do then? There were no antibiotics in sixteenth-century Verona—or sixteenth-century anywhere for that matter. I'm sure none of the surgical instruments had been sterilized and the bandage had been filthy.

"Mimi, are you listening to me? We've got to end this as soon as possible!"

"Okay, okay," I agreed halfheartedly. He was right. We were both in serious, mortal danger. But it broke my heart. I had hoped for a happy ending for Juliet.

Would her death be my only ticket home?

Seventeen

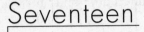

"I have not slept a wink."

WE HELPED OURSELVES to the friar's bread and cheese. Actually, we fell upon the food like refugees, which in a strange way was exactly what we were—Reality Refugees. That might make a good title for Troy's movie.

After eating the last bite, Troy collapsed onto the cot and immediately fell into a deep sleep. I scanned the upstairs for another mattress, but found none. There was a small closet that contained a closestool, which I used, and a room filled with hanging bundles of herbs and all sorts of cutting and measuring implements. A bucket of water sat on the floor and I poured some into a bowl and washed my face as best as I could, using the inside of my skirt as a towel. The water felt refreshing but I longed for a bath. I couldn't find a tub or shower. What did people do in this century?

Back in the friar's room, Troy slept with an arm stretched across his forehead. There wasn't much room on that cot. If two people shared it, their bodies would be pressed together. I grimaced. "Troy?" I whispered, trying to wake him up. If

146

he knew that there were no other beds, he might be a gentleman and offer to sleep on the floor. "Troy?" But he didn't budge. I yawned. How long could the human body go without sleep?

Maybe I could sleep in the friar's chair with my head resting on the desk. I pushed aside some rolls of parchment paper, an inkwell, and a jar of quills. But I couldn't get comfortable and I tipped the ink, staining one of my sleeves. Lady Capulet would probably put me on the rack for ruining her dress. I rested my head in my hands and watched Troy's chest as it rose and fell. He had kicked the blankets off the cot. I thought about Juliet's blankets and how she liked to crawl beneath them to think.

Juliet. Sweet little Juliet, getting ready to marry a man twice her age.

Despite my exhaustion, I unrolled one of the parchments and dipped a quill into the inkwell. The friar had said we could help ourselves to whatever we found. The possibility existed that I might never see Juliet again and I wanted to tell her a few things. Like a wiser, older sister. It didn't take long to figure out the quill and soon I was writing a letter to Juliet.

I told her about my life back in Manhattan. About how I also felt trapped so she would know that she wasn't alone. About how our mothers were kind of alike and how I had always wished for a different life. I told her about the charm and the ashes and that I wasn't really her cousin. But I was her friend. And that even if things go terribly wrong, she should never, ever consider suicide.

My head fell forward and I couldn't keep my eyes open.

Troy had rolled onto his side, freeing a narrow slice of cot. I lay next to him, not caring that his butt pressed into my thighs. Not caring about anything at all but getting some rest.

I slept long and hard and dreamed about kissing Benvolio. The kiss was soft. But then his face morphed into Troy's face and the kiss grew urgent. Troy held me so close that I could feel his heart beating. I pressed closer, wanting to kiss him forever, wanting to . . .

"Mimi, wake up. You're on my hurt leg."

At first I didn't know where I was. The room was dark except for a single lit candle that sat on a desk—the friar's desk. I was still in Verona, sharing a cot with Troy. What time was it? What day was it? I wiped drool from my chin, hoping Troy hadn't noticed. Much more to my embarrassment, at some time during the nap I had curled into the crook of his arm and had flung my leg across his body, smothering us both with my velvet party dress. I sat up.

I had just taken a nap with Troy Summer. Clarissa would be so jealous.

Troy stretched his arms. "Well, we're still in Shakespeare land." He yawned. "I was hoping that you were wrong and that this actually was a dream. Speaking of dreaming, did you know that you talk in your sleep?" He winked at me.

What had I said in my sleep? Had I called out his name?

He scooted to the end of the cot. "I have to pee." His limp was more pronounced, as were his curses each time he took a step. "I'm supposed to pee in this bowl?" he hollered when he found the closestool.

"Yes," I hollered back.

When he returned, he fell onto the cot. "I feel dizzy," he mumbled. It was difficult to tell by candlelight but his face looked flushed. I lit another candle and placed it on the windowsill above the cot. He closed his eyes. Beads of sweat sat on the bridge of his nose and above his upper lip. His blond hair, usually blown-dry and gelled, lay flat against his forehead. Even so, he was still gorgeous. His white shirt was unbuttoned, exposing a tanned chest speckled with reddish blond hair.

"See something you like?" When had he opened his eyes? How long had I been looking at his chest?

My voice rose defensively. "What is that supposed to mean? I suppose you think that just because I'm a girl . . ." I folded my arms. "You should stop assuming that everyone is in love with you."

"Whoa," he said, wiping his forehead with his sleeve. "Touched a nerve, did I? Who *are* you in love with, Mimi? That freak, Benvolio? You like the way he kisses your fingers?"

As if my feelings were any of his business. "I don't know any *freaks*, Troy, except for the hundreds that you date."

He forced a shallow laugh. "Hundreds is a bit of an exaggeration. Besides, I'm expected to date lots of girls. My fans expect me to act a certain way. It's all about appearances—you should know that. The private person and the public persona are two different things entirely."

"Oh, please. You expect me to believe that you're forced to date a different girl every week? That you do it just to sell music?"

His voice grew defensive as well. "I don't expect you to

149

believe anything I say, Mimi. You've hated me from the moment we met. I saw that look on your face the first time we kissed. Total disgust."

Disgust? He thought his kiss had disgusted me?

"You've always acted like you're so much better than me," he continued, clearly insulted. "New York society meets California beach bum. You ignore me at the theater because you assume that Troy the pop star is all there is to me. If you think that's who I really am, then you're a hypocrite." He sat up against the wall and pushed the pillow under his wounded thigh.

I glared at him. "Hypocrite? What are you talking about?"

"You might think that you're better than me, but we're no different. We're both marketable products and people use us to advance their own careers. But is the product who we really are?" I tried not to turn away from his intense gaze, even though it felt like he could see right through my clothes. "I watched you come to rehearsal every day. I saw the way you nervously fidgeted until the rehearsal started. The way you always stood off to the side, by yourself, until your mother came into the hall. Then you'd turn into Mimi Wallingford, theater princess." He mimicked my mother's voice, surprisingly well. "Turn your left side to the audience, Mimi, it's your best side. Wear the padded bra, Mimi, it will make you look sexier. Stand center stage, Mimi. You are a Wallingford, after all." He raised his eyebrows. "You don't want all that, do you? That's why you're faking the whole stage fright thing."

I wanted to slap him. I wanted to throw both wooden

shoes right at his thick head. How dare he say such mean things to me. *Faking* the stage fright thing. "I *have* stage fright. It's very real and it's horrible. Dr. Harmony says it's like post-traumatic stress disorder."

"Post-traumatic . . ." Troy wiped his upper lip. His neck glistened with sweat. "Think about it, Mimi. The stage fright serves a purpose, doesn't it?"

There was that smirk of his, spread right across his know-it-all face. I felt completely naked. What possible purpose could my stage fright serve besides making me totally miserable? I sat down at the desk, turning my back to him. Who was he to psychoanalyze me? Troy Summer was a bubble-gum musician who knew nothing about the pressures of my life.

"Good evening, children." Friar Laurence entered the room carrying a tray of food. "You slept the entire day." He set the tray on the bedside table. "I rely on the kindness of my flock for all my meals. Tonight we are very fortunate because Emmaline, the cobbler's wife, brought vegetable soup." He handed me a bowl and a half loaf of bread. I inhaled the soup, not caring that it was badly in need of salt or that I didn't recognize some of the "vegetables." I shoved a chunk of bread into my mouth. The friar offered Troy a bowl. "Eat this, my son, for it will help speed your recovery."

Troy waved the bowl away. "I'm not hungry," he moaned.

"What's this?" Friar Laurence set the soup aside and pressed his hand to Troy's forehead. "He is still feverish. Mimi, come and hold the candle while I check the wound." Troy didn't object this time, watching worriedly.

Clutching the candle, I almost gagged as the friar opened the tear in Troy's tights. The skin around the stitches blazed red. Pus oozed at the edges. I thought I might faint just looking at it. Some doctor I'd make.

"Oh my God!" Troy exclaimed. "It's totally infected. I'm going to get gangrene."

I wouldn't wish gangrene on anyone, not even Troy. "Do you have any medicine?" I asked.

"The tainted blood should be cleansed. I'll fetch the leeches."

"No!" Troy cried. "Not the leeches!"

"My son, it is possible that the wound will heal and that your fever will pass. But without treatment there is also the possibility that your leg will blacken. The only remedy for a blackened leg is to cut it off."

Troy clenched his fists and his face turned beet red. A vein bulged in his neck. I thought he might stroke out at that very moment. "This is all your fault," he snarled. "You've infected me with your barbaric surgery. You're looking at a huge malpractice suit, buddy."

Threatening was not going to help. Something had to be done, but what? If we were in New York, we'd have antibiotic cream and sterile bandages. Then I thought about the cowboy movie where the old drunken doctor pours whiskey onto his patient's gunshot wound. "Friar, what's in that jug?" I pointed to the blue jug on his desk.

He looked sheepish. "Just a bit of medicinal tea, for my aching knees."

I picked up the jug and smelled its contents. The alcohol

fumes shot straight up my sinuses. Some tea. "Perfect," I said. "Troy, I think we can sterilize your wound. It's the only thing I can think of that might help."

"Sterilize?" the friar asked, rubbing his bald spot. "Is this something you do back in Manhattan?"

"Yes." My stomach turned queasy as I glanced at the glistening pus.

You can't even look at an accident scene, my mother had said. *You're too sensitive.*

I clenched my jaw. "I'm going to need boiling water. It must reach a full, rolling boil. Can you do that?"

The friar nodded. "I have a small oven and cooking pot out back. It will take some time, though, to get the fire started."

So we set to work. The wound was such a mess that I figured we should start all over and do it right. When the water was ready, I convinced the friar that we needed to wash our hands. I sterilized a knife and a tweezerlike tool. The friar was curious about the entire process and asked all sorts of questions. I told him about bacteria and he listened intently, fetching more water when I needed it. I cut the stitches. Then, using the sterilized tweezers, I pulled all twelve stitches free. Since there were no clean bandages, I cut the bottom half of my underskirt into strips. It was unbleached linen and since it had been stuffed under the velvet dress, it seemed fairly clean. I used these strips, soaked in hot water, to soften the scabs and clean away the pus, reopening the wound. Troy kept wincing but kept very still. This wasn't rocket science, obviously. Everyone knows how to clean a wound, though I had never cleaned one as deep as that. I became very focused. The friar watched my every move. It didn't seem disgusting as I got caught up in the process. "This is going to hurt," I told Troy when I picked up the jug. He nodded and clenched his entire body as I poured the alcohol onto the wound.

Having never stitched anything, I turned this part over to Friar Laurence, but only after sterilizing his needle and thread. Troy gulped down some of what was left in the jug, which I later learned is called grappa, an intense alcoholic drink made from grapes. He pressed his head into the pillow and groaned each time the needle pierced his tender skin. I took his hand and held it. He almost squeezed my fingers off.

Finally, it was over. I dried the wound and tied the rest of the linen strips over it. "Hopefully that will buy us some time," I told him.

"Thank you," he said, smiling weakly. "Have you ever considered becoming a doctor?"

I returned the smile. Maybe Dissection 101 wouldn't be so bad after all. "It's the least I could do," I said. "I'd probably be dead if you hadn't saved me from Tybalt." Candlelight reflected in his green eyes. Reddish stubble sandpapered his square jaw. I sighed. "You wouldn't even be in this mess if I had just handed my mother the necklace."

Troy drifted back to sleep. Friar Laurence and I shared the rest of the bread. It was chewy, with seeds sprinkled throughout. My letter lay on the desk. "Friar, I wrote a letter for Juliet Capulet. If anything happens to me, or if I suddenly disappear, will you make certain that she gets it?"

"Of course, my child. But why would you disappear?"

"That charm I mentioned, I think it brought me here. I think it's magic. Do you believe in magic?"

"What you call magic, I call divine intervention. So yes, I believe." He wiped crumbs from the front of his robe. "I am a man of faith, Mimi. I struggle with the impossible every day. When I first saw you standing in the square, I knew you had come from someplace else. And all your talk about medicine convinced me further." He chuckled. "And I listen to confession every Sunday. You'd be amazed by some of the *impossible* things I hear."

I decided to make my own confession. "Friar, Juliet is supposed to fall in love with Romeo. They are part of a story that a man named William Shakespeare wrote, but their love is doomed from the start because of the feud."

"Ah, the feud." He frowned and shook his head. "It is a plague on this city."

"Why are they feuding?" I asked. Shakespeare never explains that in his play.

Friar Laurence stroked his cross. "It's no secret, so I shall tell you the tale." He sat back in his chair and rested his hands on his belly. "Lady Capulet was born Veronique Valdiza, a member of a wealthy, merchant-class family. But they were not nobles and her father desired a title of nobility more than anything else. Just before Veronique turned thirteen, she attended her first formal ball, where she met a bachelor by the name of Alfonso Montague, heir to a titled Verona family. He was none other than Romeo's future father. And, as you may have guessed, she fell passionately in love with him."

155

Lady Capulet, in love with a Montague? This was just like my second cousin Greg's soap opera.

Friar Laurence continued. "Though Alfonso Montague was beyond her class, Veronique wanted to be his wife and her father wanted his daughter titled. So Valdiza tried to entice a proposal of marriage by offering half his Venetian fleet to the Montagues, but only if Alfonso married his daughter. The Montagues would not agree to marry their only son to a merchant's daughter. They made this proclamation while standing on the church steps, for all the eavesdroppers and gossips to hear.

"The Valdiza family was shamed and Veronique was heartbroken. People whispered when she passed by and pointed fingers at her in church. They said she did not deserve a titled marriage. They said that she should never have dared to rise above her station. She refused to eat, refused to leave her house. She began to waste away. Her father almost went crazy with worry because he truly loved his only daughter. Fortunately, word of the generous offer spread so it wasn't long before other suitors came calling and one of them had a noble title—a Capulet title. Hoping to save his daughter's reputation, Valdiza agreed to the marriage on one condition: For Veronique's hand and access to half of Valdiza's fleet, this man would seek revenge, forever more, on the Montagues. All was agreed and Veronique married Lord Capulet."

"Did she want to marry him?" I asked.

"I cannot say. Her father arranged the marriage. Initially, Alfonso Montague felt no hatred toward the Capulet family, but as the years passed and the Capulets continued to attack his men and vilify his name, his heart began to rage and he, in turn, vowed to seek revenge on all Capulets. While the feud thrives, many have forgotten the cause. But Lady Capulet has not forgotten."

Even those who appear evil and wretched have feelings hidden beneath their powdered skin. Lady Capulet had loved and had lost, badly. She had been humiliated and her desire for revenge had blinded her.

"Who goes there?" Friar Laurence called out. Troy's eyes flew open and he sat up. Someone was coming up the stairs.

I turned toward the doorway as a small, robed figure entered. Troy hurled himself from the cot, grabbing the surgical knife from the bedside table.

The front of the figure's robe bore a golden Capulet crest.

Eighteen

"The miserable have no other medicine
but only hope."

"FRIAR, I NEED your help." The visitor lowered her hood.
"Juliet," I said, overjoyed to see her.

The friar eased the knife from Troy's outstretched hand.
"You won't need that, my son. She is a friend."

Juliet's mask of desperation melted into a smile.
"Mimi!" She rushed to me and squeezed the air out of me
with an ecstatic hug. A hint of onion still lingered on her
skin. "Tybalt returned this morning and said that you were
still in Verona, cavorting with Montagues. Mother ordered
Tybalt to find you and to arrest you for disobeying the exile
and for stealing a dress. I am so sorry. I fear this is all my
doing."

"It's not your doing," I assured her, trying not to focus on
the fact that I was a fugitive. Did they put up wanted posters
in the sixteenth century? "How are you? What happened
after I left? Did your father beat you?" I was happy to see
that there was no sign of her mother's slaps. Except for dark
circles beneath her eyes, her face looked as cute as ever.

She shook her head. "He told me that he would not mar my body since the wedding night was fast approaching. He was afraid that Paris would refuse me if I had whipping scars." That statement sickened me. Her body was a mere possession to be handed over to a new owner. "But he locked me in my room. No one but Nurse is allowed to see me until tomorrow. I told Nurse that I was taking to bed early. Then I climbed down the balcony and ran here to seek the friar's help."

"My child," the friar said. "Disobeying your father is a sin."

"Is it not a sin to sell your daughter to the highest bidder?" Juliet asked, her voice desperate. "I overheard them. Father is almost bankrupt and my marriage is his way out of debt. And Paris has promised Tybalt a titled position in the royal guard once we are married. I am to finance my family's future with my body and soul. Is that God's will, that I should marry a man I despise?"

Friar Laurence wrung his hands and frowned. "The Fourth Commandment is to honor thy father and mother. *That* is God's will." He scratched his overgrown ears. "Yet I have sat in the confessional with your future husband on many occasions. While I can't divulge the confessions themselves, I can say that they were of a most *inappropriate nature*. It is clear, in my heart, that the two of you are not a good match. But your parents . . ."

"Forget them," Troy said, returning to the cot. "If you don't want to marry the guy, then don't marry him."

"It's not that simple," Friar Laurence explained. "If Juliet were to refuse a marriage that her parents had arranged, the

Capulet name would suffer. Great shame would befall the family."

"I do not wish to bring dishonor to my family," Juliet said.

"And, if Juliet refused the marriage," the friar added, "she would be breaking the law of Verona."

"So?" Troy said.

"So, my son, she would be imprisoned, perhaps even put to death."

"Put to death?" Troy folded his arms. "That's the stupidest law I've ever heard of. What kind of people would put a girl to death? In my country, we barely even put murderers to death, and I'm talking about those scum-of-the-earth serial killers who slaughter prostitutes and drug addicts. Most of them get to spend the rest of their lives in a comfortable cell with free health care and television. What kind of place is this anyway where girls get put to death?"

Juliet took a hesitant step toward Troy, looking at him the way a child looks at a new toy. "I've never heard a man speak in such a manner. Who are you?"

"I'm . . ."

"That's Troy," I said, stepping between them. The less Golden Boy said the better. "He's from Manhattan, just like me. And yes, he's a Montague, but we don't have the whole feud thing in Manhattan."

She stepped around me. "Do you really believe it's a stupid law?"

"Of course."

Juliet smiled, then sighed. Then smiled again. Uh oh. I

knew that dazed expression. And Troy knew it, too, because women bestowed it upon him constantly. "You're so nice," Juliet said, stepping closer. "Did you get that wound in battle? Does it hurt much? Are you an actor, too?" She moved closer still. "Do you have any interest in marriage?"

Troy raised an eyebrow and stepped away. "Mimi?" he said between clenched teeth.

The last thing anyone needed was for Juliet to fall in love with Troy Summer. Time to nip this in the bud. Time to get back on track. "Friar, you said that it's God's will that we honor our parents. But isn't it also God's will to help those in need?" I asked. "Haven't you taken a vow to do just that? And wouldn't it be a terrible sin to break that vow?"

"Indeed, it would be." He placed his palms on his fat belly. "But how can I help?"

"Isn't there a third option, besides marriage or death? Couldn't she leave Verona? If she . . ."

"Leave Verona?" Troy interrupted. "I thought we were going to *end* this story, Mimi. You want to get out of here, don't you?" He bumped into the wall, retreating from Juliet's amorous gaze. "Don't you?"

"Troy, can I talk to you in the other room?" I asked. Troy eagerly slipped past Juliet and followed me to the friar's workshop. We stood beneath the hanging herbs, glaring at each other. "Of course I want to get out of here. There's a price on my head. But I promised Juliet that I would help her, and that's what I intend to do. She's such a nice girl, Troy. She's so young."

Troy leaned on the table. I expected him to argue with me, to tell me I was an imbecile, to tell me I should get a lobotomy or something. "You may need a vacation from your life, Mimi, but I can't afford to take one. I have to shoot this DVD. My sales were way down last month, and if I don't keep moving forward, I'm going to become one of those pathetic, washed-up teen idols. I've got to get back."

"Oh," I mumbled, stunned by his confession.

"And don't forget the whole gangrene thing." He raked his fingers through his blond hair, pushing it off his forehead. "I don't pretend to understand any of this but I know one thing for certain. We're the real people here. They're just characters. Don't forget that."

I sighed. My mother was a real person and she would be worried sick. Troy was a real person who needed to see a doctor, and I certainly needed to deal with my own problems. Maybe he was right. But maybe he was wrong. "If these people aren't real, Troy, then how did one of them manage to do that to your leg? I think they're as real as we are."

"You're so pig-headed." His blue eyes turned stormy. "You know the play as well as I do. Romeo and Juliet kill themselves. It's the way it has to be."

"Why? Why can't it be different?"

"Because Shakespeare didn't write it different," he insisted, folding his arms. "Juliet's destiny is already mapped out."

"But she didn't get to choose her destiny."

"Huh?"

"Why does everyone else get to choose our destinies?

That's what I want to know." Feelings began to bubble—feelings I thought I could control. But they came fast, shooting to the surface like a geyser. I was going to blow. I clenched my fists. "Why does everyone think they can tell us what to do? That they know what's best for us?" I took a deep breath then wagged a finger at him. "Just because Shakespeare created this world doesn't mean that he gets to decide Juliet's fate."

"Uh, yes it does, actually," he said sarcastically.

"Well, I say it doesn't." Rage took over. "She has her own desires and she doesn't have to die if someone gives her a chance to get away from her horrid life. Away from that horrid mother. Away from her name. Do you hear me? She needs to get away from her name!"

Have you ever had one of those lightbulb moments? Just like in the cartoons when you felt like you had actually reached up and flicked on the light switch? That you had achieved some sort of enlightenment? Rage can do that. Like an eruption it can clear away all the clutter we layer over our true feelings. We were in the same boat, Juliet and I, riding down the same tumultuous river with our parents at the helm. Our choice was to stay on board or capsize the whole thing!

Juliet's destiny could be changed. I was going to stick to my promise because I knew, to the core of my being, that I had been sent to help this girl. Our fates were linked in some kind of cosmic, otherworldly way.

"I'm going to help Juliet find that happy ending and I'm going to get us both home. Somehow, I'll do it." I didn't give him the chance to reply.

I returned to the friar's room. He and Juliet were eating the last of the soup.

"Juliet," I said. "It's true that only death will free you from this situation."

She straightened her back and tried to look brave. "I'm ready to face death."

"But she won't have to, will she, Friar? There's a way that death can be faked, isn't there?" I waited for his reply. He knew what I was talking about because he stared at his soup bowl for a very long time. The friar helps Juliet fake her death in Shakespeare's play, but who knew what he'd do in this upside-down version.

Juliet threw herself on the floor at his feet, clutching the hem of his brown robe. "Please, Friar Laurence. Do you know of a way?"

He clutched his silver cross and nodded.

Nineteen

"Delays have dangerous ends."

FRIAR LAURENCE, JULIET, and I sat in the herbal room while Troy sulked on the cot. A light breeze drifted through the open window, carrying the sickly sweet scent of a jasmine vine. We didn't have much time to pull everything together since the wedding was scheduled for the following evening.

Friar Laurence mixed up a batch of sleeping potion. "We are not so different," he told Juliet. "I also wish I could leave Verona."

"Truly?" she asked.

"Yes. I would like to travel the countryside, taking my medicines to the poor. The patrons of St. Francis are wealthy. They can hire apothecaries and surgeons. My talents would better serve those of lesser means." He poured the brown potion into a small glass vial. "But I am tied to this place. I cannot leave here unless the church's governing body releases me." He corked the vial and tied a string around it. "This potion mimics death by turning the skin cold and slowing breathing to the point of imperceptibility. Upon drinking this you will have only ten minutes of consciousness." Juliet tied the vial around her neck and tucked it into her bodice. "I will arrive a few hours before the ceremony. A servant will notify you of my arrival. Take the potion immediately. When I come to your room to offer a wedding prayer, I will declare that you are dead."

"The potion's perfectly safe?" I asked.

"Yes." He paused to rub his chin. "I have never actually used it. But others before me have."

"Then what?" Juliet asked.

"Then your nurse will dress you for burial and I will escort your body to the tomb," the friar said.

"How long will she sleep?" I asked.

"Half a day, not much more than that. I can make a stimulating potion if we should need to wake her up earlier."

Juliet scrunched her face, as if suddenly pained. "This will not work at all. The Capulets always host very long visitations, for days and days. How can I lie still for days and days? It is impossible." Her shoulders dropped and she flung her head back. "Oh, how can we make this work?"

"Why would she have to lie there for days and days if she's inside the casket?" I wondered.

"Juliet will be laid *atop* her casket as tradition dictates. This could be our undoing," the friar fretted. He started pacing. "If Juliet's body disappeared, the Capulets would suspect foul play on the part of the Montagues and that would be certain to escalate the violence."

"They might even guess the truth, that I had faked my death." Juliet frantically wound a lock of hair between her fingers. "They would go looking for me. And they would know that you had something to do with it, Friar."

"Lord have mercy."

"Then we have to make sure that no one comes for the visitation. How can we do that?" I tapped my fingers on the table. "How?" I tapped faster, straining my brain. The friar thought so hard that it looked as if he was having a bowel movement. Juliet started pacing, too. Her hair, formerly flattened by the hood, had regained its spring and bounced against the herb bundles as she paced.

Troy peered into the room. He had been so quiet during our planning that I had forgotten all about him. "Your plan stinks. I'm going to get Romeo," he announced.

I stopped tapping. "But Troy . . ."

"It's the only thing that makes sense." He leaned against the wall, taking the weight off his hurt leg, and started tying his shirt. "Friar, where can I find Romeo?"

"He should be at Montague House. It lies at the opposite end of this very street."

"But Troy . . ."

"Don't try to stop me, Mimi," he said, adjusting his tights. "I'm going to go get Romeo and bring him back to meet Juliet so they can fall in love and do what they were meant to do, before you doom us both. I have no intention of losing my music contract. Nor do I intend to lie on that cot and die of an infection." He started down the stairs.

That was it!

I leaped off the stool. "Friar, if you told everyone that Juliet had died of plague, what would happen to her body?"

The friar's mouth fell open. He looked at me, dumbfounded. "Plague? The family would panic. No one would dare go near Juliet. She would be placed in her casket and it would be set afire."

"Who would set her casket on fire?"

"Why, I would." His eyes lit up and he clapped his hands. "Holy St. Francis, you have solved the riddle."

Juliet stopped pacing. Needles of dried rosemary speckled her hair. "Then you will take me to Manhattan? I'd love to be an actor, just like you, Mimi. Will you take me there to be an actor?"

"I wish I could but I don't think it's possible. I don't even know if I can go back."

She stuck out her lower lip and sighed. "I so want to be an actor."

If she only knew the realities of the acting life. But I wasn't about to crush her dream. If she wanted to be an actor, then let her be an actor. More power to her!

"Juliet must not travel alone. The world is far too dangerous for a girl on her own," Friar Laurence pointed out. "There are bandits and rapists at every bend in the road. And I am not prepared to leave Verona, not with my obligations to the governing board. Besides, I have no money for travel. Perhaps you and Troy could escort her."

"You can't count on us," I said. "We don't know how long we'll be here. Besides, we don't have money either."

Juliet slumped over the workshop table. Her eyes filled with tears. "I have no money either, except a few coins. Without money I shall have to go straight to a nunnery." She started to cry. "I cannot be an actor in a nunnery." A nunnery meant living in solitude, totally shut away from the world. That would protect her from the Capulets, but it would simply be exchanging one prison for another. She had way too much spunk for a nunnery.

"We can figure this out," I insisted. "We just need to find an escort and we need to get our hands on some money."

"Or, we need to find an escort *with* money," the friar said cleverly.

Of course! Who else but the very person who is supposed to be with Juliet in the first place? He wasn't doing anything, anyway. Just sitting around, moaning about that stupid Rosaline. It wasn't like he had to fall in love with Juliet, or vice versa. He just had to help her get out of the city, to a safe new life. And he had told Rosaline that his chests overflowed with gold coins.

I ran back to the bedroom and opened the window, hoping I could catch him. "Troy!" I called. It was early evening and the moon had not yet risen. In the dim light I could barely see Troy standing in the road. He was looking up at me. "Troy," I yelled again. "Wait for us. I want to take Juliet to meet Romeo. He'll help her get out of this wedding, I'm sure of it."

"Mimi!" Troy stumbled into the bedroom, his eyes wild. The guy I had been yelling at was still standing in the road. "Tybalt's outside," Troy said. "He saw me. I bolted the door but it won't keep him out for long." Juliet and the friar rushed into the bedroom.

Tybalt? I jumped back from the window. Oh God, what had I done?

"Juliet!" Tybalt yelled from the street. "I know you are in there with that Montague scum. Come out or I shall break down the door."

Juliet gasped. "He must have followed me. Oh Mimi, I've put you in danger."

"Friar," Troy said. "Is there a back door or something?"

"Heaven have mercy." Friar Laurence took a lamp from the desk and lit it. "There's an old passageway that leads under the church. But it hasn't been used in many years. Friar Hugh built it for secret visits to his mistress."

"Juliet!" Tybalt hollered.

"I must go to Tybalt," Juliet said. "If I do, perhaps he will leave the rest of you alone." That did not seem likely. Troy and I had totally pissed him off.

"What will happen when your parents find out that you left your room?" I asked. "When they find out that you were with a Montague?"

"They would not dare to hurt me, not on the eve of my wedding. I shall be safe, Mimi. Do not worry."

I pointed to her bodice, where the potion was hidden "Don't drink that until you get word from Friar Laurence, just before your wedding. In the meantime, we'll work out all the other details." I tried to sound confident, to mask my growing fear. "I'll see you when you wake up." We hugged again. Her shoulders felt as tense as mine. This whole situation was a complete mess. What had I started and where would it end? Oh please let it end happily. If time had permitted, I would have fallen to my knees and prayed to St. Francis.

But Tybalt started ramming the church door.

"Come," Friar Laurence said. I slipped my feet into the wooden shoes, my toes screaming with each step. We followed the friar down the stairs and into the sanctuary. The altar stood aglow in candlelight. Tybalt screamed Juliet's name, hurling himself at the door. Friar Laurence hurried to the statue of St. Francis, kissed its feet, then pushed at its base. The entire statue slid back effortlessly, revealing an opening in the floor with stairs that led beneath the church. "We will need you to close the opening," the friar told Juliet. Then he made the sign of the cross over her head. "May St. Francis see you safely home."

I was the last to enter the dank stairway, turning as the statue slid back into place. As Juliet's freckled face disappeared from view, doubt gripped my entire body. I waited and listened, not wanting to leave until I knew she'd be okay. Juliet unbolted the church door.

"Traitor!" Tybalt cried. "I will drag you back to the house for all to see. You will be disowned. Where is he, the one with the wounded leg? Is he your lover? I will kill him for having led you astray."

"You will do no such thing." Juliet's assertive tone surprised me. "You have as much to benefit from my marriage as everyone else. You will take me back home, Tybalt, and deliver me safely to my room so that the wedding may proceed, as much for your neck as for mine." Well said. I gave her a mental high five.

"And then what? Romeo will come and rescue you? Is that what you are planning?" There was a long silence. Friar Laurence, Troy, and I held our breaths. "You are a fool with a little girl's mind," Tybalt said. "You cannot avoid this wedding. If anyone tries to stop the wedding, they will have to do so over my dead body." There was a shuffling sound. I think he grabbed her. "I will deliver you safely. But then I will send my men to search this church and to search the entire city. We shall find the bastard with the wounded leg, and we shall find Mimi of Manhattan and Romeo. I shall personally kill all three."

Jeez. Enough with the death threats.

"She seems capable of handling him," Troy whispered. "So, are you coming with me to get Romeo?"

"Yes." But I didn't mention my latest plan.

Walking through a sixteenth-century tunnel is not for the faint of heart. First of all, things dripped on me. Don't ask me what kind of things because I didn't have the stomach to investigate. The air was cold and dank. If there's anyplace where that poisonous black mold might grow, this was the place. I imagined microscopic spores infiltrating my lungs.

Another downside to the whole sixteenth-century tunnel experience was that things squeaked and squealed. *Living things* and they occasionally brushed against us as we walked. I screamed a few times and I'm not proud of that fact. Rats bring out the distressed damsel in me. Even Troy reacted with curses and groans. He started humming his song, "Girl, oh, oh, oh, oh, oh, oh, girl," either from nervousness or as a way to warn the rats that we were coming. I started humming it as well. Even the friar took up the mind-numbing melody. I bumped into Troy twice during our songfest. The first time he ignored me. The second time he snapped, "Watch out for my leg."

Last, but not least in the list of horrors, was the fact that the stone floor was under about three inches of standing water. I don't know what color the water was, but it slopped into my shoes. A headache throbbed at my temples, brought on by the lack of oxygen and the probably toxic mold. A scalp massage, à la Benvolio, sounded lovely, just like the one he had given me in the alley. But did I really want him touching my hair again? I hadn't washed it in days, hadn't brushed my teeth either. I probably had a half-dozen pimples from that oily party makeup and I was pretty sure all the BO in that tunnel wasn't coming just from Troy. Okay, so I was being vain, even with multiple death threats hanging over my head. But I was hoping to see Benvolio again and I didn't want to smell like a sixteenth-century gutter.

"Almost there," Friar Laurence said, his lamp bouncing with his short steps.

The tunnel slanted uphill for about thirty paces then dead-ended. The friar handed Troy the lamp. "Our exit is up there." He pushed at the ceiling and grunted until it gave way. Dim light filtered through, as did strands of straw. "This barn belongs to the church's neighbor. He is a friendly man, but still, we should attempt quiet." Troy pushed the friar's wide rear end through the exit. Then Troy struggled out. Both he and the friar took my outstretched arms and whisked me into fresh air.

A full moon had begun to rise. A cow gave us a curious look. Some chickens stirred, then tucked their beaks into their feathers. Friar Laurence extinguished the lamp and left it in the barn. "We will take the side street to Montague House," he whispered.

"We have to get to Romeo before Tybalt does," I urged.

"But Tybalt is *supposed* to fight Romeo," Troy said, poking me in the arm. "And Romeo kills him. That's a good thing because then Tybalt won't kill us."

True, Romeo kills Tybalt in the play, but as much as Troy wanted it to be, this was not the play. *This* Romeo was a tender guy whose heart overflowed with love and whose mind was weighed down by depression. *This* Tybalt was a bulging hulk whose heart overflowed with hatred and whose mind craved revenge. This Romeo was no match for this Tybalt.

I quickened my pace. "Holy St. Francis," I mumbled. "I hope we're not too late."

Twenty

"Romeo, Romeo, wherefore art thou Romeo?"

WE ARRIVED AT an imposing stone fortress. Men in black and orange uniforms flanked the entryway—a set of carved doors lit by mounted torches. The friar bowed and spoke to a guard, who in turn told us to wait. Troy and I scanned the street. Thankfully, no one had followed us. Though I guessed it was around dinnertime, the surroundings lay in deep silence. Working folk seemed to tuck themselves away early. That made sense, I supposed, in a world without electricity or television.

A man emerged from Montague House. Long and lean, he wore checkered tights, red shorts, and a puffy blue shirt that billowed as he sashayed toward us—certainly not Montague colors. His shoulder-length hair could have been a color swatch for Fire Engine Red. He tipped his feathered hat and bowed. "Friar Laurence, a delight to see you as always."

"Good evening, Mercutio," the friar said.

I had forgotten all about Mercutio. Neither Capulet nor Montague, he's a very good friend of Romeo's. Actors really love the role because Mercutio has these huge monologues and a gloriously melodramatic death scene at the hands of Tybalt. "May I introduce Mimi and Troy of Manhattan," the friar said. "They have come to speak with Romeo."

Mercutio bowed again, then repositioned his hat. The feather caressed his powdered cheek. "My young friend has locked himself in his room and will speak to no one. I have exhausted myself trying to tempt him forth. Come, maybe you will have better luck."

Friar Laurence took me aside. "I must return to my church. If I am not there when Tybalt's men arrive, they might do great damage."

"But what will you tell them about Troy and me?"

"I will tell them that my church is a place of sanctuary and those who come seeking medical attention, be they Capulet or Montague, will receive care." He smiled. "I leave it to you to work out the rest of the details. Romeo is well familiar with the streets beyond Verona so he will have no trouble guiding Juliet out of the city. When you hear the bells chime tomorrow eve, you will know that Juliet has drunk the potion. Soon after, we must all meet at the Capulet tomb." I must have looked terrified because he took my hand and squeezed. "God works in mysterious ways, my child. I believe that your magic charm is one of those ways. Your arrival serves a greater purpose. We must have faith, but we must also have courage." He squeezed again, then waddled off.

Like Capulet House, dozens of paintings lined the inner Montague hallway, and a winding staircase led to Romeo's room. Mercutio rattled on and on about the house's design.

He was a total bore. He walked on tiptoe and whipped his hands around like a hyperactive conductor.

"Is Benvolio around?" I asked. Right on cue, Troy snorted.

"Benvolio is on patrol but he's due to return shortly. Ah, here we are," Mercutio announced with a graceful flourish.

A servant stood outside Romeo's bedroom, hovering over a basket of laundry. "Young master will not be moved," the old man told us. "I am to bathe him and change his clothing but he refuses."

"More stubborn than an ass," Mercutio said, pounding his fist on the door. "Romeo! Madman! Lover! Speak to me, friend. A song will suffice. Perhaps a sonnet. Recite one simple rhyme and I shall be satisfied."

"Go away."

"Go away. That, my friend, does not rhyme." Mercutio folded his arms and leaned against the door. "How about, go away until another day? Or, go away and eat some hay."

"Go away, I say!"

"A true poet, yet he does not know it." Mercutio tilted his hat to the side. "Come out and charm us with your verse."

"Not until Rosaline loves me."

"Dear boy, if a woman does not wish to love, then she will not love. Women can control their hearts in ways that men can never imagine. Wouldn't you agree, Mimi?"

This particular woman had no idea how to control her heart. It thumped one minute for Troy and the next minute for Benvolio. Well aware of Troy's stare, I shrugged. "I'm the wrong person to ask."

"I will never come out!" Romeo cried.

I had hollered those exact words when, just before the first rehearsal of *Romeo and Juliet*, I had locked myself in my room. Mother had gone ballistic. "You have a contract with the theater. Don't make me call the doorman. I'll have him unscrew the hinges and carry you out of there." Even the black-and-white cat across the street had known that my situation was hopeless. He had mouthed a little *meow* before stretching out on his window ledge.

"I will never come out. I don't want to be in *Romeo and Juliet*. I don't want to act anymore."

"You have no choice. The only thing that will get you out of your contract is a debilitating illness," my mother had said as she paced outside the door. "Mimi Wallingford, are you listening to me? You come out of there this instant."

Debilitating illness. Oh my God, could Troy have been right? Had I conjured up the stage fright on purpose? Was I so pathetic that I couldn't admit it even to myself?

"Romeo," I said. "It's Mimi and Troy."

"Mimi from Manhattan? And Troy, the wounded singer?"

"Yes."

"Singer?" Mercutio asked, sweeping his long, flaming hair off his shoulders. "I sing as well, mostly my own compositions. You are likely familiar with my love song 'Girl, Come Hither and We Shall Dither.'"

"Uh, no," Troy said, rolling his eyes. "Hey, Romeo, buddy, let us in. We've got to talk to you about something."

"Please, Romeo."

"Lady Mimi?" A quiet voice floated through the crack

under the door. I knelt and dipped my head as close as possible. "Have you come to speak of love? Do you know why Rosaline will not love me?"

Talk about a one-track mind. "I do," I lied. "Let me in and I'll tell you."

"Romeo, Romeo," Mercutio said, kneeling next to me and pressing his face close to the door's crack. "Rosaline will not love you because she is a thick-headed bolt of linen. Come join us in the garden for a late feast. We shall sing and be merry. Troy has agreed to sing my song 'Girl, Come Hither and We Shall Dither.' "

"Uh, not really," Troy said.

"Perhaps you would prefer 'Girl, Come and Handle My Candle'?"

The latch rattled, then the door cracked open. Mercutio and I scrambled to our feet. "Only Lady Mimi," Romeo said, holding out a beckoning hand. "I only want to see her."

Mercutio patted Troy on the back. "The Montagues possess a renowned selection of instruments. Let us go down to the courtyard to compare songs. I have a few new verses that I should like to put to music."

"Go ahead," I told Troy. "I'll take care of things here."

Troy didn't look convinced and he pressed his mouth close to my ear. "Remember, it's a story, Mimi. A story that we need *to end*." His breath warmed the inside of my ear. I closed my eyes for a moment. Benvolio's breath had tickled me like velvet fingers. Troy's tickled me as well, only it ran down the length of my spine. I opened my eyes and he was staring at me. I couldn't convince myself that I hated him.

He had saved my life. He had trusted me enough to let me clean his wound. He had shared secret worries with me.

As soon as Troy and Mercutio had left, Romeo opened the door wide enough for me to slip inside.

"Clean clothes, young master," the servant said, lifting the laundry basket. Romeo thanked him and took the basket. "But master . . ."

"I will dress myself. That is all."

The Decorator from Hell had left his mark on Romeo's room. Montague black and orange covered everything, like Halloween had exploded. It made me dizzy. That horrid room had to be one of the causes of Romeo's gloom.

"Welcome to my home, Lady Mimi. But while you are here, you can never tell my parents that you are Capulet. They despise all Capulets and have vowed to run them out of Verona, or kill them in the attempt." He wore an expression as woeful as a basset hound's. "A raging river of hatred flows here. Can you feel it?" He hugged himself. "Hatred, hatred, everywhere. My parents speak of nothing else but this hatred. It consumes them."

I think I could actually feel the hatred, or maybe it was the ugly room that put me on edge.

"Only love can free me from this prison of hatred. Only love."

"Only love?" I gasped. "Is that a bathtub?" A large porcelain tub sat in the corner of Romeo's room, next to a screen and a closestool. The tub was filled with water—clean water. Rose petals floated at the surface. I dipped my fingers in. It was lukewarm. "Romeo, are you going to use this water?"

"I am too tired for that bath," he said, draping himself over his bed.

"May I?" I didn't wait for his reply. I pulled the screen around the tub and kicked off my shoes. The dress's cinched waist wouldn't budge so I tugged at it and broke the lace. Not bothering with the sleeves, I yanked the entire dress over my head and threw it on the screen. Off came the shirt, underskirt, bra, and panties. I stepped in and melted. Never had lukewarm water felt so good. I dunked my head, then reached for a bar of soap that smelled like lemon.

"Romeo," I called, lathering my hair. "When we were in the orchard, you said that you had a chest overflowing with gold. Is that true?"

"I have more gold coins than I can count."

I wiggled my toes gleefully. "And just now you said that only love can free you from this prison of hatred. Did you mean that?"

"Yes, only love. Rosaline's love."

"What about someone else's love?"

"But I love Rosaline."

I worked the soap down my arms. "Yes, but that's not really love. I know you think it is, but take it from me, it's just a crush. I felt the same way once. I couldn't stop thinking about this one guy, and I dreamed about him every night." Okay, I still dreamed about him but Romeo didn't need to know that. Bending the truth is perfectly acceptable when one is trying to save a life. Two lives. Maybe more.

"Yes, I dream about Rosaline, too."

"Uh huh." I dunked again, wondering if Benvolio liked

the scent of lemon. "But those feelings fade quickly when you meet someone else." Listen to me. I sounded like a mature, experienced woman. What a laugh.

"My feelings for Rosaline will never fade."

A stack of folded towels sat next to the tub. I had started to shiver so I wrapped a towel around my hair and another around my body. The water had turned gray. How embarrassing. The last thing I wanted to wear was that heavy dress, which was filthy, stained, and marked me as a thief. Romeo and I seemed about the same size. "Romeo, can I borrow some of your clothes?"

"Take whatever you'd like," he mumbled. I peered over the screen. He had turned toward the wall and was stabbing it with a small knife, chipping off flakes of plaster. I hurried out and grabbed the clothes basket. His black tights and white shirt fit perfectly. The puffy orange shorts were a bit loose but I cinched them with a woven belt. What a relief, to be able to walk around without two hundred pounds of velvet weighing me down. A pair of boots stood against the wall, made of soft, well-worn leather. I slipped my feet into them and sighed. Like being reborn.

Romeo scooted to the end of his bed and hung his head over the edge. "Tell me why Rosaline refuses to love me."

I worked my fingers through my wet hair. "Rosaline is not meant to love you. Someone else is."

He slid off the bed and sat on the floor, tucking his knees tightly to his chest. "Who?" He stared at me with eyes so heavy with hurt he could barely hold them open.

I sat beside him, feeling strangely maternal. I wanted to

tousle his downy hair but didn't. Only two years separated us and in many ways I was as immature as he in matters of love. But I knew what it felt like to be depressed and lost. "Romeo, you had a chance to meet someone and I messed it up. She was at the Capulet party and if the two of you had met, I'm pretty sure you would have liked each other." I didn't say that I was pretty sure they would have fallen in love. At the time, I had major issues with the whole destiny thing. My mother always told me that my destiny had been decided before I was born, stamped with a golden Wallingford seal. One could look at Romeo in the same way, created by Mr. Shakespeare for a single purpose. But Shakespeare wasn't running this show. Who's to say that Romeo and Juliet couldn't just be friends?

"There's a girl named Juliet who lives across town. She's a Capulet and her parents are forcing her to get married. She doesn't want to because she basically hates the guy and he's a pervert anyway, according to Friar Laurence. So, she's going to leave Verona, but she can't do it without money and she can't do it without an escort."

"Why do you tell me this?"

"Because I'm hoping that you'll volunteer to be her escort."

"Help a Capulet? I'm supposed to hate Capulets."

"Do you?"

He sighed. "No. I've never hated anyone." I believed him. It's a rare person who doesn't feel hatred. I began to realize that beneath the whining exterior lay a true gem of a man.

"Juliet needs your help, Romeo. Will you help her?"

I waited for his answer. He had to agree. He just had to. I didn't know squat about the world outside Verona. Juliet and I would be caught as easily as blind chickens. But all my hopes were dashed with a single, sad shake of his head. "No, I cannot leave. What if Rosaline changes her mind?"

I got to my feet. He needed a wake-up call. "What are you saying? That you're going to lie in this room, moping over a woman who will never love you? She's dedicated her life to God. Don't you get it, Romeo? You're wasting *your* life in a totally dead-end relationship." How could I get through to him? I felt the walls of the orange and black room closing in on me. Time was running out. "You said that you were trapped. That's a terrible way to feel. I know the feeling all too well. We might all be trapped."

"Trapped?"

"Totally and completely *trapped*," I said. "I don't even know if Troy and I can get home. We might have to start a new life here or outside Verona. But what I do know is that Juliet *can't* stay here. She has a chance for freedom." I turned to him. "Anyone who helps her might be in danger, and who am I to ask you to take such a risk? I just thought you might like to get away from this place for a while. Get away from all the heartache and all the feuding." I folded my arms around my knees. "She's not even fourteen, Romeo. They are selling her body and she's not even fourteen."

"Rosaline is only fourteen." Romeo stood, straightening to his full height. I hadn't realized he was so tall or broad shouldered. "I would kill the man who tried to sell her body." He walked over to a trunk and took out a velvet bag, then filled it with coins. He tied the bag to his belt. "I shall help this girl. When do we leave?"

"Really?" I leaped to my feet. "You'll help?" He nodded and I threw my arms around him. At that moment, Romeo Montague, a secondary character of little appeal, was promoted to heroic leading man. "We need to leave right away. Let's go find Troy."

Thanks to Mercutio's voice I knew where to find the guys. His falsetto waltzed down the hallway as he reworked Troy's song.

> Girl, thou hath me ringing, girl, thou hath me dinging
> The bells of love, the bells of love.
> Girl, thou hath me sharing, girl, thou hath me swearing,
> The vows of love, the vows of love.
> Girl, oh, oh, oh, oh, oh, oh, girl.
> I'm speaking of thee, girl.

Mercutio had completely transformed the song, slowing down its original hip-hop rhythm. He stopped singing to play a flute solo while Troy strummed a mandolin. I felt so much better in my clean clothes and soft boots. With Romeo at my side I had a good chance of pulling this off. I hummed as I stepped into the courtyard.

Suddenly, it felt as if someone had stabbed me in the gut. For there sat Benvolio, on a bench at the edge of the courtyard, with a woman on his lap.

And he was kissing her.

Twenty-one

*"The course of true love
never did run smooth."*

T ORCHLIGHT SILHOUETTED BENVOLIO'S classical profile as he whispered in an ear that was not mine. The woman giggled.

I just stood there, hoping that I was staring at a man who simply looked like Benvolio. Maybe his identical twin, but not *my* Benvolio.

He didn't notice me at first, since I was dressed like a man. But others noticed. "Romeo, you have emerged. And who is this?" Mercutio asked, twirling his flute like a baton. "A lamb in wolf's clothing."

"Mimi?" Troy asked.

Benvolio roughly pushed the woman away. "Go," he told her. She stopped giggling and ran from the courtyard. Rising on his long legs, Benvolio strode toward me. He took both my hands in his and kissed them. I let him because I could feel Troy's eyes burning into my back. I decided to play it cool.

"Mimi," Benvolio cooed. "Your beauty makes the torches burn brighter."

Hello? You already said that to me. That must have been his standard pickup line.

Mr. Shakespeare once wrote that "jealousy is a green-eyed monster that doth mock the meat it feeds upon." In other words, it can make a perfectly rational person act like an idiot. I controlled my urge to scream at Benvolio. Maybe even to slap him. Did I have a right to be jealous? We hadn't made any kind of commitment, had we? Of course not. Talk of marriage isn't the same thing as actually agreeing to marriage. Marriage wasn't what I wanted anyway. I just wanted a boyfriend, even if he was from the sixteenth century. A nice, loving, loyal boyfriend. Was that too much to ask?

"I did not see you come in," he explained. Obviously. "Why are you dressed in that manner?" He circled me like a tiger. Hadn't he ever seen a woman in pants?

"Mimi," Romeo whispered. "I need to get a few things for our journey. I shall return momentarily." He left the courtyard.

Benvolio placed his hand on my waist and guided me to his love bench. A trellised lemon tree climbed the wall behind us. "Mimi," he said, sitting so close I could feel the heat of his thigh. His words were entwined with the scent of warm lemon peel. "Cupid pierced my heart the moment I first saw you in the apricot orchard." What might have sounded flattering before I had found him in a liplock now just sounded slick and rehearsed. "Have you given any thought to my proposal?"

"Uh, can we talk?" I asked, hoping to go someplace where Troy couldn't hear. Though he pretended to be absorbed in his music, his gaze kept darting my way.

Benvolio's smile was stiff. "Of course." He led me around the garden wall and under an archway to a room lined with shelves of linens. "We haven't much time. I must lead the guard on night duty."

"About your proposal . . ."

"Mimi," was all he said. Then he kissed me.

Okay, so I was mad at him, but I had also been lusting after him since the moment we met. I couldn't help myself. I kissed him back, and he kissed me back, and we kissed and kissed and kissed until I thought my lips would swell up like balloons and burst.

Until I thought my eyeballs would roll backward, not from ecstasy, but from sheer boredom.

That's right—sheer boredom.

Surprised? So was I! What in the world was wrong with me? How could I find a man like Benvolio—a man with black curly hair and chocolate eyes and the face and body of a Roman god, boring? But the kisses felt empty. I don't know how else to explain it. Add to my growing list of things to discuss with Dr. Harmony, the possibility that I'm a total lesbian. That would just about kill my mother.

"You will become my wife then?" he asked, taking a quick breather.

Uh oh. I supposed that kissing in a linen closet in the sixteenth century meant that we were officially engaged. I put my hands against his chest, trying to force some space between us. "I'm not ready to get married, Benvolio."

That seemed to amuse him. "You're as ready as any woman." He grabbed my butt with one hand and began kissing me again. His other hand started untying my shirt. I tried to pull away but he pressed against me with his weight, pushing me into one of the linen shelves. I tried to yell at him but his mouth completely covered mine. He was hurting me. I had to get away. I raised my knee, hoping to drive it into his crotch, but he twisted sideways. That twist gave me an opportunity. "Stop!" I cried. His hand clamped over my mouth and he pushed me onto the floor. Then he kicked the door shut.

"Don't fight, Mimi," he whispered. "There's passion between us. You can't deny it. We don't have to wait until our wedding night." And then he was on top of me, and I realized that I was about to be raped. How could this be happening? My mind raced, my hands searched the air for something to grab on to, something I could use to fend him off.

Please stop, I begged with my eyes.

"You can't kiss me like that and expect me not to want you."

Oh God, he was all over me, his weight pressed on my hip bones. I couldn't breathe. He started struggling with my pants. I couldn't get out from under him. I couldn't *push him off*!

And then he was rising up in the air, and Troy was shoving him against the shelves, with a tight grip on his neck. My heart pounded in my ears as Benvolio tried to fight Troy off, but Troy tightened his grip. "Damn you!" Troy said, spit flying from his angry lips. Troy might have strangled Benvolio if Mercutio hadn't entered the room.

"Gentlemen," Mercutio said, sizing up the situation. "It does not bode well for Montague to fight Montague." I scooted into the corner, trying to disappear.

"If you touch her again, I'll kill you," Troy threatened. Benvolio gasped for air.

Mercutio calmly placed his hand on Troy's outstretched arm. "You must release your grip, sir."

"I want him to swear he will not touch her again."

"He will reply if you release your grip." Mercutio patted Troy's arm. Troy released his grip and stepped back.

Benvolio rubbed his neck, then narrowed his eyes. "I don't have any intention of touching her again. She is all yours."

All yours? I'm not anyone's! But I was trembling so hard I couldn't speak, let alone defend myself.

"There, that is settled." Mercutio patted both men on the back, though neither relaxed his stance. "Seems there has been far too much drink tonight."

"Yes," Benvolio said through clenched teeth. "Too much to drink." He straightened his clothing and left the linen closet, without a single glance my way.

Mercutio frowned. "There goes a hotheaded fool. I'm glad to see you are both in one piece. Not everyone survives an encounter with Benvolio."

Mercutio returned to the courtyard but I stayed in the corner, still dazed. Troy knelt on his good knee and closed my borrowed shirt. I couldn't bear to look at him. "Don't say I told you so," I pleaded, my eyes filling with tears.

"Mimi, I would never say that." He reached out to touch my arm, but stopped short. "I'm sorry."

I tried to compose myself. I brushed dust from my pants, trying, as well, to brush away the sensation of Benvolio's groping hands. Troy had saved me again. I looked into his green eyes. "I . . . I . . ." Stammering was all I could manage. What was I trying to say? Was I going to blame myself by saying that I shouldn't have kissed Benvolio? Or was I going to say something even more stupid like I shouldn't have worn pants in a time when women's butts were hidden beneath heavy skirts? Troy wrapped his arms around me as I fought back tears. "I . . . I should have poked him in the eye. They always teach that on *Oprah*."

"I should have poked him in the eye, too," Troy said, trying to ease the tension.

We sat that way for a bit. His hug was comforting, as if I had been wrapped in a towel fresh from the dryer. I no longer felt lemony clean. I wanted to jump back into the tub and wash Benvolio's saliva from my neck and face. "How's your leg?" I asked.

"Better. I think you did a good job. I could use some Tylenol, for the pain, but it's not too bad."

Romeo peered in. "What happened?" He noticed my tears before I could wipe them away with my sleeve. "I went to the kitchen to get some bread for our journey. Did I miss something?"

"No. Everything's fine," I said. Troy and I got to our feet.

Romeo opened his mouth, about to say something. Then he cocked his head toward the doorway. "Did you hear that? It sounds like fighting."

"Capulets!" a voice cried.

We stepped out of the linen room. The sleepy house had erupted in chaos. Servants in nightgowns scurried past, clutching each other in fear. A group of guards almost knocked me over. "The Capulets have attacked," one of the guards cried. "To the front gate, men!" Romeo dropped the bread and dashed across the courtyard. Troy and I followed him until we reached the portrait hallway. We stopped beneath a towering painting of some long-dead Montague and watched as Romeo charged out the front door.

"We can't go out there," Troy said. "The Capulets are looking for us."

"But I haven't told Romeo that Tybalt is looking for him, too." The long-dead Montague stared at me with a down-turned mouth, judging me, blaming me, for the mess I'd made. "Tybalt wouldn't be looking for Romeo if I hadn't yelled his name out the window. What if Tybalt's out there?"

"Tybalt and Romeo are supposed to fight." Troy's voice was steady and calm. "Romeo will kill Tybalt like he's supposed to and we'll all be better off. Then we won't have to worry about him trying to kill us."

Of course things would be easier without Tybalt constantly threatening to arrest and execute us. But what were the chances that Romeo would actually succeed? While I wouldn't shed a tear for Tybalt, I had come to like Romeo. I had never met anyone who was so honest about his emotions. "But what if Tybalt kills Romeo?"

"That's not the way it happens. Just let things fall into place so the story can get back on track." Troy leaned wearily against the wall. "I'm begging you. Enough with the 'Mimi to the Rescue' thing. It's a story. Let it end."

A servant ran past and raced up the marble stairs just as

a man in a long, orange and black robe appeared at the top step. "What's all the noise outside?"

The servant jumped up and down as if his feet were on fire. "Lord Montague, the Capulets are attacking."

"Damn them to hell!" Lord Montague bellowed, reaching for the banister. The servant took the old man's arm and helped guide him down the stairs. Montague, fair and thin like his son, counted each stair as he awkwardly made his way down them. "Hurry, man," he told the servant, stumbling when they reached the floor. As the servant guided him toward the front door, Lord Montague took no notice of Troy and me, his eyes staring blankly into space.

"He's blind," Troy whispered. "But Lord Montague isn't blind in the play."

"Exactly. Now do you get it? This isn't the play," I said, throwing my hands in the air. "Shakespeare's been completely erased. Face it, Troy. Nothing's predictable. It hasn't been since we arrived. There's no way of knowing if Romeo will kill Tybalt or the other way around." Shouting erupted outside. "I've got to see what's going on. Come on." He followed me up the stairs to Romeo's room. Romeo's door stood wide open. Once inside, Troy closed it and slid the bolt.

We leaned across the sill of Romeo's window. A full moon floated in a cloudless sky, casting soft white light on the scene below. For the first time since arriving, the surroundings felt artificial, as if I sat in a box seat, staring down at actors on a stage. Yet the Wallingford troupe had never achieved this gut-wrenching level of tension.

Lord Montague stood on the steps, flanked by his

guards. Servants nervously crowded near the entryway. "Where have they gone?" he demanded.

"We know not, sir," a guard replied. "Mercutio and Benvolio took off after Tybalt, along with Benvolio's men."

"And my son?"

"He followed."

"Did he take a sword?" Montague asked. "Tell me, man, did Romeo take a sword?"

The guard looked down at his feet. "No, sir. He said he was going to try to persuade them to cease fighting."

"Send out the troops!" Lord Montague began to pace, wringing his hands and cursing. "I'll not have that lovesick boy killed by Capulets!"

"Halt!" one of the guards ordered, peering into the distance. "Who goes there?"

Benvolio emerged from the shadowy end of the street, carrying a body in his arms. A cascade of Fire Engine Red hair swung with each heavy step. Benvolio laid Mercutio's body at Lord Montague's feet. "Mercutio is dead, my lord," Benvolio said, his face clenched with anger. "Killed by Tybalt Capulet."

"Where is my son?" Montague asked desperately. "Where is Romeo?"

"Romeo lives." Troy and I let out huge sighs of relief. Benvolio addressed the gathered crowd of servants, guards, and woken townsfolk. "Romeo tried to stop the fighting. He pleaded with Tybalt but Tybalt lunged and slew Mercutio. As honor dictates, Romeo grabbed Mercutio's blade and pierced Tybalt's heart."

"He fought? My son fought?" Lord Montague smiled with pride and puffed out his chest. Then his stance deflated and he reached out, waving his hands. "Benvolio, come to me. I must speak to you in private."

Troy and I hid behind a curtain as Benvolio led Lord Montague to a spot just beneath the window. "Were there Capulet witnesses?" Lord Montague asked.

"Yes. Tybalt's men. They have taken the villain's body back to Capulet House."

Lord Montague clutched Benvolio's shoulders. "Then Romeo has broken the prince's law."

"Tybalt was a murderer," Benvolio said. "Romeo did his duty by avenging Lord Mercutio's death."

"The prince does not care about the circumstances. It is only a matter of time before Romeo is arrested for Tybalt's murder and executed. Where is he?"

"He is ashamed of his actions. He is hiding."

"Go to him. Tell him that he must leave Verona immediately. Tell him that I will publicly declare him forever banished to buy some negotiating time with the prince." His voice cracked with emotion. "Tell him I have never felt so much pride and that I love him. Tell him this."

"Yes, sir."

"My heart breaks tonight, Benvolio."

"As does mine."

"Come on," I whispered to Troy. "We've got to get to Romeo."

Twenty-two

*"Men at some time are
masters of their fate."*

B ENVOLIO HAD A head start but I had already guessed
where Romeo was hiding. By the time we reached Friar
Laurence's church, Benvolio had delivered the bad news.

"Banished," Romeo said, clutching Mercutio's bloodied
sword. "Never to see Verona again."

"Never. Your father has commanded it."

"Mercutio is dead. Dear Mercutio." Romeo spoke softly.
"Our friend is dead, Benvolio. Dead."

Troy and I stood just inside the sanctuary, keeping a dis-
creet distance. I had come to rely on the Montagues for a
sense of security but that had been shattered. Benvolio had
turned against me and Romeo had joined me on Verona's
Most Wanted list. We shared the uncertainty of homeless-
ness, uprooted by forces beyond our control. Crazy, incon-
ceivable forces unleashed from a tiny vial of ashes.

Friar Laurence wrung his hands and gazed sympatheti-
cally at Romeo. "Holy St. Francis. What a tragedy."

"Before Mercutio died, he cursed both the houses," Romeo said. "A plague on Montague and Capulet, those were his last words. He died because of our hatred."

"He died because Tybalt was a bloodthirsty monster," Benvolio snarled.

"Mercutio is dead and I am banished, never to see Rosaline again." Romeo hugged the sword to his chest.

"Banishment is far better than execution," Benvolio pointed out. He peered through one of the windows, then moved to another. "They'd not spare an ounce of mercy."

"Yes, my child, far better than execution."

Benvolio checked another window. "No sign of pursuit. But the prince and Lord Capulet will search, come morning light."

"I am a murderer," Romeo said. The sword fell to the floor. The clank of metal echoed off the stone walls and made my heart skip a beat.

Benvolio smacked his palm on the sill. "Forget about that woman," he said angrily. "You must leave immediately." He untied a coin pouch from his belt and handed it to Romeo. "Take this." Romeo stood lifeless, staring into space, into the unknown future. "Take it! You must leave now."

"I'll hold it for him," I said, stepping forward. Though it sickened me, I didn't look away when Benvolio handed me the purse. I held my chin up and met his espresso eyes with a determined glare. Troy stepped forward as well, his body tensed like a lion ready to pounce—like a guy ready to protect *me*.

Benvolio did not flinch or back away, keeping his gaze steady. "Lord and Lady Capulet will not forget your exile, Mimi. You are also in grave danger. I suggest you leave for Manhattan immediately and take Romeo with you." He raised his voice, as if he wanted everyone to hear, even the church mice. "Romeo acted honorably when he avenged Mercutio's murder. So, too, shall I act honorably by apologizing to you, Mimi. I am sorry for having treated you most unkindly."

"Unkindly?" Troy still sounded furious.

I didn't tell Benvolio that I accepted his apology because the feelings of betrayal were still fresh, but I appreciated the gesture.

Benvolio strode to Romeo's side and embraced him. "Go, cousin, and may this bloody feud never cross your path again." He unsheathed his sword and hurried from the church, the heavy door slamming behind him with an imposing finality. I knew I'd never see him again.

"Good riddance," Troy hissed.

"Benvolio speaks the truth. You must all leave before dawn's light," Friar Laurence advised.

There seemed to be no way around it. Troy could no longer argue that the story had to get back on course. Staying meant certain death for Romeo and me. Troy wouldn't be welcome back at Montague House, not with Benvolio running the show. I was filled with fear and uncertainty. Leaving Verona was now our *only* option, but what did leaving mean? Would that bring an end to this crazy adventure or were we doomed to stay in this world for the rest of our lives? My mother and aunt were probably sick with worry. How many days had passed? I couldn't remember.

"Where will we go?" I asked the friar.

Friar Laurence stuck his hands into the sleeves of his brown robe. "Do not go east toward Venice. There are too many Capulets there. Avoid the papal states as well, for the Capulets have loyal allies. You could go to England, but the journey would be long."

"Juliet would hate England," I said. "Women weren't allowed to be actors in England. I mean, *aren't* allowed."

The friar scratched his bald spot. "Since Troy's wound may slow you down, I suggest you venture west to Milan and possibly hire a carriage there, or buy passage on a merchant's wagon. Or you could travel south to Genoa, then take a boat to Spain. I know not which way is less dangerous."

"This just totally sucks," Troy said, sitting on one of the benches. "How are we supposed to get home? Running for our lives across Europe can't be the way."

"I know of no roads to Manhattan," Friar Laurence said. "And God has not provided you with another charm."

A conundrum that we couldn't wrap our brains around, the way home eluded us. We had gone back to the cobbler's shop but had found no magic portal. Verona's only quill merchant had never heard of William Shakespeare. Even if I had wanted to, events had strayed so far from the original story line that there was no way of putting them back on course. Neither of us said what we were thinking—that there might not be a way home. Ever. Plague, giant rats, bad shoes, and sleeping in barns were about to replace leading roles and number one hits. My old, faraway life, the one that had tormented my heart and soul, seemed so benign. At least no one in Manhattan was trying to execute me!

An image of Lady Capulet's face, with that creepy plucked forehead, loomed in my mind. "We'd better get going," I said. "They'll look here for sure." Romeo continued to stare at the church wall. His feelings had consumed him, again. I tucked the coin purse into my boot. "Romeo, come on," I urged. "We still have to get Juliet. She's relying on us." Troy started to say something but I didn't want to hear his objections. "It's Romeo *and* Juliet, Troy. Remember?"

For the zillionth time since our arrival, Troy totally surprised me. "I think you're right. We shouldn't leave her behind." He shrugged. "She's a nice girl."

"We can't wait for tomorrow's wedding," I decided. "Juliet has to take the potion tonight. Romeo, are you with us?"

The friar took one of Romeo's delicate hands, clutching it between his own. "My son," he said gently, looking into the vacant eyes. "Today you took a life and that is a great sin, even if it was a murderer's life." A single tear rolled down Romeo's soft cheek. "But God, in His wisdom, has given you an opportunity to redeem your soul by helping to save another's life. Juliet needs you, my child. Go, and God will watch over you."

"Redeem my soul?" Romeo lifted the friar's silver cross and kissed it. Then he turned and looked into my eyes. "If I am to be banished, then I welcome any and all refugees of this feud who wish to join me." He picked up Mercutio's sword. "Let us go and rescue Juliet."

The friar hurried to his room, stuffing a bag full of things he said we'd need. "Your letter!" he exclaimed, stumbling back down the stairs. "I could not find it. Tybalt's men must have taken it when they searched."

"If the Capulets read that letter, they'll know I lied about being a Capulet."

Friar Laurence swung open the front door. "All the more reason for haste."

We slunk along the back roads like the criminals that we were. Romeo carried the friar's bag. Despite Troy's limp and the friar's short steps, we made good time. I could have run a marathon with all the adrenaline that pumped through me. Fortunately, we didn't encounter anyone, just more of those delightful, well-fed rodents. As we hurried, I filled Romeo in on the sleeping potion plan. He didn't say a word, and appeared to be deep in thought. I could only hope that he had been listening.

Like Montague House, Capulet House was a frenzy of activity. The Capulet guards had gathered at the front and were brandishing their weapons and cursing the enemy. They weren't actually beating their chests but were close to it. "The Montagues must die!" one of them shouted as a jug was passed around.

"Romeo murdered Tybalt. Romeo must die!" A rousing cheer followed. A shiver ran through me when I realized that they were getting ready for a good old-fashioned lynching.

"The girl who disobeyed her exile must also die."

"Mimi of Manhattan must die!"

Imagine hearing a group of drunken warriors shouting your name and following it with a *must die*. Suddenly I missed my superspecial tagline: *Great-granddaughter of Adelaide Wallingford*. The tagline Must Die totally sucked.

Staying out of view, we crept around to the side of the house. Stone walls muffled the guards' ruckus. The errand boy's crate sat empty and the little courtyard beneath Juliet's balcony was awash in moonlight. Juliet stood on the balcony, her frizzy hair tumbling over the shoulders of her white nightgown. I was about to call up to her when Romeo touched my arm. "Who is that?"

"That's Juliet," I whispered.

"Juliet," he repeated. He dropped the bag and took a cautious step forward. Right then and there I knew, as sure as I knew my heart was beating, as sure as I knew my lungs were expanding, that once again, something amazing was about to happen. And it did.

Sweet, sad Romeo, severed from his family and from Rosaline, grieving the murder of a friend and his own act of murder, took a deep breath and came to life. It seemed as if the air in that courtyard contained a higher concentration of oxygen. As his lungs filled he began to glow. It looked like someone had painted him with liquid moonlight. The dull eyes that had imprisoned sorrow ignited, as if backlit by a Wallingford lighting technician. Moonbeams danced through his brown hair. Troy and the friar were breathing the same air, yet neither of them glowed. It had nothing to do with oxygen. Romeo had fallen in love.

"Hello," he said.

Juliet gasped and leaned over the railing. "Are you an angel?" she asked, squinting from his glow. Okay, so she might have squinted because of the glare bouncing off his sword, but believe me, the guy glowed.

"I am Romeo," he said.

Even if you haven't read *Romeo and Juliet*, you're probably familiar with the balcony scene—the most famous scene in the entire play. Troy and I had acted this scene countless times. The lines played out in my mind. *Romeo, Romeo, wherefore art thou Romeo? Deny thy father and refuse thy name, and I'll no longer be a Capulet.*

"Go on," Troy whispered to Romeo. "Say it." He was playing out the scene just as I was, expecting Romeo to begin reciting Shakespeare's line, *What light through yonder window breaks?*

But Romeo did not recite Shakespeare's line. In fact, he didn't say anything for a full minute—an uncomfortable span of silence. Neither did Juliet, who gazed down from her perch with a shy smile.

William Shakespeare might have given his young lovers all sorts of sophisticated things to say, but in this version, *my* crazy version, they were just a couple of kids. Romeo, still in shock from the night's horrors, and Juliet, terrified by what the next day would bring, were as surprised by their sudden attraction as any two people would be. They stood mesmerized, floating in the moment of knowing that they were more attracted to each other than to any other person on Earth.

Finally, Juliet broke the silence. "Why have you come?"

Romeo moved into the courtyard. Troy, Friar Laurence, and I stayed in the shadows, shameless eavesdroppers. "I have come to escort you out of Verona."

"Where would you take me?"

"I would take you wherever you should like to go." He rested his hands on his hips. "You do not wish to go to a nunnery, do you?"

"Never." She smiled and leaned farther over the railing. Her nightgown rustled in the faint breeze. "I wish to become an actor. I might even write a play."

He broke into a huge grin. Wow! That was the first time I saw him smile. "That is a great wish." He didn't take his eyes off of her. I don't think he even blinked.

Suddenly, Juliet became self-conscious. She straightened up and tried to flatten her hyperactive hair. "If you have heard any rumors that I have boils on my bottom or that I have onion breath, they are not true."

"I would never believe such rumors."

"Does it bother you that I am a Capulet?"

"No. Does it bother you that I am a Montague?"

"No." She draped herself over the balcony again, resting her chin in her hands. "My mother once loved a Montague. Have you ever been in love?"

"Not until this very moment." He gazed and gazed and gazed some more. Like Copernicus staring at the sun, realizing that he had discovered the center of the universe.

Troy took my hand and whispered his line, "Did my heart love till now? Forswear it, sight. For I ne'er saw true beauty till this night." I didn't pull away, but I felt very confused. I wanted to curl into his arms, but was it because he had saved my life? Was it because I was scared? Was it because I had never really gotten over him? Or was it because of this place, electrified by Romeo and Juliet's mutual attraction?

They could have stared at each other all night but time was of the essence. I slipped from Troy's grasp and stepped out of the shadows. "Hi, Juliet." Troy and the friar followed.

"Mimi? Is that you? Why are you dressed like a boy?"

"It's a long story. There's been a change of plans."

And that is when the balcony door burst open.

Twenty-three

"To sleep, perchance to dream . . ."

FRIAR LAURENCE, ROMEO, Troy, and I darted into a
thicket of vines directly beneath Juliet's balcony. Lady
Capulet's sinister voice shattered the romantic atmosphere
and squeezed my stomach into a knot. To this day her voice
occasionally comes back to me, permanently stuck in my
head like shrapnel.

"Tybalt is dead!" she announced. "Murdered by Romeo,
son of Montague. Oh, the horror. Such terrible tidings on
the eve of your wedding." Wooden shoes paced above our
heads. "The guards have gathered and will seek revenge at
dawn's light. They have orders to kill the boy on sight."

"On sight?" Juliet asked.

"I hope they kill every Montague they find. Even that
little liar who pretended to be one of us. She made me look
like a fool." She had read the letter. Juliet said nothing. The
pacing ceased. "My daughter, I know you were fond of your
cousin Tybalt, but do not allow these circumstances to weigh

heavy on your mind. We shall proceed with the wedding tomorrow, as planned. Then Paris's men will be added to our own to avenge Tybalt's murder. I must go comfort your father. Tybalt was his favorite nephew."

"Yes, Mother."

"Come inside and sleep. You must be beautiful and fresh for your wedding."

The balcony door closed. We waited for Juliet to reemerge but she didn't. "Do you think the coast is clear?" Romeo asked. "I shall go to her."

"No," I decided. "I think I'd better do it." It was totally crazy of me to volunteer to put myself back in the viper's den. But someone had to. Romeo would slow things down with all his gawking and gazing. "I've been inside her room and the house. I know where to hide if I need to."

"Mimi," Troy objected.

"I'll be fine."

I started to climb the vine. I had never climbed anything in my life. It wasn't like I had spent my summers at camp, mastering the obstacle course and rope ladder. To my surprise, the climb was fairly easy since the vine had grown on a wooden trellis. I swung my legs over the railing and lowered myself onto the balcony without a sound. If Lady Capulet found me, I'd be slain, my body left in the gutter to be eaten by sixteenth-century, troll-sized rats. I listened at the door, then cautiously cracked it open.

Nurse stood at the table, folding laundry. "It's her ladyship's orders. Get yourself into bed."

Juliet cast a quick glance my way. She jumped into her bed and pulled the covers to her chin. "I'm in bed. Now be gone, Nurse. I cannot sleep with you fussing about."

"Such a beastie," Nurse said. She lifted a dress from the laundry basket—my costume from the play. "Don't know why you wanted me to clean this. Her ladyship will have a fit if she sees it."

"Give it to me," Juliet demanded. Nurse did and Juliet shoved the dress under her pillow.

"Such a vile mood. Can't blame you, though. I was married once. Did you know that? Nervous as a pig in a slaughter house the night before me wedding." Nurse cleared her throat and her ruddy face turned even redder. "Has her ladyship discussed the matter of wifely duties with you?"

I winced. Last thing we needed right then was a sex education lecture.

"Nurse, please go," Juliet urged.

But Nurse kept folding. "You've a right to be nervous. That man is foul, he is. This wedding breaks me heart." She began to sniffle. "You may be a beastie, but you're me beastie, you is. And I can't stand the thought of him locking you away in that palace, which is what he'll do. A man like that treats a woman like she's no better than an obedient dog." She dabbed her puffy eyes with her grimy apron hem. "I wish this wedding would never happen."

Juliet leaped from the bed. "Do you speak the truth, Nurse?"

" 'Course I speak the truth." She blew her nose on the edge of her apron.

Juliet clapped her hands together. "If I had a way to escape this wedding, would you keep it a secret?"

"Escape?" Nurse let go of her apron. "Why, Juliet, child, I've prayed to God every night that you might escape."

"Swear it, Nurse. Swear you will keep the secret."

"I swear. On me old heart and me mother's grave, I swear." Juliet waved at me and I stepped into the bedroom. "Heavens," Nurse cried. "It's a Montague!"

"No," Juliet said, clamping a hand over Nurse's mouth before she could scream for help. "It is Mimi. She has come to help me." Juliet lowered her hand, and Nurse gawked at my clothing.

"She's a boy?"

"No, only dressed as one." Juliet opened her bedroom door and peered down the hall. Then she shut the door. "The coast is clear. What is the new plan?" she asked worriedly. "Why are you early?"

I tried to explain calmly and succinctly. "Romeo's banished from Verona and, as you know, I'm exiled. Troy is no longer welcome at Montague House. The three of us must leave before morning light, so if you're coming with us, you must take the sleeping potion right now."

"Sleeping potion?" Nurse asked. "What nonsense is this?"

"It is the only way I can avoid bringing dishonor to the family," Juliet explained. "Tell me, Mimi. Is it true that Romeo killed Tybalt?"

"Yes, but it was to avenge Mercutio's death. Tybalt murdered Mercutio." Juliet nodded, for she didn't need to be convinced of her cousin's violent nature.

"Are you still coming with us?" I asked.

"Yes," she replied.

I ran onto the balcony and leaned over the railing. "Friar Laurence," I whispered. "She's ready."

The friar was not built for climbing. His stout legs had zero flexibility and his fat gut kept pressing against the ivy, throwing him off balance. Troy and Romeo gave him a push to get him started. After much grunting, he crash-landed onto the balcony. His robe twisted around his legs, exposing lily white calves. "Heavens," Nurse said as I helped the friar to his feet. "Me old heart can't take so many surprises."

"My good woman," Friar Laurence said, smoothing his robe into place. "My old heart concurs."

"Nurse has sworn to help," Juliet explained.

"Where is the potion?" the friar asked.

Juliet pulled it from her sleeve and held it up for all to see. "Shall I drink it now?"

"You don't have to do this," I reminded her. "You can just leave and not fake your death. That is still an option."

"I cannot shame my family."

"Then drink the potion, my child," Friar Laurence said gently.

It was a momentous occasion. Juliet raised the vial as if to make a toast. In the play, Juliet says, *Romeo, I come! This do I drink to thee.* But this Juliet did nothing of the sort. "To freedom," she said with a blinding smile. "To sweet, sweet freedom!" The friar, Nurse, and I held our breaths. There was no going back now. We stood on a slippery precipice. What could go wrong? What hadn't we considered? What if we couldn't wake her? What if it didn't work? Tipping the vial to her lips, she drank the potion in a single gulp. "Horrid," she complained, scrunching her face. Then she frowned and stumbled sideways. "I'm dizzy."

The friar and I steadied her before she tipped over. "I thought you said she'd have ten minutes."

"It must work quicker on one so young," Friar Laurence guessed. We led her to the bed and helped her lie down. Her eyelids fluttered.

"Me poor little lamb," Nurse said. "Her face is so pale, it is."

"The potion is working," Friar Laurence said. "It creates a mask of death."

"I am so dizzy," Juliet mumbled. "The room spins faster and faster."

"When you wake up, I'll be by your side," I told her, taking her hand. It had already turned cold. A blue tinge spread across her lips. I could actually feel her body shutting down.

"I am sorry to make my parents sad," she said, her voice drifting away. "I never wanted to make them sad." I wanted to remind her that her parents had imprisoned her, had sold her body to a total creep just because he had money and power. But I didn't. She knew those things yet she still loved them. She didn't want to bring misery to them, the misery that all parents feel, be they wicked parents or not, when a child is lost.

Her lids stopped fluttering.

Nurse began to cry again. "She's dead, she is. Me poor little lamb."

Friar Laurence bent over the bed and gently opened one of Juliet's eyes. "She is sleeping yet she appears dead. Do you understand?" Nurse shook her head and cried even louder. The friar took her by the shoulders and spoke to her with a calm, reassuring voice. "All will be well. It is time for you to go tell Lord and Lady Capulet that you have discovered Juliet dead. If you say anything about the potion, Juliet will not be free and we will all die. Do you understand this?" Nurse nodded. "Go now."

Nurse took one more look at Juliet, then shuffled from the room. Friar Laurence and I rushed to the balcony, closing the door behind us. Troy waited at the top of the vines to help the friar. He had an easier climb down, thanks to gravity. Standing in the courtyard he brushed a few ivy leaves from his robe. "I will go to the front of the house and claim that I have come to bless Tybalt's body," the friar explained. "Most assuredly I will be summoned to Juliet's room. Once the Capulets have seen and touched their daughter, once they are certain that she is dead, I will pretend to discover the sign of plague—swellings under her arms. I guarantee that everyone will flee the room and action will be immediately taken to remove the body from the house."

"What do you want us to do?" Troy asked.

"Wait at the tomb. Romeo knows its location. I will bring Juliet there as soon as possible." Friar Laurence stroked his silver cross. "May St. Francis bless us all." He picked up his bag and hurried on his way.

It was to be another long, sleepless night. I hoped that, when it was over, Romeo would have his love and Juliet would have her freedom. But what would Troy and I have? Were we to become imprisoned in this place or would this bring about an ending?

I told you at the beginning of this story that one year had passed since these events. Certainly it is no secret that Troy and I made it back to the twenty-first century; otherwise you would not be holding this book in your hands. But we almost didn't make it back. I shudder to think how close we came.

Turn the page for the grand finale.

Twenty-four

"Thus with a kiss . . ."

THE WAIT SEEMED an eternity as I worried about everything that could go wrong. *Romeo and Juliet* is a tragedy, after all, and I was messing with its inherent elements—despair, suicide, doom. Maybe it's impossible to carve a happy ending from a tragedy, in the same way that you can't drink fire and you can't light a candle with water. It just can't be done.

Romeo had led us to the cemetery, an eerie place crowded with towering statues and ominous tombs. Built above ground, the tombs came in all shapes and sizes—one-room structures for the less prosperous, monstrosities for the mighty. Though moonlight made it difficult to hide, we found a place in the shadows between two small tombs. Fortunately, the summer night was warm so we were comfortable in our thin shirts. My adrenal glands pumped away, still in the fight-or-flight mode. Every sound became magnified as I listened for the friar's approach, but I heard only creaking tree limbs and scurrying vermin.

Dread descended, as it usually does just before something really great happens—or something really horrific. Every minute that passed meant less time for us to get ahead of the Capulet search party. I started biting my fingernails. "What if" was the theme of the moment with Romeo and I volleying it back and forth like a tennis ball.

"What if the friar can't convince them that it was plague?"

"What if the potion wears off?"

"What if Nurse chickens out and tells them about the plan? Oh God, we should never have trusted her." I bit through to the quick of my index fingernail.

"Okay, let's all just calm down," Troy said. "It's in the friar's hands now. Worrying isn't going to help anyone."

"He is right," Romeo said. "We must have faith." He rubbed dirt onto Mercutio's blade, trying to rub away the dried blood.

"What's that thing you always chant when you're freaking out?" Troy asked.

"Om ya."

"Yeah. Om ya. Om ya. Om ya." We chanted together. Even Romeo joined in.

Sure, worrying wouldn't help anyone, but it was my nature to worry, especially when a horde of thugs was preparing to disembowel me.

"Romeo," Troy said. They sat on either side of me. "I just wanted to tell you that I'm sorry about Mercutio. He seemed like a really nice guy and a great musician. He worked a miracle with my song."

"He was one of our finest musicians," Romeo said sadly. "He taught me to play the mandolin." Though the place was dead, pun intended, they kept their voices hushed.

"It's a cool instrument. I learned to play it when I was a kid," Troy said. "I used to be totally into classical music, which didn't exactly make me the most popular kid at school. But then my father introduced me to this talent agent and, voila, Troy Summer was born."

"That's not your real name?" I asked.

He grimaced. "Are you kidding? My real name's William Jones. How boring is that?" He didn't seem like a William or a Bill. But the Troy I was getting to know didn't seem like an arrogant pop star either. This Troy had agreed to help Juliet, even though he believed it might ruin our chances of going home. This Troy was courageous and kind. But would this Troy still date every woman he came in contact with?

We fell into silence. My butt went numb so I shifted, brushing against Troy's arm.

"Juliet is so beautiful," Romeo said. "I have never met a girl who wanted to be an actor." He sighed. "What is her favorite color?"

"I don't really know," I replied.

"What kind of music does she prefer? Does she like to take walks at sunset?" He sounded like one of those personal ads. "What is her favorite flower? Is it the rose? Did you notice that her lips are like roses?"

"Actually, Romeo, she isn't crazy about roses. In fact, don't compare her to any kind of flower, trust me." The last thing he needed was to remind her of Paris.

"I just want to know everything about her."

"Easy does it," Troy said. "You'll have plenty of time to learn all those things. That's the fun part."

"Really?" Romeo asked. He leaned across my knees, eager to learn from a dating master. Here's where the old Troy would reveal himself. I rolled my eyes, preparing for his womanizing wisdom.

"Once you start spending time together, you'll learn things about her that no one else could have told you. Things that you never would have suspected. Like the fact that she snores and has cold feet." He folded his arms and I caught his smile in my peripheral vision. Why was he smiling at me? Hey, was he referring to our nap on the cot? "Maybe you'll learn that she'd make a great doctor or that she has the capacity to care about people she barely knows." He took a dramatic pause, leaning against the wall. "Maybe you'll learn that *she's* not the spoiled princess you thought she was."

"Maybe you'll learn that *she'd* rather have someone speak directly to her than about her," I said, folding my arms and leaning against the wall.

"I'd be happy to speak directly to her," Troy said. "If *she'd* promise not to run off."

"Fine. Go right ahead. There's nowhere for her to run off to anyway."

Romeo gave us each a puzzled look. "Are you angry with each other?"

Troy cleared his throat. "Romeo, would you mind checking for the friar?"

"I'd be happy to." Romeo got to his feet and left the cramped hiding spot.

Troy began to fiddle with his bandage. "Well, it seems that Romeo and Juliet were meant to be together after all."

"Is that what you wanted to tell me? You wanted to say I told you so?" I really hated how defensive I always got around him.

"I just thought that maybe some people are destined to meet." He moved closer. Dirt smudged his face and he didn't smell like his cologne, Summer's Scent. He smelled and looked like a guy who had never heard of marketability. "Maybe *we* were destined to meet."

I pursed my lips with apprehension. Was he the kind of guy who would try to take advantage of me at my most vulnerable hour—thrust out of my own time and place, possibly forever homeless, nearly raped, with a death sentence hanging over my head? But Troy's expression wasn't the least bit predatory. God, how I wanted to trust him.

He stopped fiddling and looked at me, his gaze traveling across my face as if tracing my features. "I wish I could go back to that first day we said our lines. I never meant to hurt your feelings. I really screwed things up."

"I don't know what you mean," I lied. He was talking about the kiss, of course. Why didn't I have the courage to tell him how I really felt? If I had learned anything from this adventure, it was that I could do whatever I set my mind to. I had cleaned an infected wound, had climbed an ivy vine into an enemy fortress, and had even chosen to wait in a cemetery when I could be fleeing the city. But I couldn't admit my true feelings to the guy who sat next to me.

"That first time we kissed, you thought I was making fun of you, didn't you?"

Oh crap! Why did he have to keep bringing that up? It was painful enough without having to talk about it face-to-face. Was he going to offer me kissing lessons again? But he placed a hand over mine and entwined our fingers.

"I loved the kiss. That's why I smiled at you. I loved it. I was embarrassed by how much I loved it."

Was he playing me, the same way Benvolio had?

"The kiss surprised me, and that's why I said that stupid thing. I didn't mean to hurt your feelings. I guess I was just trying to hide my own. I was a total ass."

"Yeah, you were," I said, withdrawing my fingers from his warm grip.

"I'm just going to be totally honest with you, Mimi. I've always been crazy about you. But you never gave me a second chance."

"I was hurt!" I blurted. "You should have said you were sorry."

"I tried, believe me, I tried. But you totally avoided me. Every time I tried to talk to you, you hurried away." He was right. I had done my best to avoid him. "I thought I disgusted you."

"You did! Because then you went out with Dominique." I hated how jealous and whiny I sounded. But there was nothing slick about this conversation, nothing rehearsed or memorized. We were raw and wounded, exhausted, and quite possibly soon to die.

"All we did was have dinner," he said, throwing his hands in the air.

"What about Lauren?"

"Just dates. All of them, just dates. My agent doesn't want me seen alone in public." He was getting angry. So was I.

"But what about Clarissa?"

"What about her? I was trying to make you jealous." He was close to yelling, clenching his jaw.

"Well, it worked!" Oops. That slipped out.

His features softened, as did his voice. "Damnit, Mimi. I'm crazy about *you*. Even with all your snooty looks, even with your neurotic stage fright, even though you got me into all this mess, I'm still crazy about you. I can't get you out of my head."

Now was the time. Say it! Admit it! Tell him that I felt the exact same way, that try as I might I hadn't been able to get him out of my head either. Tell him, tell him, *TELL HIM*.

"Friar Laurence comes!" Romeo cried.

We crossed the lane to the Capulet tomb as a horse and cart pulled up. Romeo took the reins and Troy helped Friar Laurence from the driver's seat. "Fortunately, no one else wanted to accompany me," the friar explained. Clutching a small lamp, he waddled to the back of the cart. "The memory of last year's plague is still fresh. It exacted a horrific toll on this city. Many questioned their faith, myself included."

Juliet lay in the cart, her body draped with a linen sheet. "Any problems?" I asked.

220

"None. But the household's grieving nearly broke my heart." He pulled the sheet aside. Juliet's skin was as colorless as her nightgown. "I will do penance until my dying day to make up for this. Come, let us get her inside." He looked at the sky. "Dawn is almost here. We must hurry."

Romeo easily scooped her up. No longer weighed down by depression, he carried her with ease.

Friar Laurence took his bag from the cart and slung it over his shoulder. Using the lamp, he lit a pair of torches that flanked the tomb's door. Out of the bag came a ring of keys, which he used to unlock a heavy metal gate. "To keep out thieves," he explained, returning the keys to his bag.

We passed through death's door. Cold air enveloped us, along with the stench of rot. "There are separate rooms for the different generations," Friar Laurence told us. He led us to a smaller room off the main entry. "That is Juliet's casket." He pointed to an ornately carved coffin. "It was made for her at birth."

"Freaky," Troy said.

"The casket in the corner is Tybalt's. I'll have to prepare that later. So much to do, so much to do."

The combination of lamplight, caskets, and spiderwebs gave me the creeps. Gargoyles watched our every move from their perches along the ceiling. I imagined that they came to life when no one was around. I wouldn't have been a bit surprised if someone had started playing the organ.

The ribbons and bows of Juliet's nightgown cascaded over Romeo's arms as he held her. Friar Laurence handed the lamp to Troy, then he reached into his bag and took

out a vial. "Lay her atop the casket. It's the only place."
Romeo did, then took hold of her hand.

"She's as cold as river water," he said worriedly.

"Do not fear, my son. This stimulant will wake her."
The friar's hands trembled as he uncorked the vial.

I tilted Juliet's head as the friar dripped the vial's contents onto her tongue. He closed her mouth. Nothing happened. I tilted her head again and he fed her some more.
Still nothing. "That's strange," he said, sniffing the vial. "It
usually works immediately."

Oh my God, we had killed Juliet Capulet. The elements
of tragedy had prevailed.

"Wake up," I begged. "Juliet. Juliet. Yoo hoo. Wake up."

Troy bent over and hollered, "Hey, Juliet! Wake up!"

"I don't know what could have gone wrong," the friar
said, shaking the vial. "Holy St. Francis, there's nothing left."

"Juliet!" we all screamed.

Romeo took her shoulders and started to shake her gently.
"Don't die," he said. "Please don't die or I shall die, too."

"Don't say that," I said. "No one's going to die."

"Let's try mouth-to-mouth," Troy said, setting the lamp on
Tybalt's casket. He tilted Juliet's head back and was just about
to place his mouth over hers when Romeo pushed him away.

"What are you doing?" Romeo asked. "She's my love. I'll
kiss her." He didn't give us time to explain the mouth-to-
mouth concept. He bent over Juliet and said, "Love's first
kiss," then tenderly pressed his lips to hers.

Actually, it all makes perfect sense now that I've had time

to think about it. How does one traditionally wake a sleeping princess? With a kiss, of course.

Juliet's lashes fluttered and she took a huge breath. Romeo smiled as she opened her eyes. She didn't ask where she was. She just threw her arms around Romeo's neck and kissed him back.

"Thank God," Friar Laurence said.

Juliet and Romeo kept kissing. All their pent-up passion heated up that tomb, I can tell you that. It got a bit embarrassing so we turned away. "One of you had better break that up," the friar whispered. "Dawn is almost here."

"Okay, you two," Troy said, pulling Romeo off of Juliet. "You can get a room later. We've got to get out of here."

Friar Laurence reached into his bag again. What would he pull out this time? A magic carpet? He handed Juliet a dress. "You can't travel in that nightgown. I found this in your bed. And these slippers as well."

"That's my dress," I said, taking the lavender and gold costume and the little backstage slippers. "It's too big for Juliet. I'll wear it and she can wear these pants. They cinch at the waist."

"Help me move the casket into the cremation chamber," Friar Laurence said. Romeo and Troy lifted the box and followed him out of the room as Juliet and I exchanged clothes. Once again I was wearing that dreaded costume. Juliet tucked the coin bag into one of the boots. The boots were a bit big, but they'd work. She looked adorable. Color bloomed in her cheeks and excitement made her hands tremble. She had a new life ahead of her. I envied that. What Troy and I had was still unknown.

We stood outside the cremation chamber. Friar Laurence placed the nightgown in the open casket, then threw in the lamp. "This chamber saw a great deal of use during last year's plague. The Capulets wouldn't burn their dead in the public pyres." The nightgown instantly caught fire. The friar closed the cremation chamber. "Time to go."

We rushed to the tomb's entrance, almost knocking Lady Capulet off her feet.

Twenty-five

"Parting is such sweet sorrow."

LIKE A GHOSTLY apparition, Lady Capulet blocked our exit with her willowy frame. Her powdered skin was blotched and streaked from crying. "How dare you," she hissed.

"Mother," Juliet gasped, ducking behind Romeo.

"I thought you were dead. Do you know what you have put me through?" She clenched her fist over her heart. "When I saw my only child dead, I wanted to die! I came here for one last good-bye." She swayed, as if about to faint. Romeo stepped forward to help her but she lashed out at him. "How dare you touch me, you miserable Montague! You, who conspired to take her away without a single good-bye. Wrenching her from my life as if a mother's love is meaningless." She began to cry, deep sobbing that brought tears to my own eyes as I thought of my mother, worrying about my whereabouts, wondering if she'd ever see me again. I hadn't said good-bye. I had yelled at her and told her I hated her. Would she have to live with those last words for the rest of her life? I missed her.

"Please, Mother, stop crying. Truly I didn't want to cause you grief but I didn't know what else to do." Juliet started crying as well.

"You shouldn't be angry with Juliet," I said. "This was my idea."

"You," she said hatefully. She took a rolled paper from a pocket in her cape—my missing letter. "Tybalt's men brought this to me. Fortunately, no one else read it. You planned this from the very beginning. You came here just to destroy my family." She tossed the letter to the ground and turned her anger on the friar. "And you! I shall write to the pope and have you excommunicated. You will have no church to call home. How dare you assist with this attempt to steal my daughter from her family." I quickly retrieved the letter.

Juliet squeezed past Romeo. "No one is stealing me," Juliet said. She stepped forward and took her mother's hand. "No one has forced me. I know what you have tried to do for me, Mother. I know about the terrible heartache you endured and how you suffered for a love you could never have. I know you married Father for security and you wanted the same thing for me. But my marriage to Paris would have been loveless." She put her arms around Lady Capulet's waist and laid her head on her shoulder.

Lady Capulet stood rigid, her arms hanging at her sides. "Love only tears your heart apart."

"Sometimes it does, but sometimes it puts your heart back together." Juliet tightened her arms, trying her best to melt the icy exterior that her mother wore like armor. The rest of us watched in silence, no one knowing if this would be the end of Juliet's adventure or the beginning.

"You will not change your mind about marrying Paris?" Lady Capulet asked.

"I will not change my mind," Juliet replied. "I will leave with or without your blessing. But I tried to do so without bringing shame to the family."

"Your determination reminds me of my own." Lady Capulet sighed. "It is not possible to cancel the contract with Paris, not without great embarrassment and shame. Therefore we must leave everything in its place. Everyone must believe that you died of plague and were cremated this very morning." She bent her long neck and kissed her daughter's forehead. "Then so be it. You shall have your freedom."

The walls echoed with huge sighs of relief all around.

We emerged from the tomb as dawn's rays melted on the horizon like orange sherbet. With the light came a renewed sense of urgency. Friar Laurence paced nervously, glancing down the cemetery's narrow road.

"Promise me that you will send a letter, now and then. Use Mimi's name to mask your true identity."

"I promise."

"And once I know where you are living, perhaps I can come for a visit."

"That would be nice," Juliet said.

Lady Capulet had reserved a superior sneer for Romeo. "Do not expect me to ever approve of you, young man, but promise me that you will take care of her."

"I promise," he said, bowing.

"You look like your father," she added, as if she had just told him that he looked like pig crap.

"I hear guards," Friar Laurence cried, wringing his hands.

"That would be your father's men, sent to search for Romeo," Lady Capulet said. "Go now."

"Quick, get in the cart," Romeo urged as stomping boots echoed through the cemetery. It sounded like a large group of guards, though the Capulet tomb blocked them from our view.

"Forget the cart," Lady Capulet said. "Take the horse, daughter. It will get you and Romeo out of the city quicker."

"Mimi's in danger, too," Juliet said. "I can't leave her."

"She's in no danger," Lady Capulet insisted hurriedly. "I will remove the exile and personally see that she gets back to Manhattan. No one will harm her. Go. Go now!"

"But Mimi, you brought us together. You and Troy must come, too," Romeo pleaded.

We couldn't all fit on that horse. Believe me, I wanted to go with them. "I'll be fine," I insisted, showing a brave face. Of course, I didn't trust Lady Capulet for an instant. "Go on. It's what you're meant to do."

"I will never forget you," Romeo said, kissing my cheek.

Juliet and I hugged. To this day I can feel that small, warm body. I handed her my letter. "Read it when you can. I know your story, and I want you to know mine."

"Good luck, you two," Troy said, unhitching the horse.

Romeo jumped onto the horse. He reached out his hand and pulled Juliet onto the saddle.

"Go," Lady Capulet said. "Find the happiness that I never found." She slapped the horse's rump and it began to gallop away.

I felt nervous and excited at the same time. What an adventure Juliet was about to have. I wished I could go along with her, to see how she made a new life for herself.

Juliet turned and smiled at us, a smile that was both blissful and fearful, just as newfound freedom often is. And off they went—a happy ending after all.

Lady Capulet watched until they disappeared from view. Then she wiped a tear from her eye. "You are exiled from this town," she told the friar. "You know the truth so I want you to leave Verona immediately. Be gone from my sight." Then she turned to me. "You and that man wait here. I will tell the guard that you are free and have them escort you to wherever you would like to go."

Lady Capulet looked upon me, one last time, with a stare as blank as virgin canvas. Then she tipped her head, ever so slightly. Her exit was glorious, with her cape billowing behind her as she glided around the tomb's corner and out of view.

The friar picked up his bag. "I want you to take the main road to St. Luke's church. I have a friend there, Friar Martin, who will help you. Oh dear, I almost forgot to give you this." He reached into his bag and pulled out the quill. "I thought you might like to keep this. It's the quill you used to write Juliet's letter. It's all I have to offer."

I took the quill. "Thank you."

He scratched one of his big ears. "I'm curious, though. You told me that someone else had authored Romeo and Juliet's story. But you are the one who helped Juliet find freedom and who helped Romeo find love. And you've helped me as well, for now I am free of my obligations to Verona. Free to tend to the poor." He smiled in his knowing way. "It would seem, my child, that God, in His wisdom, has made you the author of all our stories." He kissed my hand, then disappeared around the tomb's corner.

"I'm the author," I whispered, staring at the quill. "Troy?"

"I'm way ahead of you," Troy said, grabbing one of the torches from the tomb's entryway. "Why didn't we think of this before?"

Why hadn't we? With hindsight it was so obvious, but sometimes we are blind to the most obvious things. Such as our true feelings. "Do you think it will work?"

"It had better," Troy said, "because even if Lady Capulet keeps her promise, I'm not looking forward to sixteenth-century life."

I thrust the quill into the flame, the heat almost singeing my skin. The flame instantly took to the feathered end, melting the fluffy white ostrich feather into a black paste. "Your ladyship," I heard a man call.

The quill's handle caught fire, burning as quickly as a piece of kindling.

"We are ordered to search the entire city."

"Search no more," Lady Capulet cried. "The Montague spy and her lover are at the Capulet tomb. Kill them!"

She had betrayed us, after all.

"Here they come," Troy said.

The flame reached my fingers. "Ouch!" I cried, dropping the quill. Footsteps came closer. I dropped to my knees, hovering over the quill. It had transformed into a snakelike coil of silver ashes. A guard rounded the corner.

"Mimi?" Troy cried, standing between the guard and me. "Hurry."

"Montague!" the guard snarled, raising his sword.

Oh please, oh please, oh please work. I took a deep breath and blew the ashes as hard as I could. They swirled in the morning air, stinging my eyes and nostrils just as they had in the theater. "Troy!" Where was he? Coughing, I squinted through the ash cloud. The guard's sword hovered above Troy's head. As I lunged through the cloud, the sword began its descent. "I wish we were home!" I screamed, grabbing Troy's hand.

At that moment, it felt as if I had plunged down a roller coaster.

Troy's hand slipped from my grasp.

Twenty-six

"All the world's a stage and all the men and women merely players. They have their exits and their entrances."

My butt felt numb. For good reason, because I was sitting in snow. A few flakes landed on my cheeks as I turned my face to the sky. Gone was the blue Verona morning. Gray blanketed the sky above the little alleyway where I sprawled like something that had just been tossed from a truck. Cold air pierced my lungs as I took a huge breath of realization. This was *my* alleyway—the one outside the Wallingford Theatre.

It had worked.

I scrambled to my feet and tried to open the backstage door. Locked, as usual. Would Troy be on the other side? I knocked, then pounded. "Hey, let me in! Troy!" No one opened it. Where was he? The image of that sword slicing through the air hit me. What if he hadn't made it back? What if that blade had killed him? I ran down the alley, around the corner to the theater's entrance. The marquee nearly blinded me with its twinkling yellow lights. Troy

Summer Stars in *Romeo and Juliet*, Final Performance, it read. Why hadn't they changed the sign? It wasn't Sunday.

Pimply-faced guy opened the lobby door. "Ain't you supposed to be backstage?"

"I'm back," I said, stumbling into the lobby. Applause echoed from the performance hall. The Coat Check Crones peered over their counter.

"Who's that?" one of them asked.

"Why, that's Mimi Wallingford, great-granddaughter of Adelaide Wallingford," another said.

"I'm back," I repeated. "I'm okay." I half expected to be rushed by FBI agents, or a police officer or two. At the very least, I expected someone to ask me where I had been. But the Crones started trying on fur coats, completely ignoring me, and pimply-faced guy shrugged.

"Whatever," he said.

Okay, so no one gave a crap about me. But surely they would have been worried about Troy. Famous, rich, popular Troy. "Have you seen Troy?" I asked. "Is he back? Where is he? Is he okay?" The guy squirmed with discomfort. That was the most I had ever said to him. "Why won't you answer me?"

"I don't know what you're talking about," he replied.

"Actors always get uppity on the final performance," one of the Crones told another. The final performance?

Hysterical girl screams erupted from the hall. That could mean only one thing. Troy was onstage. It was the final performance and Troy was onstage. No time had passed, as if we had never left. My entire body went slack. Of course Troy was onstage. He hadn't bothered to look for me. He hadn't bothered to wait on the other side of the backstage door. He had jumped right back into his Troy Summer persona. I should have expected as much.

"Mimi." Fernando rushed into the lobby, waving a foundation brush. "What are you doing out here? You make me crazy." He took my hand. "You need powder, you need gloss. Come." He led me down the hall. "You make a mess with that necklace, you go outside for fresh air, now you feel better." He led me into the dressing room. "But do you think about Fernando? No, you do not. You get snow all over your dress and ashes in your hair. This is Fernando's last chance to make up Juliet, and I'm not sending you out there looking like a street person." He pushed me into his chair.

A familiar feeling began to well in my stomach. "Fernando? How long was I outside?"

"I don't know. Five minutes, ten minutes. You make Fernando so crazy."

What if I hadn't gone anywhere? What if it had all been a dream after all? Just like Dorothy, just like Alice, a stupid dream induced by inhaling toxic ashes. Juliet wasn't free. Romeo hadn't been reborn. Troy didn't love me. My hands started shaking as I realized I was about to perform the play again. Nausea began to churn in the pit of my being.

"Oh, this is just great," Clarissa snarled. She stood in the doorway, her hands on her hips. "I thought you ran home." She stomped her foot. "I got all dressed for the part. I want to play Juliet tonight."

Bile rose in my throat and I gagged. Fernando grabbed his plastic bowl and held it under my chin. Clarissa smiled.

"Fantastic. You're too sick to do it." She leaned over me as I fought back the wave of nausea. "You're the worst Juliet ever. Everyone knows that. You'll just go out there and embarrass your mother again."

Someone was shouting. It sounded like, "We want Troy." The shouting grew louder. It wasn't just one voice, it was the audience, chanting over and over—"we want Troy, we want Troy."

The director stuck his head into the dressing room. "Oh my God, where's Troy?" he asked, waving his clipboard frantically. "He's missed his first entrance. Has anyone seen Troy?"

Clarissa intentionally bumped my chair as she left the room. "I'll help you look for him. Mimi's too sick to play Juliet."

We want Troy. We want Troy.

Troy wasn't onstage? Troy had missed his first entrance? But they had been screaming for him. It must have been pure anticipation.

Fernando shook a can of hairspray. "What's the matter with everyone tonight?" he muttered. "Everyone is crazy. Now, hold still."

But I didn't hold still. I jumped from the chair and ran out of the dressing room.

We want Troy. We want Troy.

I didn't care if Dr. Harmony labeled me a hopeless lunatic and made me sit in a little chair for the rest of my life, I knew that it hadn't been a dream. I could still feel the warm Verona air and the blisters on my big toes. I could still taste the marzipan-covered apricots and the friar's bland soup. I could still feel Juliet's hug and hear Troy's words: *I'm crazy about you.* But what if he hadn't made it back? What if that blade had reached him before the ashes? Holy St. Francis, what if?

I grabbed the doorknob and pushed the backstage door wide open. Troy stumbled toward me.

"I've been looking all over for you," he said. Standing in the alleyway, he was still a total mess, with his flat hair and his bandaged leg.

"I've been looking for you, too," I said. He stepped into the hallway. We smiled, equally relieved, equally amazed.

He took me in his arms. "It really happened," he whispered.

"It did."

"I wish I could have seen the look on that Capulet guard's face when we disappeared."

"Troy!" The director rushed toward us. "What have you done to your leg?"

"I . . . I . . . ," Troy stammered.

"He fell outside, on some ice," I said quickly.

"On some ice?" The director gawked at the makeshift bandage. "Never mind, there's no time to explain. Go! You're on!"

Troy looked confused. "No time passed," I told him. "It's still the last performance."

"Troy!" the director screamed as Clarissa glared over his shoulder.

Troy tightened his arms around me and pressed his lips to my ear. "Are we doing this? Are we giving the love scene one last shot?" His warm breath flowed into my body, igniting goose bumps in every possible place a goose bump can be ignited.

Hell yes, I was giving that love scene one last shot.

"Let's do it," I said.

Clarissa pounded her fist into the wall as Troy and I ran down the hallway. He stepped onto the stage and the crowd went wild, immediately forgiving his tardiness.

Nurse and Lady Capulet stared disapprovingly at me, as did the stage manager. How well I deserved their scorn. I had done nothing to earn anyone's respect, constantly complaining about a profession that each of them cherished. Tonight was going to be different. Sure, I wanted to get to the kissing scene, but something else tugged at my heart.

Juliet's smile flashed in my mind. There was so much more to her than Shakespeare ever imagined. Was there more to me? I had moped and whined like a spoiled brat ever since rehearsals began. I had even manifested stage fright as just another way to sabotage my career. Juliet and I shared the same feelings of being trapped, of having our lives directed by someone else. But even though she ultimately chose her own destiny, she still considered her family's reputation. She never wanted to bring them shame or dishonor.

I tiptoed to the edge of the stage and peered at the audience. My mother had said that she'd be in the sixth row, along with members of an admissions committee who expected to see a brilliant performance by the great-grand-daughter of Adelaide Wallingford. It was difficult to see past the squirming fans.

"I'm right here." I gasped and turned to find my mother standing behind me. "I wanted to check on you. You were so upset. Can we talk?" We squeezed past Nurse and Lady Capulet, and ducked into the prop room. She pulled a plane ticket from her purse. "I didn't cancel it. I may be horrid, but I'm not that horrid."

"Mom." My voice caught for a moment. I had so much I wanted to say. "I don't hate you."

"I know. But I've given you plenty of reasons to be mad at me." She sat on a bench, tucking her wool skirt under her lean thighs. "You think I haven't been listening to you, but I have. I just let all this other stuff get in the way."

I sat next to her. "You mean the debts?"

She put a hand over mine. "This theater was your father's passion. Before he died, he begged me to maintain it for you. He assumed that his first love would be yours as well." She smiled sadly. "It never occurred to him that the great-granddaughter of Adelaide Wallingford might want to do something else with her life. You were only eight. How could he have known?"

"Mom, I know you've just been trying to make things work. But at some point, we have to stop trying to live Dad's dream. How about if we compromise?" I scooted closer to her. "I'm happy to perform in the DVD version of *Romeo and Juliet*, but after that I'm going to take some time for college. But not the Theatre Institute. I still want to try pre-med."

"Okay. That's a sound plan." She squeezed my hand. "I think your father would understand your decision. He understood passion, above anything else. Believe me, that's why I married him." Her smile sweetened as her gaze drifted into memory. "Your father would want you to feel passion in your life. He would want you to be happy. And that's what I want, for the both of us. What would you think about selling this place?"

"What?" I couldn't believe the question.

"Reginald Dwill has made a terrific offer. It would cover all our debts, including the one I've incurred on your trust fund. You could go to college in Los Angeles."

"What about you?"

"I'll go back to acting. It's what I do best. Your cousin Greg said I'd be perfect for the role of Dr. Tiffany on his soap opera. She's a plastic surgeon who has risen from the dead." She rolled her eyes.

The lights dimmed, and the stagehands rushed in to collect the pieces of Capulet House. Mother and I returned to the wings as the stage was transformed. "Is that what you want?" I whispered. "To act again?"

"It's what I dream about." She pulled me into a hug. "When I'm not dreaming about you."

The lights rose and Nurse and Lady Capulet stepped onto the stage. My mother hugged me again, then hurried back to the audience. Fernando blotted my nose. I picked up my special little chair and handed it to him. "Burn this," I said.

"Where's this girl? What, Juliet!" Nurse called.

I stepped onto that stage like I had never stepped onto it before, imagining a wild-eyed, freckle-faced girl of not quite fourteen. A girl with hair that defied gravity and a thirst for freedom that is the essence of the human spirit. I stepped onto that stage with one goal—to command it like my great-grandmother, grandmother, father, and mother had commanded it before me. To honor my family name.

I think I succeeded—at least, that's what everyone told me. The admissions committee couldn't have been more flattering, and my mother's face couldn't have beamed any more brightly.

What about the kiss? Of course I'm going to tell you about the kiss. When Troy climbed the fake ivy and spoke those beautiful words of love, I let my secret feelings flow through Juliet's lines. They flowed across the stage and over the audience, electrifying the entire theater. I didn't know, until that moment, that the simple act of two people pressing their lips together could produce such an intense, physical reaction. What a kiss! It completely erased the first one. Most of the front row girls groaned. Eat your hearts out!

When the play was over, Troy and I had our first official date. We took a taxi to St. Francis's Hospital and got him a big fat shot of antibiotic, right in the butt. Then we went back to the Wallingford because I had some unfinished business. He waited in the taxi while I stood in the lobby, gazing at the portrait of my great-grandmother.

"Adelaide," I said. "I'm leaving the theater."

"*Leaving, are you?*" She pursed her painted lips. "*Acting is not your cup of tea, is it?*"

"No, it's really not. But I did my best tonight."

"Yes, I heard the applause. It was magnificent." Her eyes twinkled. "You should be very proud, my dear, very proud indeed. Applause like that comes from the heart."

Mr. Shakespeare once wrote, *Our doubts are traitors and make us lose the good we oft might win, by fearing to attempt.* In other words, a wish is a good place to start but then you have to get off your butt and make it happen. You have to pick up a quill and write your own damn story.

So I took my exit.

Om ya.

A Few More Words

So that was my story, my life-is-the-stuff-of-dreams story. I'm pleased to report that as of this writing, I'm living in Los Angeles with my aunt Mary, attending UCLA. Troy lives in the city, too. He signed with a new label and is experimenting with classical music. He's really into the mandolin. And yes, we're still dating. The soap opera role is keeping Mom busy, but she's coming out for Christmas. She and Reginald have become an item, so it feels like the theater is still in the family.

But there's one more thing to add.

Remember that little black-and-white cat, the one that lived across from my apartment with the old lady? Well, he's perched in Aunt Mary's oak tree as I write this. The old lady was happy to give him to me. She said he whined too much.

But now he's as happy as a lark.

I named him Romeo.

Acknowledgments

I would be lost without my critique group and their combined talents when working with a first draft. Deep gratitude to Susan Wiggs, Sheila Rabe, Anjali Banerjee, Elsa Watson, Dennis O'Reilly, and Carol Cassella. And endless thanks to my husband, Bob, for always reading every single page I put in front of him even though none of my stories are about aviation or mountain climbing.

I'm lucky to have a supportive and accessible agent, Michael Bourret, and an excellent editor, Emily Easton. Thanks also to the staff at Dystel & Goderich Literary Management and the staff at Walker Books for Young Readers.

Last, but not least, I'd like to thank a three-volume set of books titled *The Annotated Shakespeare*. Santa gave them to me when I was thirteen years old. That's when I fell in love with a certain playwright, without whom this novel could not have been written.

When Suzanne Selfors was cast as Mercutio in a summer stock production of *Romeo and Juliet*, she was devastated to be playing a male part. But once she realized that she would get to wear a fake beard and learn to fence, she was hooked and spent the rest of her high school years as a thespian. These days, her favorite things include organic gardening, boating in the San Juan Islands, and hanging out in coffeehouses. Suzanne lives on an island in Washington State with her husband and two children.

www.suzanneselfors.com

QUOTE LIST

"This above all: to thine own self be true." *Hamlet* (act 1, scene 3).

1. "All the world's a stage." *As You Like It* (act 2, scene 7)
2. "What's in a name?" *Romeo and Juliet* (act 2, scene 2)
3. "Now is the winter of our discontent." *Richard III* (act 1, scene 1)
4. "Of all base passions, fear is the most accursed." *Henry VI, Part One* (act 5, scene 2)
5. "Two households, both alike in dignity, in fair Verona where we lay our scene . . ." *Romeo and Juliet* (act 1, scene 1)
6. "An honest tale speeds best, being plainly told." *Richard III* (act 4, scene 4)
7. "One pain is lessen'd by another's anguish." *Romeo and Juliet* (act 1, scene 2)
8. "The lady doth protest too much, methinks." *Hamlet* (act 3, scene 2)
9. "Look like the innocent flower, but be the serpent under 't." *Macbeth* (act 1, scene 5)
10. "How stands your disposition to be married?" *Romeo and Juliet* (act 1, scene 3)
11. "Why, then the world's mine oyster." *The Merry Wives of Windsor* (act 2, scene 2)
12. "O' she doth teach the torches to burn bright!" *Romeo and Juliet* (act 1, scene 5)

13. "Holy St. Francis! What a change is here." *Romeo and Juliet* (act 2, scene 3)

14. "Though this be madness, yet there is method in 't." *Hamlet* (act 2, scene 2)

15. "A horse, a horse. My kingdom for a horse!" *King Richard III* (act 5, scene 4)

16. "The game is up." *Cymbeline* (act 3, scene 3)

17. "I have not slept a wink." *Cymbeline* (act 3, scene 3)

18. "The miserable have no other medicine but only hope." *Measure for Measure* (act 3, scene 1)

19. "Delays have dangerous ends." *King Henry the Sixth*, Part One (act 3, scene 2)

20. "Romeo, Romeo, wherefore art thou Romeo?" *Romeo and Juliet* (act 2, scene 2)

21. "The course of true love never did run smooth." *Midsummer Night's Dream* (act 1, scene 1)

22. "Men at some time are masters of their fate." *Julius Caesar* (act 1, scene 2)

23. "To sleep, perchance to dream . . ." *Hamlet* (act 3, scene 1)

24. "Thus with a kiss . . ." *Romeo and Juliet* (act 5, scene 3)

25. "Parting is such sweet sorrow." *Romeo and Juliet* (act 2, scene 2)

26. "All the world's a stage and all the men and women merely players. They have their exits and their entrances." *As You Like It* (act 2, scene 7)

A letter from Suzanne Selfors to the man himself—William Shakespeare—just to clarify that she never intended to steal his fans. She only wanted to make Romeo and Juliet *seem more applicable to the world today. You should still read the original story after finishing* Saving Juliet.

Dear Mr. Shakespeare,

I wanted to let you know that I am a huge fan of your play *Romeo and Juliet*. I appreciate how you added your own vision and style to a love story that had been published many times by many writers before you. In keeping with this revisionary tradition, I have done likewise with your play. I messed around with it a bit. I turned it inside out and stood it on its head. I'm confident you won't be offended for I have simply followed your lead. We are fiction writers, after all.

I first discovered your play during the summer of my thirteenth year. My father was running a fishing boat in Alaska. My mother had started a new career, and she needed to find ways to keep my little sister and me busy. So she signed us up for summer stock theatre. I'd been in a few school plays but not since sixth grade, so I wasn't quite sure that this was something I wanted to do. Hanging out at home and watching TV sounded so much better.

On a sunny Monday morning, my mother dropped us off at a church in town. We filed into the basement with dozens of other kids. A guy with a bushy red mustache welcomed us. He said he was our director. Then he said that for the next four weeks, we were going to live and breathe Shakespeare. In other words, you.

My reaction was dismay. My summer was going to be a total nightmare. I do not wish to offend you, but at that time in my life your writing was as unappealing to me as cod-liver oil. Your sentences were completely incomprehensible. Your plays seemed ridiculous—men in tights walking around with thick British accents, saying things like, "To be or not to be," and "Now is the winter of our discontent." Blah, blah, blah.

Our director told us that the play we were going to perform was *Romeo and Juliet*. I looked around the room. We were all kids. Was this guy nuts? How could he expect kids to perform Shakespeare? And why would we want to?

But then he told us the story. He told us about two families that hated each other and two people who loved each other, and about how they died because there was no way for them to live freely. And then he said, "And these two people were the same age as some of you." And that's when your story came alive for me.

Many years have passed, but your play still holds a special place in my heart. When I decided to put a modern twist on your story, I did it with the hope that it would help new readers discover your play. By introducing a modern narrator (Mimi), I was able to add a modern perspective. By going behind the scenes, I could highlight the aspect of your play that intrigued me the most—namely, Juliet's plight.

For the twenty-first–century Western reader, the idea of being forced into a marriage at age thirteen is horrific. The ideas that as a woman you could not speak your own mind, choose your own husband, or choose your own career go against everything we are taught as girls. Juliet Capulet was a prisoner of her family, her status, and her own body. Her choice to marry Romeo in secret was not just an act of rebellion, it was an act of social, political, and religious treachery—for she was acting against the laws of blood, state, and church. In the end, the only way she could find freedom was through suicide.

For me, then and now, the tragedy of the story is that Romeo and Juliet were destroyed by a society that wanted them to act in a prescribed way, when their souls longed for something else. Though modern teens may live under a different set of rules than fifteenth-century teens, they still feel the suffocating strain of society's expectations—to succeed, succeed, succeed! Failure is not allowed in this achievement-oriented culture. This generation of parents may not be arranging marriages, but they are setting expectations that can feel equally imprisoning.

And so, Mr. Shakespeare, though our stories diverge in some ways, at the heart of each is this powerful question: should we allow others to write our stories, or should we write them ourselves?

Your admiring reader,

Saving
Juliet

The following scene appeared in the very first draft of Saving Juliet. *The setting is a room in Capulet House. Mimi has just arrived and still believes that she is dreaming. An old serving man leads her to a room where she is supposed to wait for Lady Capulet.*

In this scene I was trying to illustrate the confinement and boredom of an upper-class woman's life. Also, I was experimenting with language—still not sure whether I should try to sound "Old Worldly" or be modern. In the end, I chose the latter.

Though this scene is entertaining, it slowed the pace of my story, so I cut it. It would have appeared in Chapter 8 of the final book had I kept it.

I stepped into a room thick with the smell of competing perfumes. Four benches sat in a semicircle in front of an unlit stone fireplace, and upon those benches sat seven women, all dressed in lavender and gold.

"Introducing Mimi of Manhattan," the old man said. "Just arrived for the party and newly robbed." He bowed to me and exited.

Seven sets of hands laid down their embroidery and seven heads turned my way. A funny pillbox hat sat atop each head, tied in place with a ribbon. I looked around, wondering if Juliet was present, but no one seemed young enough. I smiled and waited and since no one spoke, I said, "Hello."

One of the women, her neck held stiff in a high collar, patted a vacant spot on her bench. I sat beside her. My bench-mate's eyes bulged like a goldfish's. Her hair was pulled into a tight bun and golden ringlets hung in front of her ears. I never realized that a dream could include so many details.

"Is Juliet here?" I asked.

"Nay. She's in her chamber. Did he say newly robbed?" she asked in a high voice. I nodded and her eyes bulged further. "Pray thee, is that the reason thy gown is torn and muddied? Did the robbers molest you? Is thy virginity still intact?"

The other six women cocked their heads, waiting for my reply. My virginity was not a subject I wanted to focus on. Look, it's not that I was embarrassed by my virginity. Given the choice, I would choose to wait until someone loved me and proclaimed his love and I loved him back and proclaimed my love and all that good stuff. Then I'd have a decision to make. But I hadn't even come close to having to make a decision. You see the difference?

"They didn't molest me," I said. "But they took my traveling cases."

The women collectively sighed with disappointment. "Oh, how dull," one complained. "The least you could have done was to fabricate a story to entertain us."

"Aye, the least."

"Lativia," a woman with a mole on her nose said. My bench-mate looked up. "Lativia, go and see if anyone doth approach."

"You know I don't approve," Lativia told her.

"Lativia!"

Lativia got up and scurried to the door, her velvet skirts swishing as she went. She opened it and peered out. "Not a soul," she announced. Upon the door's closing, each woman reached under her skirt and pulled out a book. Without another word to me, they began to read. "I detest reading," Lativia whispered, returning to our bench. "But they read all the time. If caught, they shall be punished."

"For reading? Why?" I asked.

She scooted closer, almost killing me with her perfume. "Lord Capulet sayeth that women should only learn subjects which are womanly in nature." Lativia picked up her embroidery hoop and showed it to me. "I'm stitching a Capulet crest." Each of the other embroidery hoops held Capulet crests as well, in various degrees of completion. "To maketh his lordship proud," she told me, pulling a golden thread through the cloth.

"Oh, shut up, Lativia. You disturb my concentration. I'm reading Petrarch."

"This shall be my twelfth crest," Lativia whispered. "I waste no time with reading."

"Waste time?" An older woman with a slight mustache snapped her book shut and waved it at Lativia. "Foolish girl. 'Tis embroidery that wastes time. Petrarch wrote that 'tis the duty of each individual to strive for excellence and individuality. How shalt we accomplish this if we sit inside all day and know nothing of the world? Did God not giveth us minds, too?"

"Shhh," one of the women said. "You blaspheme."

Funny how dreams can include stuff you never knew you knew. I had never read Petrarch. But he sounded very interesting.

The mustached woman lowered her voice. "Just yesterday morn, my son asked my husband why the church doth forbid Copernicus. My husband did not know the answer because he hasn't read Copernicus. Well, I know the answer."

A few women gasped. "How? Dare you to read it?"

"Fie! What? Of course not," the mustached woman said with a guilty expression. "But I have heard others speak of it. My point being that I could not tell my son that I knew the answer to his question because I am not allowed to possess more knowledge than my thickheaded husband. So I pretend to be stupid and happy with my embroidery day after day after day. Is that what you want for your daughter? For all our daughters?"

"You protest too much," Lativia said meekly.

"Tell us, Hortense, why dost the church forbid Copernicus?" an old lady requested.

We all leaned in. Hortense looked around, then raised her painted eyebrows. "Because Copernicus asserts that it is the sun and not the earth that stands in the center of all things. That the earth actually spins around the sun."

"How indeed, if the earth is actually spinning, do we not all feel dizzy?" the old woman asked.

"I sometimes feel dizzy," Lativia said.

"If the earth doth spin, why do we not fall off?"

"Gravity," I blurted. They fell silent, putting down their books and looking to me for an explanation. I strained my brain to remember what I knew about gravity. "Gravity is a force that keeps everything in its place."

"Like the Catholic Church," Hortense said.

"Not quite. Let me show you. May I borrow your book for a moment?" I held out my hand and Hortense passed me her book. "Things can leave the earth and travel toward the sky." I stood and threw the book up in the air. "But eventually, everything comes back down." I caught the book. "Gravity."

"What about a bird?" Lativia asked.

"It also returns if it stops flapping its wings," I said, throwing the book again to make my point. "Everything eventually returns." I handed the book back to Hortense, whose eyes held a newfound respect. In my dream, I was a genius. How fun.

"What dost thou read in Manhattan, Mimi?" the woman with the mole asked.

"Mostly plays. Lots and lots of plays."

Slow yet determined footsteps echoed in the hallway and all seven heads turned to face the door. The women gasped and tucked their books into the tops of their thick stockings. The unanimous reaction made me a bit nervous, like I was about to get caught doing something I wasn't supposed to be doing. Each woman quickly retrieved her embroidery and posed with needle in hand. The door opened and a tall woman with a plucked hairline entered. Such a strange thing to do to one's forehead. Everyone stood and curtsied and said, "Good day, Lady Capulet."

Saving
Juliet

1. Mimi fights for her right to choose her own path and become a doctor. Juliet fights to avoid an unwanted marriage. Even though parents and other figures in your life try to look out for your best interests, sometimes they do not see your wants and desires. In your life, have you ever had to fight against someone in power to gain your independence?

2. When Mimi begins to have a panic attack, she chants "om ya." What do you do when you are stressed? Do you think Mimi fakes her stage fright?

3. The play's feud began when Lord Montague rejected Lady Capulet. Can you think of any other times, in history, literature, or your own life, when holding a grudge has led to a drawn-out conflict?

4. Mimi is very concerned with helping Juliet find her happy ending, even when it may mean that she won't be able to get home. If you were Mimi, would you have helped Juliet? Have you ever helped anyone even though it could have hurt yourself?

5. When Mimi kisses Benvolio, she is bored with the kiss. But when she kisses Troy, she has an intense reaction. Juliet is only revived when Romeo kisses her. Do you believe in true love's kiss?

6. How do you feel about Mimi's mother? Do you think it was fair of her to take the money from Mimi's trust fund? Do you think she changes at all in the end? How does she compare to Lady Capulet?

7. Can you think of anyone like Rosaline who has dedicated his or her life to a cause? Do you think you could ever do this?

8. Romeo and Juliet are often described as "star-crossed lovers," meaning that their fate was predetermined by forces beyond their control. Do you believe in fate, or that one's own choices determine the future? Or a combination of the two? Explain.

9. Why do you think Lady Capulet betrayed Mimi and Troy in the end? And why did she let Romeo and Juliet go? Do you think she is evil, or does she have some positive characteristics?

10. At the end of the book, Troy and Mimi discover they hadn't really known each other prior to their adventure. Their opinions were based on appearances before taking the time to get to know each other. Has this happened in your own life? Have you judged someone without knowing his or her true character? Did you change your opinion after you got to know this person?

11. Mimi says we have to pick up a quill and write our own story. What do you think she is trying to tell us?

12. If you could go back in time, what time period would you go to? Why? If you could enter a story, which one would you choose? Why?

13. If you were casting the movie version of *Saving Juliet*, who would you cast in the leading roles? Why?

14. Shakespeare's Verona is a fictional setting in both *Romeo and Juliet* and *Saving Juliet*. Which details of the setting are your favorite? Is there anything about this time period that makes you happy to be living in the twenty-first century? Why or why not?

15. How does this story compare to Shakespeare's *Romeo and Juliet*? What do you think happens to Romeo and Juliet after they leave Verona?

Katrina is one wish away from her deepest desire.
Now if only she could decide what that might be . . .

Suzanne
Selfors

COFFEEHOUSE ANGEL

by the author of Saving Juliet

Read on for a sneak peek at the next funny,
heartfelt novel from Suzanne Selfors.

Two

Last year, this guy named Aaron started calling me Coffeehouse Girl. At least it wasn't Hurricane Girl, the obvious choice, since my name is Katrina. And it was better than being called Lard Ass, or Crater Face, or Homo—delightful titles bestowed on some of my classmates.

"Hey, it's Coffeehouse Girl."

"Wanna take my order, Coffeehouse Girl?"

"Hey, Coffeehouse Girl, why don't you introduce Lard Ass to the concept of nonfat milk?"

His teasing wasn't a big deal. Neither the popular girl nor the shunned girl, I existed somewhere in the mundane middle—the perfect place for the untalented. Fortunately, the nickname hadn't spread beyond Aaron and his buddies. And it didn't feel like a malicious nickname. It was just a factual statement. That's who I was—the girl who worked in that weird old-lady coffeehouse. And that's what I smelled like, not like an old lady but like freshly ground coffee. Sometimes the grounds got caught in the hem of my shirt or on my shoes. Sometimes the percolator's steam scented my hair. Aaron's buddies would sniff me.

"Coffeehouse Girl smells *gooooood*."

"I'd like to drink her up."

"I've got a grande for you, Coffeehouse Girl."

I wonder if it's a universal law that boys become annoying turds around age eleven and slide downhill from there.

But they never said those things to me when Vincent was around.

Vincent didn't have a nickname. He could have, the way he always smelled like chlorine, the way his goggles left imprints around his eyes, the way he shaved his legs before races. But no one bothered Vincent. He had broken every swimming record held by Nordby High. Though swimming didn't draw the same kind of frenzy as basketball or football, the line of swimming trophies in the gym's trophy case couldn't be missed.

His size didn't hurt either. Half Native American, half Norwegian, he looked like the offspring of Geronimo and Conan the Barbarian, minus the killer attitude and weaponry. In other words, he was an absolute hunk. So while others bore the weight of Freak or Loser, Vincent got left alone, which was exactly how he liked it.

Vincent and his dad belonged to the Suquamish tribe, as did about a quarter of the students at Nordby High. The most famous member of the tribe was Chief Sealth, also known as Chief Seattle. The tribe owned most of the land to the east of Nordby, and it had plans to build a huge casino and resort. But until the resort's completion, there was little tribal money for higher education. And Vincent's dad didn't bring in much from his job as a security guard. So Vincent needed that swimming scholarship.

Monday morning always began with an assembly in the gym. Paper coffee cups with Java Heaven cloud logos overflowed from the trash can. Kids hung out at Java Heaven because it offered the trendy stuff like smoothies, energy drinks, and iced espresso. Senior citizens hung out at Anna's because it offered the stuff senior citizens prefer, like percolated gut-eating coffee, nondairy creamer, and sugar that comes in cubes.

Elizabeth, my best *girl* friend, waved from the bleachers. I sat between her and a freshman I didn't know. Vincent sat with the swim team a few rows lower. If this had been a picnic, or a movie, or that God-awful monster truck rally he had dragged me to, then Vincent would have sat next to me. But in high school, you gather at the watering hole with your herd. Vincent's herd all wore matching Nordby Otters Swim Team sweatshirts.

I didn't have a herd.

"Face is sitting down there," Elizabeth informed me. She always knew exactly where Face was sitting. You'd think she had stuck a GPS unit up his butt or something. "Face is *soooo* cute."

She said that at least four times a day.

Face was Elizabeth's code name for David Cord. She didn't want anyone to know that she had a killer crush on him. Face was not a member of the mundane middle. His herd wore polo shirts and spent most rainless afternoons at the Nordby Golf Course.

"Good morning, students," Principal Carmichael greeted from center court. "As you all know, winter break begins next Wednesday." Screams of glee erupted. Students stomped their feet. Mr. Rubens, the phys ed teacher, jumped out of his chair and blew his whistle. The enthusiasm settled back to boredom.

The principal cleared her throat. "We have a lot to accomplish before winter break, but guidance counselor appointments are of the highest priority. Yellow notices have been placed in lockers to remind those students who have not yet met this requirement. These appointments are mandatory."

Someone behind me hollered, "Fascist!"

Carmichael scowled. "The yearly consultation with the guidance counselor is an important part of your education, especially for those of you who are planning to go to a college or university." She adjusted the microphone. It shrieked like it always did. Elliott, the school's technical genius, ran out to fix it like he always did. No one yelled "Nerd!" Elliott was going to bring teleportation to the masses or invent liquid time or something and we all knew it.

"Thank you, Elliott." Principal Carmichael adjusted her glasses. "And now Heidi Darling has an announcement, so please give her your undivided attention."

Elizabeth and I groaned as Heidi strode to the microphone. It was the whole perky thing that made us cringe. Natural perkiness is digestible in small amounts. But she was too wide-eyed, too smiley, too bouncy. What kind of a carbon fingerprint does a person leave after maintaining that level of energy?

"Listen up," Heidi said in her clipped way. "This year, my dad's coffeehouse, Java Heaven, is sponsoring the Winter Solstice Festival, so that means that it's going to be the biggest and best festival ever." She paused expectantly. No one applauded, but she kept on smiling. "So the thing is, we need help, people. The decorations don't get set up on their own." Groans filled the gym. Heidi planted her hands on her hips. "My dad said he'll give Java Heaven coupons to those who volunteer, good for a free sixteen-ounce Mocha Cloud Frappe, which is organic because we care about the environment."

"Hey, Coffeehouse Girl." Aaron, the annoying turd, sat behind me. "You got anything free to give out? I'd like to taste your frappe."

Elizabeth jabbed him in the shin with her pencil, then leaned close to me. "Maybe I should ask Face to go to the festival."

"Go for it," I said encouragingly, even though I knew she would never ask him. Elizabeth could jab guys with pencils, she could intimidate them with her big boobs and her in-your-face attitude, but she had no idea how to ask one out. We were both pretty pathetic when it came to guys. Neither of us had ever been on an actual date.

Heidi waved one of the Java Heaven coupons. "If we show our school spirit, we can make this the best Solstice ever. *Gooooo* Otters!"

Heidi Darling was like a virus, the way she invaded everything—every school club, every committee and event. Last spring she had painted a mural on the cafeteria wall with the theme "school spirit." Why would a person want to do all that stuff? And who really cares about "school spirit"? What's the point?

"I highly advise each of you to volunteer and help with the festival decorations," Principal Carmichael said, taking the microphone from Heidi. "Volunteering will look good on your college applications."

And there's the point.

Our main focus as teenagers, according to just about

everyone, is to jam-pack our lives with activities so that we can get into an Ivy League college and therefore succeed in life. Because that's the way it works. Weak application = crappy college. Crappy college = crappy job. Crappy job = crappy life. In other words, poverty, alcoholism, obesity, and depression. It's enough stress to make your hair fall out. By the time Heidi Darling graduated, her college application would be the size of an encyclopedia. She was on the fast track to Har-friggin'-vard.

"Thank you, Heidi," Principal Carmichael said. Heidi speed-walked back to the bleachers. "So, students, remember to see your guidance counselor before—" The principal stopped speaking as the gym's double doors slammed open.

A strange guy entered. He wore a khaki kilt, a ragged sweater, and sandals with no socks. A satchel hung from his shoulder and his long brown hair was all messed up, as if he'd been *sleeping in an alley*.

"May I help you?" the principal asked. "Young man, may I help you?"

"I apologize for the intrusion, madame." He walked toward the bleachers. Maybe he was a new student, but that still didn't explain why he had been sleeping in our alley.

"He's *sooo* cute," Elizabeth whispered. I usually ignored Elizabeth's declarations of "cute." With each boyfriendless month that passed, her standards lowered. She was dangerously close to substituting "cute" for "alive." However, the guy did look much better under the bright gym lights than that yellow alley light.

"Excuse me," Principal Carmichael said. "You're not a student here. We have strict security codes."

"I won't be but a wee moment." He stopped walking and

scanned the bleachers. "I've come seeking a lassie. I mean, a young lady." A roar of student laughter broke the tension.

"You're not *seeking* anyone until you check in at the office," the principal said. "Mr. Rubens will show you the way. Mr. Rubens?"

Mr. Rubens put his hand on the guy's shoulder. "Come with me, young man."

The guy calmly slid from Mr. Rubens's grasp and walked right up to the first row. "I must reward her good deed." Then he pointed. "There she is."

Oh God.